# BLACK★BULLET

## THOSE WHO WOULD BE GODS

**SHIDEN KANZAKI**

ILLUSTRATION BY
**SAKI UKAI**

C000001865

## KISARA TENDO

A former rich girl who was born into the prestigious Tendo family, but for her own reasons, she left home to become independent. Although she attends school and runs the Tendo Civil Security Agency at the same time, she's has been forced into poverty. She is the girl Rentaro yearns for.

## RENTARO SATOMI

Second-year at Magata High School. An employee of the Tendo Civil Security Agency run by Kisara Tendo. With his Initiator partner, Enju, he fights against the Gastrea, parasitic organisms beyond human imagination.

## ENJU AIHARA

One of the Cursed Children, who have the Gastrea virus inside their bodies. A precocious ten-year-old hiding superhuman powers. She's very attached to her partner, Rentaro Satomi, treating him like a lover, and she views the well-endowed Kisara Tendo as her rival in love.

## KIKUNOJO TENDO

Aide to Lady Seitenshi. He holds the political post with the greatest authority and is Kisara Tendo's grandfather. He intimidates those around him. He also has a profound connection with Rentaro Satomi, who was taken in by the Tendo family in the past.

## SEITENSHI

Ruler of Tokyo Area, one of the five areas Japan was divided into after the Gastrea War. Sixteen years old. With her otherworldly beauty, kind heart, and noble will, she has much support from the masse

## KOHINA HIRUKO

Kagetane Hiruko's daughter. Like Enju, she is one of the Cursed Children. To people other than her father, she acts very belligerently. She boasts that she is unrivalled in close combat with the two short swords at her hip, and she is Enju's worthy opponent.

## KAGETANE HIRUKO

A mysterious man who fights against Rentaro and Enju, plotting the destruction of Tokyo Area. He is clad in a ridiculous outfit of a tailcoat, a silk hat, and a mask for a ball, but his fighting ability is immeasurable.

## SHOGEN IKUMA

Promoter with the Mikajima Roy
Guard. Using an enormous basta
sword as his weapon, he is a hig
ranking fighter who relies on ins
to crush his opponents. He char
Rentaro and the others to elimir
them even though they all have
same goal.

## KAYO SENJU

Initiator paired with Shogen Ikur
Although she is a Cursed Child li
Enju and Kohina, her abilities are
as helpful for combat. Instead, sl
possesses extreme intelligence a
supports her partner, Shogen Iku

### SUMIRE MUROTO

Someone who often gives Rentaro advice, she used to be in charge of the New Humanity Creation Project. A shut-in and a mad scientist. She is a genius, and she loves to tease Rentaro.

## BLACK BULLET
## CONTENTS

| P. 001 | PROLOGUE | DEFEAT |
| P. 007 | CHAPTER 1 | THE TENDO CIVIL SECURITY AGENCY |
| P. 073 | CHAPTER 2 | THE CURSED CHILDREN |
| P. 123 | CHAPTER 3 | THE GASTREA THAT DESTROYED THE WOR |
| P. 161 | CHAPTER 4 | THOSE WHO WOULD BE GODS |
| P. 197 | EPILOGUE | PUTTING ON A BOLD FRONT |

# BLACK★BULLET

## THOSE WHO WOULD BE GODS

### SHIDEN KANZAKI

ILLUSTRATIONS BY SAKI UKAI

YEN ON

NEW YORK

BLACK BULLET, Volume 1
SHIDEN KANZAKI

Translation by Nita Lieu

This book is a work of fiction. Names, characters, places, and
incidents are the product of the author's imagination or are
used fictitiously. Any resemblance to actual events, locales, or
persons, living or dead, is coincidental.

BLACK BULLET, Volume 1
©SHIDEN KANZAKI 2011
All rights reserved.
Edited by ASCII MEDIA WORKS
First published in Japan in 2011 by KADOKAWA
CORPORATION, Tokyo.

English translation rights arranged with
KADOKAWA CORPORATION, Tokyo,
through Tuttle-Mori Agency, Inc., Tokyo.

English translation © 2015 by Yen Press, LLC

All rights reserved. In accordance with the U.S. Copyright Act
of 1976, the scanning, uploading, and electronic sharing of
any part of this book without the permission of the publisher is
unlawful piracy and theft of the author's intellectual property.
If you would like to use material from the book (other than for
review purposes), prior written permission must be obtained
by contacting the publisher. Thank you for your support of the
author's rights.

Yen On
1290 Avenue of the Americas
New York, NY 10104
www.yenpress.com

Yen On is an imprint of Yen Press, LLC.
The Yen On name and logo are trademarks of
Yen Press, LLC.

The publisher is not responsible for websites
(or their content) that are not owned by the publisher.

First Yen On Edition: August 2015

ISBN: 978-0-316-30499-3

10 9 8 7 6 5 4

LSC-C

Printed in the United States of America

## PROLOGUE    DEFEAT

The boy sat hugging his knees in a corner of the cracked road, watching people pass by. The rain had turned the narrow road muddy, and there were a surprising number of people traveling on it, or sitting in protest and making a fuss about something.

If the boy strained his eyes, he could see an elderly man who had not received rations and was staving off hunger by gnawing at the roots of trees. The man's eyes bulged, and his throat was extremely swollen. The boy could not look directly at the scene, since like most people who had once had no choice but to eat grass and bark, he knew that it would make him sick.

There was a man selling small pieces of crushed biscuits at an exorbitant price whose pockets were stuffed with ten-thousand-yen bills that were basically useless scraps of paper. But the man in question was skin and bones himself and seemed to be the one most in need of nutrition.

Behind him, at a hastily made barricade, the protestors were a mountain of black, carrying placards and yelling. The placards were not quite visible from where the boy sat, but they undoubtedly said "Let us live."

They had all abandoned their possessions and homes, making a reverse evacuation into Tokyo. But not even Tokyo had the capacity to accommodate the entire nation's refugees. Despite the plentiful open land, everyone pitched their tents close together in dense formations. The most certain method of keeping off the wind and rain was to take shelter inside a building, but it took a lot of courage to live inside half-destroyed office buildings and department stores that could collapse at any moment.

Before the boy's eyes spread a scene he'd once thought existed only on TV: the end of the world. What everyone had in common were their dirt-covered faces and the despair and hopelessness that ate away at their hearts. The many who rejected this pitiful way of life had long since ended their lives to hold on to their dignity. Who in the world would believe that this moment was the present and that this place was the area around the capital of Japan?

Suddenly, the boy was overcome with a great listlessness, and his consciousness faded away. He didn't know what he should do. He didn't have a place to go home to, either.

Every day, countless numbers of people died, and the war just kept getting worse. The dead were either piled on top of one another and burned, or recently, to save fuel, they were being thrown into a mass grave and covered with dirt. These past few days, there wasn't a day that went by without the smell of burning protein or rotting flesh.

The boy was sure he had been lucky. However, even if he tried to believe that he should be grateful that there'd even been a funeral, the sadness that oppressed him didn't let up one bit, and blood continued to flow.

When he closed his eyes, the first thing that came to mind was a low, repetitive, monotone voice.

The boy had been made to sit in the front row of a room where the sound of chanting, cicadas, and a faraway wind chime mixed together. Two caskets were stretched out in front of a monk chanting prayers to Amitabha, and in front of those were a large number of flower wreaths offered in tribute. Almost buried beneath the flowers were pictures of the deceased smiling brightly.

The boy's stomach twisted with pain, and he squeezed the fist on his knee so hard that his whole body shook. He hung his head in shame as the teardrops he tried to hold back dripped down his nose. The stain spread on his already-soaked pants.

It was only a week earlier that the area where the boy lived had become the site of a bloody battle with the invasion of the Gastrea. As jet engines of missiles and the flames of mortars dyed the night sky crimson, the boy's father desperately pushed the struggling boy unwillingly onto the night train so that he could be taken care of by his father's friend in Tokyo. Just before the train doors closed, his father said with a serious look on his face, "Mom and I will be there soon, too."

Indeed, a mere five days after the boy had been taken in by the family in Tokyo, his parents arrived. As ashes.

*Joint funeral.* It took many hours of explanation for the boy to understand what those two simple words meant. At first, he couldn't believe what had happened and grabbed at the dark ashes with his hands. The clumps were unbelievably easy to crumble with his hands, and they fell like fine pebbles through his fingers. The boy opened and closed his blackened palms, trying to connect with reality the explanation he'd received, but it was no use. There was just no way he could believe that those ashes had been his mother and father just a few days earlier.

Ashes could not laugh with him, sleep next to him, or cook him delicious food. Before he knew it, he had bitten the chanting monk and kicked off the lids of the caskets, going wild. Showing the people who had come to the funeral the empty caskets, he screamed, "Mom and Dad aren't dead!" and ran outside, bumping into the black-and-white curtain used for funeral services.

And then two days later, the boy ran out of the large residence with many servants and ended up where refugees had set up their temporary tents. But because the boy did not have any ration tickets, there was no way anyone would bless him with food. With no other choice, he chewed on tree roots and sucked on the juice of grasses. He ended up with violent diarrhea and became dehydrated from food poisoning.

Overcome by dizziness with his vision narrowing, he could not stand any longer, and let his body sink to the ground while leaning on a wall in the street. Looking in front of him with his vision blurring, he saw many legs in his field of vision. The legs of the thousands of refugees walking on the street passed in front of the boy's eyes. Thin legs, old legs, children's legs, men's legs, women's legs. His mouth was so dry that he didn't even have any spit left. Even when he stretched out his hand in supplication and called out with his thin, weak voice, none of those legs stopped.

A single tear ran down the boy's cheek. He didn't want to go back to that house—the Tendo house—again. The boy didn't think he could stand living any longer with the new parents and many older brothers and one younger sister he had had for one week.

Even though he was a child, he knew. It was the end for this country. Over eighty percent of its country's land had been taken by Gastrea, and land, sea, or air, the self-defense force had suffered devastating losses. It was unbelievable how many people had been killed.

He was sure it would hurt less if he just died here and now. But— the boy put strength into his hand and scratched at the earth. If he were somehow able to survive this, he would spend the rest of his life searching for his parents to the ends of the Earth.

Suddenly, a long rumble like distant thunder echoed through the area. The people going to the road stopped their feet and tilted their heads. The man who guessed the situation first climbed the bell tower attached to the church and rang the bell with a desperate look on his face.

The boy slowly followed everyone's gazes toward the sky and saw a gigantic shadow flying over the ridge of the mountain range in the distance. The moment everyone realized that it belonged to a creature with gigantic wings, the camp descended into chaos. Raising their voices in screams, pushing and shoving, stepping on fallen old women and children, they all started to panic and run, trying to get just one step farther away from the thing.

The boy's hazy consciousness kept him gazing at the sky as he put strength into the hand holding his knee, but with his empty stomach and in his dehydrated state, he could not move another step from where he was.

Behind the being by a few seconds came a mass of machines that appeared from beyond the mountains—the self-defense force's support fighter aircraft.

As the fighter aircraft pursued the giant creature, their engines roaring, the creature tried to shake them off. They almost seemed to dance as they drew an acrobatic path through the air. It was a scene that could have only been seen on TV just a short time ago.

Finally, seeing a good opportunity, a fighter aircraft in the back fired an air-to-air missile. The creature twisted its body in midair in an attempt to avoid the Sparrow missile that rocketed toward it, but the missile impacted its flank nonetheless, and a blaze of fire bloomed in the sky.

Seeing the creature let out a long scream as one wing was broken off in midair, the crowd stopped and cheered loudly. But the next instant, those cheers became screams.

"It's coming this way!" someone yelled.

The falling giant changed its course as it fell, and eventually it came to fill the boy's field of vision. The rising shouts and bellows mingled until all that could be heard were screams.

As the giant being scraped the ground, severe tremors shook the earth, and the crowd of people fell one after another like dominoes as they screamed. The monster took a path to the ground like an airplane trying to land on a runway, but the impact of the large body was not so easily reduced. Cutting down a swath of buildings and temporary tents with a loud destructive reverberation, the creature made a hard landing, heading directly at the boy.

*I'm going to be crushed*, thought the boy, shutting his eyes tightly.

The air resounded with the sounds of cracking and crumbling and screaming as large bits of rock and clods of earth hit the boy's face. Then, there was the choking smell of the earth, and all he could hear was a sound of ragged panting that was not his own.

He was alive.

Opening his eyes, through the thick cloud of dust, he saw the head of the giant creature before his very eyes, close enough to touch if he stretched out his hand far enough.

"Gas...trea...," the boy murmured without thinking.

It was probably about fourteen meters in length, and it looked like a dinosaur from prehistoric times. Its reddish wings looked like a bird's, but it had two eyes that stuck out like half-moons, sparkling like lumps of crystal. They seemed like a dragonfly's compound eyes.

It was an avian-insectoid Double Factor. From its pointed beak flowed a great volume of venous blood, and from within its heaving chest was a glowing red light. Thanks to this... No, *because* of this...

As if responding to the boy's hate, the Gastrea strained its whole body to raise its head. Blood dripped in long, flowing threads. The monster suddenly opened its beak and let out a shriek in front of the boy's eyes and nose. A mixture of saliva and blood splattered on his face, and a blast of beastly smelling wind played with his hair. His whole body shook, and a scream almost escaped from his throat. He drew back his body, thinking he was done for.

At that moment, someone pulled the boy's arm with an explosive force, and he just barely escaped the Gastrea's sharp beak. "Huh...? S-sir?" said the boy.

Though the man was easily sixty, he had the solid body of a martial artist and a tall frame that towered over the boy. This was Kikunojo Tendo, the head of the Tendo family that had taken the boy in.

*He came to look for me? All the way here?* thought the boy. As he stuttered, trying to thank the man, the extremely late Special Forces surrounded the nearly dead Gastrea, holding their rifles ready.

The boy's savior, without looking in his direction, told him: "If you do not want to die, survive, Rentaro."

At the captain's signal, empty shell casings flew into the air as the dry sound of gunfire filled the sky.

Two months later, Japan declared its de facto defeat to the people, and each region closed their Monolith barrier and took a stance of autonomous defense. Following Japan's lead, the major powers of the world also closed their Monolith barriers as a temporary measure. The majority of Japan's land had been taken over, and there were a vast number of casualties, with tens of times more missing.

In the year 2021, mankind lost to the Gastrea. Ten years later...

# BLACK BULLET CHAPTER 01

## THE TENDO CIVIL SECURITY AGENCY

1      *SPRING.*

Beneath an evening sky dyed red, the square-jawed, rough-faced senior inspector of the homicide department approached the fine-featured, thin young man threateningly. "Huh? *You're* the civil officer who's here to help us? Even stupidity has its limits. You're just a kid!"

The young man who was being approached with such derision, Rentaro Satomi, let his listless eyes slide up to the side, looking idly at a crow cawing as it returned to its nest. All he wanted was to go home.

Rentaro answered the inspector evasively, grumbling, "Doesn't matter what you say. I can't do anything about it. I'm the civil officer who's here to help. I have a gun and a license. My boss told me to come here, so I did, because I had to, but if you're going to doubt me, I'm going home."

Clucking his tongue, the inspector started walking around Rentaro, narrowing his eyes as if appraising him. "That uniform... You a student?"

Rentaro looked down at his uniform. On the chest of his pitch-black uniform that looked just like a suit was the embroidered insignia of Magata High School. "What's wrong with that?" he said.

"So these days even kids can play at being civil officers, huh?" said the inspector. "Show me your license."

When Rentaro pulled out his license, the inspector looked at the picture on it and compared it to Rentaro's face. He snorted. "That's an unlucky mug. Not real photogenic, are you?" he laughed, his stomach shaking.

*This is work, too. Just deal with it,* Rentaro said to himself as he glared at the inspector.

The inspector, who introduced himself curtly with nothing more than "I'm Tadashima," threw the license back at Rentaro. "Tendo Civil Security Agency, huh? Never heard of it."

"It's 'cause we aren't that well known," said Rentaro. "Uh, sorry to rush things along, but can we talk about work now?" Rentaro lifted his face and looked up at the dilapidated apartment building in front of them. Cracks, filth, corrosion, and damage made it stand out, but it was an extremely normal six-story apartment building. It was called the Grand Tanaka. "This is really where the trouble is?"

"Yeah, that's right," said Tadashima. "The guy in Room 102 called screaming, saying there was blood leaking down from the room above. Putting all the info together, there's no doubt it's a Gastrea. Anyway, let's get in there already. Friggin' finally." At the *finally*, Tadashima raised his voice, as if intentionally trying to be overheard, and walked into the building.

Civil officers and inspectors not getting along wasn't anything new, but it was so obvious that rather than being angry, Rentaro was just disgusted. He stopped in front of the building, seriously considering going home, but then reluctantly followed the man in.

Shortly after the defeat, a law was put in place stating that no one was to enter the scene of a crime involving Gastrea without a civil security officer, or "civsec" for short. It was a necessary step in the efforts to try to slow down the skyrocketing rate of police officer deaths, but there wasn't a police officer to be found who welcomed with open arms the civil officers who were stepping into their jurisdiction.

At that moment, Tadashima put his rough face close to Rentaro's, as if realizing something. "Hey, where's your Initiator partner? You civil officer fighters come in pairs, don't you?"

"Oh, I didn't think this was bad enough to need her," said Rentaro. He was startled on the inside, but he couldn't admit that he'd accidentally left her behind. Thinking that maybe it was a bad idea to not have her after all, he looked back down the dim hallway they came from, scratching his head.

When he heard about the Gastrea incident in their neighborhood from the agency president, his one and only boss, he remembered pedaling his bike seriously for once, trying not to let another agency get the job before them. He must have left his partner behind at that point, too. He just hoped she didn't get lost.

When he got up to the scene, room 202, there were already a bunch of officers gathered near the door.

"Has there been any change?" asked Tadashima.

At Tadashima's words, one of the squad members looked back with a pale face. "S-sir. Just now, two point men went in through the window. After that, we had no further contact with them."

The atmosphere at the scene froze.

"You idiots! Why didn't you wait for the civil officer to arrive?!"

"We didn't want the guys who always come and run wild on the scene stealing the credit from us! You know how that feels, don't you, sir?"

"Who cares about that?! Anyway—"

"Outta the way, you idiots! I'm gonna break in!" Rentaro interrupted.

Tadashima looked into Rentaro's eyes for a second and jerked his chin with an order. Two of the fully equipped police squad members waiting behind them were stationed in front of the door, holding shortened door breacher shotguns at the hinges of the door.

Rentaro also pulled out his gun, a Springfield XD, from his belt, cocking the slide as he did so he could fire if necessary. He took a deep breath to clear his mind. Wiping the sweat from the palm of his hand on his pants, he clicked his tongue. This had really turned into a troublesome case. "Do it," he said.

The two shotguns fired at almost the same time Rentaro kicked down the door. His eyes narrowed for a second as the brightness of the setting sun flooded his vision. As if rising out of the sunset, the small, six-tatami-mat room was dyed with the setting sun. However, something redder than the setting sun was spilled out all over the floor of the living room. There was also the rich, unmistakable smell of blood. Two police squad members had been thrown against the wall, dead.

Rentaro saw something he found hard to believe there. In the middle of the room, a tall man was standing still. He was probably over

190 centimeters tall. His too-skinny arms and legs were attached to a too-skinny torso. The mysterious figure was outfitted in a wine-red pinstriped tailcoat, silk hat, and to top it all off, a *maschera* mask, like you'd wear to a masquerade.

The Gastrea was gone. But who was this man…?

Eventually, the masked man turned around and gave a faint smile. From behind the mask, he turned his sharp gaze to Rentaro. "You're rather late, civsec, my boy."

"What…? Are you…in the same business?" said Rentaro.

"It's true that I was also after the Gastrea that was the source of the infection. However, I am not in the same business as you. Why, you ask?" The man spread his arms in front of him as if performing on stage. "Because I am the one who killed the two police officers."

The instant Rentaro realized the man was an enemy, his body reacted. He closed the gap between them in an instant and hit the man with the heel of his hand, not waiting for an answer. The angle and timing of the attack were both good.

"Oh, you're rather skilled," said the man.

Just as Rentaro thought the masked man looked like he was having fun taking the attack, there was an impact on his chest. The punch made Rentaro's chest cave, throwing him across the room. He crashed onto the glass coffee table in the living room on his back, winded.

*What in the world is this guy?* Rentaro thought. His face twisted in extreme pain, he opened one eye and saw the masked man winding up his fist for another close-range punch. As he hurriedly rolled off it, the glass table splintered with a shrill crash. Rentaro was able to jump out of the way and stand up, but a roundhouse kick came right at the side of his head, as if his evasive position had been anticipated. Both he and the arm he put up to block the attack were sent flying into the wall with the terrible force of the kick.

The masked man sniffed contemptuously.

Rentaro was dizzy with despair at the vast difference in their abilities even as he took a firm stance.

Then, an out-of-place ringtone echoed through the room, and the masked man picked up the phone. "Kohina? Um, yeah. I see, okay. I'll go meet up with you."

"Look over here, you monster! This is for my friends!" shouted a voice.

When Rentaro turned to look, standing in the door were a number of police squad members holding carbine rifles.

The masked man quickly drew a gun from the holster on his hip without even looking in their direction. Blood suddenly erupted from their blue tactical vests and splattered on the wall. The masked man kept firing, and three people who used to be human were shot down in the blink of an eye. The officers waiting outside became agitated.

Rentaro closed the gap with all his strength and stepped firmly on the floor. "Tendo Martial Arts Second Style, Number 16: *Inzen Kokutenfu!*" The round kicks that he fired off in return were avoided by neck movements from the masked man, but Rentaro stepped quickly into his second attack and unleashed his *Inzen Genmeika*. Rentaro fired off high kicks that didn't miss their mark this time, and hit the masked man's *maschera* directly.

Rentaro started to yell "Yes!" but the man put a hand on his neck—which had been twisted back with the force of the kicks—and forced it back into position with a strange sound. The most surprising part was that the man did not once let go of his cell phone. "Oh, it's nothing. I'm just a little busy. I'll be there soon." Flipping his cell phone closed, he didn't move, looking intently at Rentaro.

Rentaro felt chills freeze his blood.

The man let out some short laughs as he held his mask to his face. "Oh my, that was wonderful. Even though I was not paying attention, I didn't think you'd actually get a hit in. I would love to kill you right here, but there's something else I must do right now."

He stopped talking for a moment, and his piercing eyes looked at Rentaro from the depths of the mask. "By the way, what's your name?"

"Rentaro…Satomi."

"Satomi…Satomi, huh?" the man mumbled to himself, sidestepping the pieces of glass from the broken window and going out to the balcony, putting his leg on the handrail.

"Let's meet again sometime, Satomi… Or should I come find you?"

"You… What are you?"

"I am the one who will destroy the world. No one can stop me." The man jumped down from the balcony in a single bound.

For a while, Rentaro's stiffened body couldn't move, as if it had been sewn down. He opened his sweaty palms and closed them hard. Could such a powerful being exist in this world?

He heard a groan and looked back with a start. The men who were shot by the mysterious masked figure were seriously injured and were being carried out on stretchers, their friends calling desperately to them.

Rentaro's fist shook. Then, he felt a hand on his shoulder give him a strong shake.

"Get a hold of yourself, civsec! We've been prepared for this since starting this job. What you need to do right now is—"

Rentaro clucked his tongue and shook Tadashima's hand off. "I know! I have to stop the Pandemic first!" Looking at the clock on the wall, he gathered his thoughts and gave himself a pep talk. He had lost a lot of time, but his work wasn't over yet. Shutting out thoughts of the strange man from his consciousness for the moment, Rentaro, gun in hand, cautiously checked the bathroom and inner Japanese-style living room, opening all the closets. Finally, he opened the only thing left to check—a large wooden closet.

Inside, there was nothing but clothes.

"Hey, what's going on? Where's the Gastrea?" said Tadashima.

Rentaro was a little confused hearing Tadashima's voice behind him, but he put his gun away and went back to the living room.

The problem was a puddle of blood that had spread on the floor where the masked man had been standing. It was not the man's blood. He had not been injured. And even though Rentaro didn't want to think about it, this was enough to be fatal.

Rentaro looked at the picture frame on the low table. It was a picture of a family, with the daughter tucked in between the loving embrace of the husband and wife. "The guy living here was living by himself, wasn't he?"

"Yeah, it was a man living by himself," Tadashima answered.

Rentaro checked the ceiling. "What the…?"

Tadashima made a face, following Rentaro's gaze. There was an object stuck to the ceiling with green gel. Rentaro jumped and touched the thing stuck to the ceiling. He rubbed it with his fingers, and it felt extremely sticky.

"There's no mistake that the victim was attacked here," said Rentaro. "But the victim probably escaped from the window of the living room looking for help. And then, I don't really wanna say it, but moving around after losing this much blood, he's probably..."

Tadashima nervously groped around in his pocket and pulled out a cigarette. "Let me get this straight. Not only is the source of the infection still walking around somewhere, but the infected person is, too?"

Rentaro nodded. "Inspector Tadashima, please evacuate the neighborhood immediately and request a blockade to seal off the area. They couldn't have gone far. We should look outside, too. If we wait until it becomes a Pandemic, demotion's gonna be the least of your worries."

It was like drifting between being awake and being half-awake. There was a reassuring floating bridge connecting the two, but just as the man realized what it was, it would disappear.

Before he knew it, he had stopped his wandering around in the sunset. He looked to his right and to his left. Why was he walking around this place? Even though it was at some remove from his home, the view in the distance looked familiar, so this had to be be somewhere in the Tokyo area. He couldn't say exactly where he was, but he had a faint memory of the scene around him. He thought maybe he was so drunk that his senses had gotten confused, but his thoughts were clear and he had not lost his sense of balance, except for the slight languidness left in his body.

He shook his head slightly. What was his name? It was Sumiaki Okajima, of course. After having the name for forty-five years, he wasn't going to forget it that easily. It was fine up to that point. But then why was he in this place? No matter how hard he thought, he could not come up with a single explanation.

It didn't seem like he was sleepwalking. This was a residential area, but he didn't have any friends who lived in the area. He couldn't possibly have trekked all the way out here, then. Or perhaps he had just set out on an aimless walk, and the inertia of his feet had carried him here. *Inertia*, he repeated inside his head and couldn't help but smile bitterly.

Ever since the company he worked for had gone under, it was as if he'd just kept living through inertia. Tired of having his savings get lower and lower, he'd tried to compensate for their loss through gambling and poker, but that was the beginning of the end. By the time his delirium died down and he was able to objectively see how stupid he had been, he had already paid an immense fee to learn his lesson.

After the Gastrea War, Sumiaki had looked with scorn on those people who had lost their purpose in life and were slowly killing themselves, but he had now turned into exactly what he had scorned in the past.

He could not bring himself to blame his wife and daughter, who had washed their hands of him early on. When he lost money, he would get drunk and violent. No one could call him an excellent father by any standard. His ability to barely maintain a clear head was, pathetically, because he had run out of money to buy alcohol. His house had been foreclosed upon, and now that he spent all day in his cramped apartment spacing out, he'd grown uneasy at not being a productive member of society, and was occasionally so overwhelmed with emptiness that he wanted to scream.

Sumiaki bought a sports drink from a vending machine by a utility pole and put it to his mouth. Maybe it was because the flavor was too light, but it didn't taste like anything to him. He downed the five hundred milliliters in the blink of an eye, but it just seemed to make him even thirstier. "Seriously, why am I here—"

At that moment, Sumiaki was taken aback, hearing someone yelling in a loud voice.

"Rentaro, you insensitive imbecile!"

In front of him, he saw a girl with a long shadow walking toward him. She seemed about ten years old, wearing a short skirt and a fancy coat lined with a checkered fabric. She had thick-soled lace-up shoes, and her hair was tied with largish hair ties into pigtails that swayed slightly left and right.

As he passed her, he heard her furious voice saying, "You bastard, you've got some nerve abandoning me, your fiancée, like that!"

It seemed like someone had left her behind, but she passed Sumiaki without noticing his presence. Thinking she lived in the area, he called her from behind. "Miss, can you give me some directions?"

He himself was surprised at how suspicious he sounded, so it made sense that the girl was surprised. She lifted her face, suddenly jumping and backing away.

"W-wait, please. I don't mean you any harm. My name is Sumiaki Okajima, and I think I live around here, but I don't know how to get home."

The girl looked at him without moving a muscle. As he was thinking about what else he could say to clear up any misunderstanding, the girl seemed to realize something and looked at him in bewilderment. "Sir... You don't know what has happened to you?"

"What do you mean?"

"There's nothing I can do for you. Of course, there's nothing anyone else in the world could do for you, either. But... Well, is there anything you have left to say in the end? To your family or friends? You have someone, right, sir?"

"What in the world are you saying?"

"I'm not saying this because I want to. But Rentaro says it's my duty to tell the person, so that's why I'm telling you, sir."

Their conversation wasn't meshing properly. Sir? This girl that barely came up to Sumiaki's chest was looking at him with what seemed like pity in her upturned eyes.

"You have not realized, after all? Then you should take a look at yourself. But do it slowly, so as not to fall into a panic. Then you will understand my words."

Overpowered by the mysterious resignation the girl emitted, Sumiaki looked at himself. "What the... What is this?" His abdomen was dyed red. No, it wasn't just his abdomen. He had a large wound that looked like he was ripped open up to his collarbone or throat, and there was still fresh blood flowing from it. His blood was dripping and forming a puddle on the paved road where he was standing.

Gingerly touching his abdomen with his hand, he felt a slippery, unpleasant sensation. Why didn't he notice until now? Why didn't it hurt, anyway? What had happened to him? Just then, his vision took

a turn for the worse, and it looked like the sky and the earth switched places. The next thing he knew, Sumiaki had collapsed on the ground. "I...remember. That's right, I became penniless, and then..."

In the countless job interviews Sumiaki had gone to, his character would occasionally be attacked, and he would be tormented by frustration that made him grind his teeth. Eventually, he was hired as a solar cell module cleaner. It was hard work, but he was guaranteed a certain wage, so once his life settled down, he might even be able to bring his wife and daughter back to live with him. It was still just a dream, and his goal for the time being was just to put his life back together, but once he realized there were still things that he could do, his body was filled with excitement.

He wanted to at least hear their voices. Thinking that, he had gone out to the balcony of his apartment to call his wife's parents' house. In the few rings it took for the other side to answer, Sumiaki looked up suddenly, which might have been the most unfortunate thing he did in his life.

There was a giant, human-size organism stuck to the wall on the fourth floor. It seemed to choose the moment Sumiaki noticed it to move, and its two eyes flashed red like fresh blood as it climbed down.

"I ran away after almost being killed by that Gastrea, and got all the way here."

"You have infectious Gastrea in your bodily fluids," the girl said in an emotionless voice.

Sumiaki looked at the marks left by two fangs on his collar. "Oh," a resigned sound leaked out of his throat.

He remembered what he saw many times on TV during the war. A lab rat was injected with the Gastrea virus, and minutes later became a terrifyingly strange-looking creature that scared audiences out of their wits when it gave a cry.

After the girl pointed it out, his calf started to itch, and his body grew hot, tormented by a pressure that was bursting out from the inside. His DNA was probably being rewritten at high speed that very second. The next thing he knew, his eyes welled with tears. "Then you're a civil officer's...?"

"Yes, I am an Initiator. My name is Enju Aihara. I'm ten, and old enough to be a real lady."

He tried to smile, but his face twisted with a spasm. His body was already starting to move on its own. "I have a favor to ask… Will you apologize to my wife and daughter for me? Tell them I'm sorry for everything I did."

"I will."

That was the last of the world Sumiaki saw. Just like that, he passed the critical point where he could stay in human form. Just as it seemed like his arms and legs were shriveling faster than common sense would allow, long, thin, pitch-black legs sprang out from his body as if piercing through it. Hair sprouted from the legs, and four pairs of glowing red eyes appeared on the head. His abdomen swelled up like a ball, and from the corners of his mouth, two glistening fangs grew in. The yellow-and-black spotted pattern would fill a human with a visceral disgust. This was a giant spider.

The petite girl didn't scream or run away. She just quietly readied herself. Then, she was interrupted by a voice from a completely different direction. "Gastrea—Model Spider, Stage One, confirmed. Entering battle with it now!"

"Rentaro!" said the girl.

"Enju, you okay?"

Enju ran to him. Rentaro also ran toward her with his arms spread wide. Even if it was just for a short time, the two had been apart, and under the slowly setting sun, in a flood of emotions, they reunited with an embrace—an embrace Enju would under no circumstances allow, as she let loose a kick straight at Rentaro's crotch.

"Owwwwww…" Holding his crotch, Rentaro went to his knees and put his forehead to the ground. Writhing with an intense pain unknown to any woman, Rentaro clenched his teeth and lifted his face. The girl, Enju Aihara, 145 centimeters tall, was looking down arrogantly at him with her hands on her hips.

"You have some nerve shamelessly showing your face in front of me again after throwing me off the bicycle."

"A-are you mad?"

"Of course I am."

"I-I had no choice. If I didn't get this job, Kisara would have kicked my butt, you know!"

"I would do the same if you abandoned me."

"Then what am I supposed to do?"

"You should just offer your buttocks quietly. Then the only remaining problem would be who is going to kick it. You can choose who will kick it."

"Dummy, who wants to choose between two options like that?"

The two were interrupted once again by the roar of a gunshot. Arriving late to the scene was Tadashima, holding a smoking revolver in his hand. "Hey, you two! Are you ignoring the enemy to do a comedy sketch? Do your job, civsec!"

The newly born Gastrea's skin spurted blood when the bullet hit it, but in the next instant, it began healing with terrifying speed, and finally spit out the .38-caliber bullets that Tadashima had fired from the healed wound. The Gastrea turned its head toward Tadashima and let out a shrill cry. Not good.

Rentaro decided it was faster to rush over and knock Tadashima to the ground than it was to yell at him to duck.

"*Oof!* What're you doin—"

The giant spider lowered itself and jumped, scraping the area the two had just been with incredible force. Tadashima's face paled.

"Inspector, this is a single-factor Jumping Spider Gastrea."

"J-jumping spider?"

"The original is a spider that can jump tens of times its body length to get food. You can tell from the characteristic coloring on its body. Also"—Rentaro took Tadashima's revolver—"regular bullets are not that effective against Gastrea. If you shoot at them, you'll just make them excited, so you're not supposed to use them."

"Then how are you supposed to defeat them?!"

Just then, a dark shadow covered them, and Tadashima let out a short scream.

The smell of rotten eggs hit their noses, and Rentaro turned around slowly after feeling a chill run up his back. There was the giant spider with all eight legs opened wide. Opening and closing its mouthparts and fangs with venom glands on them, its stomach faced him. Its physical form and flashy coloring brought on a visceral feeling of disgust, and its spinnerets made a grating sound.

Seeming to suddenly notice something, the Gastrea quickly turned its body to face the small girl. Pointing its spinneret at the girl, it trembled and suddenly covered the girl's body with something that looked like a casting net, and changed positions.

"Eww, what is this? It's rather sticky."

The girl tried pulling at it with her hands, but whenever she did, the viscous threads wound themselves around her more.

At that moment, Rentaro glanced sharply at the glowing, slimy green strands, completely unlike a normal spider's silk. It was the same as the stuff he had seen in the victim Sumiaki Okajima's house.

"Get down, Enju!"

"Huh?"

The girl couldn't react to the quick order. Her frail body was thrown to the side, and she flew almost twenty meters, scraping the ground so violently that she left a mark.

"Enju!" Rentaro shouted as he quickly drew his gun from his belt and pulled the trigger. His arm jumped with the recoil from the intense discharge. The second the bullet hit, the Gastrea let out a loud scream and tried to protect itself with its eight legs as it retreated. There was no sign of the wound starting to heal itself.

*All right, this is good*, thought Rentaro to himself. He fired again. He fired bullets continuously at the spot where a leg had been blown off and its body was shaking violently off balance. Its hard exoskeleton ripped open, its bodily fluids gushed out, and the .40-caliber bullet drilled a black hole in its mark.

Rentaro fired about ten shots before the gun's slide release stopped, telling him that it was out of bullets. In the distance, the Gastrea's body was curled into a ball, and it didn't even twitch. Approaching it carefully, he saw that one shot had taken one of its venomous fangs off, along with part of its face. But then Rentaro stopped. *Oh?* he thought. Not only had less than half of his bullets hit, but there was also no trace of any bullets hitting the vital organs. He gulped. He had a bad feeling about this.

In that instant, the spider jumped up and uncovered its venom glands, rushing straight at Rentaro. His body couldn't react quickly enough to the surprise attack. Rentaro was hit, and his body stiffened.

Just then, with the sound of a fierce impact, the Gastrea's body was thrown alongside the ground, bouncing once, crashing into the stone wall next to him, destroying it and making the utility pole collapse along with it, blowing up a great pile of dust. For a second, he didn't understand what had happened. "Oh, was that you, Enju?" he said finally.

Enju stood where the Gastrea had just been a moment ago, a proud look on her face. "Hah! You're always letting down your guard too soon, Rentaro. I cannot bear to watch you."

Tadashima's mouth opened and closed, but no sound came out. He surely couldn't believe that this slight girl's kick had sent flying the sixty-kilogram Gastrea that had been there a moment ago.

On the outside, the girl didn't really look any different from a normal girl—except for one thing. Her eyes, black until just a moment ago, were now shining red. She had crimson eyes, just like the Gastrea.

The shock on Tadashima's face slowly turned to understanding. "Ah, so this kid's the Initiator."

"I'm Rentaro's partner, Enju Aihara. Remember that, you public servant," she informed him deliberately, with a triumphant look. Her arrogance was improper for her age, yet at the same time charmingly beautiful.

Rentaro had learned his lesson after the ten-year-old girl pointed out his worthlessness, and reloaded before he approached the Gastrea with his gun out. Stretching its many legs up toward the sky, the spider gave a final spasm, and then was really dead.

Rentaro turned toward Tadashima and bowed his head seriously. "Sorry, Inspector. I let my guard down because it was a Stage One."

"Hey, wait, weren't you going on earlier about how regular bullets weren't effective on Gastrea?" asked Tadashima.

Rentaro turned to face Tadashima. It wasn't really a secret, so Rentaro didn't say a word. He just showed his spare magazine—or rather, the bullets in it.

Tadashima's small eyes widened in understanding. "I see, they're Varanium bullets."

Rentaro nodded and took one out, rolling it on his palm to show him. The tip of the golden cartridge—the Varanium-black bullet—reflected the setting sun sharply. "As you know, this is made of the metal Varanium, which inhibits the Gastrea's ability to heal wounds."

*And it's because we have this that mankind has barely been able to avoid extinction*, he thought inwardly. The Gastrea hated this metal vehemently, and if they were thrown into a room lined with it, they were said to waste away and die.

"There are things you can do to a bullet, too, huh?" asked Tadashima.

"There are civsec officers who stand out more with swords and spears made of this metal, but mine is a bullet. The bullets are special, but the gun is just an ordinary gun," Rentaro said. "Look." He held out the XD he used to show him, and Tadashima put his hand on his chin and looked impressed.

Suddenly, Rentaro felt a few light tugs on the sleeve of his uniform and turned to see Enju smiling and vigorously pointing at herself. "I know, I know. You were amazing. Good job. And you saved my life. That's what you wanted to hear, right?"

"I also have something to say to you." Enju beckoned him, so Rentaro had no choice but to lean in to her eye level. He figured she just wanted to tell him that his finishing move was too weak, or that he should get stronger, which made him want to sigh.

Then, he found his head being quickly rotated, and like a surprise attack, something soft pressed against his lips.

*Wha—?!* His body stiffened, and Enju moved away in a flash, hands clasped behind her back bashfully.

She laughed. "Thanks, Rentaro. You still have a long way to go as my partner, but when I let my guard down, you stood in the way of the enemy alone. That was kind of cool."

"Y-you…"

"What, did you want to do it more? If it's you, you can do some other things, too."

Rentaro felt the blush rising in his cheeks. "I… Idiot! Don't even say that kind of stuff as a joke! What'll you do if there are people around who misundersta—"

Feeling a sudden chill on the back of his neck, he turned and saw Tadashima pull handcuffs from his hip and sidle over.

"You've got some strange tastes, you pig," said Tadashima.

Rentaro broke out in a cold sweat. Tadashima continued glaring at him.

"Recently, there's been an idiot playing pranks on girls in the area. His physique is about the same as yours, and his weight is about the same as yours, too… What do you think about that?"

"Y-you've gotta be kidding me. It's a misunderstanding, a false accusation! I plead not guilty!"

"I'll hear what you have to say at the station."

"Y-you bastard!"

Rentaro and Tadashima chased after each other around Enju.

"E-Enju, please! Say something!"

Enju puffed her chest out as if to tell everyone to listen to her. "We have a deep relationship that cannot be summed up in one word."

Tadashima cocked his revolver. What? Was he going to be shot dead?

"She's a freeloader!" said Rentaro.

"He's always so amazing at night that I can't sleep," said Enju.

"I toss and turn in my sleep!"

"Our futures are sworn to each other."

"No, they're not!"

Tadashima looked back and forth from Rentaro to Enju, comparing them. Finally, he put the handcuffs away. "Man, I was gonna put a pair of shiny bracelets on you, too."

"P-please stop, Inspector. Your joke's going too far."

Rentaro drew a deep breath as his gaze dropped to Enju's back. The skin on her back was peeled off, and it was completely red. It must have happened when she took the blow from that thing's body earlier and scraped her back against the ground.

"Does it hurt, Enju?" he asked.

The girl snorted with triumphant eyes and looked at him unwaveringly. "I'm fine. It'll heal soon. I'm more angry about my clothes being ruined. It even broke one of the straps of my camisole."

As if to back up the girl's words, what she said came to pass. The painful-looking scratches that covered her back got smaller as they all watched. Eventually, the wounds healed as if nothing had happened, and all that was left was the beautiful, smooth skin of a young girl, along with her ripped clothes.

Looking at Tadashima's gaping mouth from the corner of his eye, Rentaro thought, *That's the normal reaction.*

An ordinary human would first get a scab over the wound, and then the wound would slowly heal over time under that. The fact that she skipped that process when her wound healed emphasized the fact that she was no ordinary human.

Superhuman powers of healing. That was one of the benefits they had as Initiators—girls who could control the Gastrea virus under certain conditions. The extraordinary muscular strength and agility they possessed also fell into that category. And when she was not using her powers, like now, her eyes were always black.

Rentaro was a Promoter, someone who supported the Initiators, and he had the responsibility of directing her onto the right path. "Oh yeah, Enju. You talked to the victim before he experienced shape collapse, right? Did he say anything?"

"Yes, he said to say 'hi' to his wife and daughter."

"I see..." Rentaro looked at his watch, straightened his back, and gave Tadashima a salute. "On April 28, 2031, at 1630 hours, Initiator Enju Aihara and Promoter Rentaro Satomi eliminated the Gastrea."

"Good work, civil officers."

Even if it was ritualistic, Rentaro bowed back at the highest-ranking officer on the scene. Exchanging glances with Tadashima, they both let smiles escape.

At that point, an innocent voice that didn't understand what it meant to read the situation broke the mood.

"Hey, more importantly, are you going to make it back in time for the sale?"

"Huh...? Oh!" Rentaro hurriedly pulled out the day's insert flyer from his pocket. The blood drained from his face.

"Oh, you're going already?" asked Tadashima.

"Yeah, if you've got more work, let me know."

Tadashima seemed to be mumbling something for some reason. "Well, you know, that...when you, uh, helped me earlier... Oh, never mind. Anyway, what's the important business you're rushing off to?"

"Bean sprouts are six yen a bag!"

Watching the young man's shadow as he ran away, followed by the playful smaller shadow following him like a puppy, Shigetoku Tadashima grumbled. "Bean sprouts...?"

He had thought about thanking him for protecting him earlier, but it seemed silly now.

"You made it out in one piece, Chief?"

Turning around, he saw his subordinates who had split up to search for the Gastrea start arriving late to the scene.

"They looked like new faces. Do you think we can use them?"

"Who knows. Speaking of which, I forgot to ask for their IP Rank." Tadashima pulled out a cigarette from his chest pocket almost unconsciously and lit it. Seeing that, his younger subordinates gazed at the cigarette without a word.

"You gonna work with the cigarette in your mouth?" one said.

"Don't be so stuffy. I almost died just now." Ignoring his subordinate's knit eyebrows, he took a deep puff into his lungs and blew it out. It had been clear all day, so even the Monoliths standing far in the distance could be seen in one glance. The enormous rectangular walls standing 1.618 kilometers high and one kilometer wide dotted the scene like steel towers at regular intervals. Even though they seemed out of place in the natural landscape, there was also a feeling of reverence for them for some reason.

Within the Monolith barrier that completely surrounded a portion of the Kanto Plain was one of the last paradises left for mankind. What looked like a forest of black chrome stone blocks were actually slabs of metal made of Varanium. They were the same as what surrounded the Kanto Plain, extending into Old Tokyo, Old Kanagawa, Old Chiba, and Old Saitama.

Gastrea hated Varanium. With the special magnetic field given off by Varanium acting as a natural barrier, Tokyo Area was able to avoid large-scale Gastrea attacks. To put it another way, outside of the five remaining areas in Japan including Tokyo, the rest of the land was teeming with nonhuman monsters and nonhuman monsters that used to be human. If a mere human were to take one step outside of the Monolith, he would either be devoured in an instant or end up as one of them.

And this wasn't just happening in Japan.

Before Tadashima knew it, forensics and other police had gathered, gathering evidence and putting up caution tape that said KEEP OUT.

Ten years ago, these Gastrea began to appear around the world, and with their infectious capacity, their destruction of humanity accelerated with incredible momentum. One infected person became two, two became four, four became eight... When humanity finally began to worry about the multiplying Gastrea, it was already too late. There was nothing they could do.

All the countries that suffered damage during the large-scale war used the Monoliths, which were barely good enough for practical use, to build barriers. Now, ten years later, they continued to desperately barricade themselves with them.

Humanity lost the Great Gastrea World War.

The cigarette smoke that rose into the air soon dispersed in the setting sun.

In those ten years, Japan had healed the wounds of its defeat and finally gotten its cultural compass back to the levels of the early 2020s.

Tadashima crushed the shortened cigarette butt with his foot and looked out of the corner of his eye at his subordinate, who was moving briskly to the scene.

Occasionally, to prevent a Pandemic, they would have to hunt an early-stage Gastrea that had wandered in. At first, that was the job of the police and the riot squads under their command, or the self-defense force, but now, civsec had a firm hold on a large share of the fighting jobs. The police were left to deal with the aftermath.

Feeling the thick spring air on his skin, Tadashima looked at the two disappearing backs with uncharacteristic sentimentality. Initiator and Promoter. Fighters who came in pairs. They used the power mastered by their bodies to fight the Gastrea.

They were mankind's last hope.

2

"Do you have anything left to say before you die, Satomi? Do you?"

Cold sweat ran down Rentaro's cheek, and he backed away from the voice, but his back was soon against the wall.

The girl with the dangerous-sounding voice had a frown on her face and her arms crossed, and her foot tapped impatiently. He knew that this would happen. She was extremely angry.

In front of Rentaro's eyes was a beauty in black. In sharp contrast with her smooth skin white as light snowfall, her long straight hair was jet-black. The only places where her skin was exposed were her face, the nape of her neck, her hands, and the part of her thigh that could be seen between her skirt and her high socks. Everything else was covered in black with the school uniform of Miwa Girls Academy, and other than the red ribbon tied at her chest, it could be said that she was completely black and white. Her turned-up almond eyes were sharp. She was cute when she smiled, but she was usually in a sullen mood, which seemed like kind of a waste.

Rentaro was trying his best to protest while being overpowered, but he kept his voice low. "Wh-what's done is done, right?"

"You moron!" Her shouting echoed in the small, cramped room, and when Rentaro avoided her sharp punch at the last moment, she seemed to snarl as she glared at him.

"Why did you dodge? You're making me angry."

"Don't be unreasonable!"

When Rentaro made a move to escape, the girl followed, fists flying, chasing him around the reception area's furniture.

*Damn it, the whole day's been like this.*

"The only thing…you're good at…is running…" The girl had no stamina and shortly fell back, her shoulders heaving as she caught her breath.

"C'mon, I'll work hard when we get a new job, all right, Kisara?" said Rentaro.

"Don't be stupid! This was our last chance!" the girl said. "And," she continued, glaring at Rentaro, "at work, you are to call me 'President,' not Kisara." Flipping her long hair, she briskly returned to her work desk. "Useless thing," she said as she sat in her office chair.

Rentaro sighed. When he got back to the office, it wouldn't be a mere butt-kicking waiting for him, it was an iron-fisted punishment that knew no moral bounds.

There was a large ebony work desk about the size of a grand piano and a well-tanned leather office chair. Seeing a girl wearing a sailor school uniform sitting there looked very strange.

Kisara Tendo. The youngest daughter of the Tendo family that took Rentaro in ten years earlier, and the president of the Civil Security Agency, that Rentaro worked for.

"In other words, is this what happened? You rushed off to buy the sale items that are sitting on that desk right now, and didn't realize until you were halfway there that you had forgotten to get paid by the police?"

"Yeah...," Rentaro mumbled brusquely as he averted his gaze.

He had hurriedly called Tadashima, who said, "What? I thought for sure that it was a pro bono service you were doin' for us. Well, what's done is done, so why don't we just call it a free trial? If more jobs come up, I'll make sure to work you good and hard!" he said, laughing as he hung up.

Kisara rested her chin on her knee and continued with a look of displeasure on her face. "And then all you bought were two bags of bean sprouts?"

"Y-yeah! It was limited to one bag per person, so I brought Enju and bought two!" Wondering what kind of report he was giving, he searched for something else to talk about. "Do you want some, too?"

A bag of bean sprouts flew right into his face.

"Come on, Satomi, we've had zero income this month. Whose fault do you think that is, you useless, good-for-nothing fool? Besides, is the supermarket time sale more important to you than your report to your boss?"

Suddenly, Kisara started trembling with her hand still in a fist. But instead of a punch, she put both hands on the table and stood up. "Most importantly, why didn't you tell me about the limited-time sale?!"

As if on cue, Kisara's stomach growled, and the girl collapsed on her chair, holding her stomach. Her eyes were blank. "I can't take this any longer. I want beefsteak..."

"I do too, you know," said Rentaro.

Kisara was currently living on her own, separated from the Tendo family, so even though she looked rich, her wallet was empty. "Hey, Satomi," she said.

"What is it?" said Rentaro.

"Get to work."

"Ugh, I'm getting spasms from my chronic disease."

"They'll stop if you work."

Kisara looked down at the rush-hour traffic from the third-floor window of Happy Building, where the Tendo Civil Security Agency was a tenant. She shook her head gently and sighed. "Owning a business is harder than I thought it would be."

"Did you think it would be easy?"

"Playing the stock market or foreign exchange is easier. Just moving things from the right side to the left side results in a profit margin. But a business is completely hopeless. That's also because you're an unreliable moron, Satomi."

"You don't think it's because the second-floor tenant is a cabaret and the first floor is a gay bar? The fourth is a loan shark, you know."

"You don't get it, do you? Location doesn't matter to a truly good company."

*Was that how it was?* Rentaro thought. "We should just pass out flyers or tissues and advertise on the streets," he said aloud.

"Boring. Doing average things will only bring average results. If we're going to do something, we need something with more impact."

"Then why don't you wear a maid outfit and pass out flyers?" He meant that because Kisara had extremely good raw material to work with, ten out of ten people would turn to look at her, but apparently Kisara did not get that. Her face turned red and the vein on her temple bulged.

"I am a Tendo! Are you telling me to imitate those lowly waitresses and hostesses? I will do no such thing! You should run into a crowd and shout 'Tendo Civil Security Agency is right here!' while setting yourself on fire or blowing yourself up!"

"That's terrorism…" Rentaro was half-shocked as he looked around. "But, President, seriously, let's hire another employee."

Even if it was small and cramped, the Tendo Civil Security Agency rented out a whole floor for its offices, and having just Rentaro and Enju as its only two employees was too much of a waste.

"I will if there's someone I think I can use," Kisara said curtly and snapped her fingers to change the subject. "Satomi, make some tea."

"Do it yourself," he said.

"Oh my, what idiot was it that forgot to get paid again?"

"Damn it. Okay, okay. I shall bring it directly, Miss."

Wondering how she could still put on such airs when she was so poor, Rentaro poured hot water into the teapot and put it on Kisara's desk.

"Oh, thanks," Kisara said, but didn't look as she continued typing on her laptop with her delicate white fingers, but when she looked up for a second, their eyes met. "Hey, the Gastrea you defeated was an infected, right?"

"Yeah," he said brusquely, and continued, answering what she left unasked. "We couldn't find the source of the infection, but it was probably the same Model Spider Factor. Since it wasn't a bird or winged insect type, another company probably found it and took care of it already. If it were above Stage Three, we would've been called in to help. Besides, the biohazard alarm didn't go off, either."

The single-factor Gastrea that Rentaro had defeated was just a scaled-up version of an animal on Earth, so it was still almost cute. With two or more factors, and especially with four or more, the DNA was so mixed up that the resulting Gastrea could only be called a monster.

For Gastrea in Stages One through Four, as their stage numbers increased, their strength rose exponentially. So even though the employees of the various civsec companies were by no means friends, if they were in a situation they felt was more than they could handle, they would work together to exterminate it. Because there was no request for help, the source Gastrea must have been easily exterminated.

Dropping her gaze to the computer display, Kisara rejected Rentaro's opinion. "There are no reports to that effect, or any eyewitness reports at all."

"What?" said Rentaro.

Kisara turned her laptop 180 degrees. On the screen was a map. It was from the civil officer agency website, and it showed where there had been fights with and sightings of the Gastrea over the past ninety days.

"This is…" Rentaro scowled and looked at Kisara, who nodded slowly.

"There aren't any reports, are there?" she said.

"But there's no way there wasn't a single eyewitness report of a source, right?"

"There isn't one here." Kisara brushed back her hair and looked at him provocatively with upturned eyes.

Rentaro narrowed his eyes and looked at the map and the words on the website again. "Why isn't the government sending out a warning to the whole region? This is a serious matter."

"Satomi, the government is not incompetent, but they hardly ever use coercive means like evacuation orders, so there's no point in getting your hopes up. I mean, that's why we civil officers exist."

*It really is a terrible job*, he thought, clucking his tongue. He shook his head lightly. "I need an expert opinion on this. I'll go talk to Doc after this."

"I'll also try asking other civil officers indirectly about it. We'll be hunting the remaining source, too, as soon as possible."

"Roger."

Kisara lowered her beautiful eyelashes and sipped her tea. Rentaro looked sideways at his boss with respect. No matter what she said, she understood that human lives needed to be put first.

Having no way of knowing Rentaro's inner thoughts, Kisara finished working on her computer and closed it, clasping her hands together and stretching. Rentaro could hear her back cracking satisfyingly. He noticed that he was accidentally looking at her generous chest pushing up her sailor school uniform and hurriedly averted his gaze.

"Oh, come to think of it, where's Enju?" asked Kisara.

"Huh?" said Rentaro. "Oh, she said she was getting sleepy, so I took her home first. If you're going home soon, I can walk you partway."

"Sorry, I have hemodialysis today, so I have to go to the hospital."

"Oh yeah, I forgot."

Taking a sip of the half-cooled tea, she surveyed the inside of the office. Rentaro followed her gaze. The reception area furniture for meeting with clients faced the plain desk used by the only employees, Rentaro and Enju. Because there were times when they had to stay overnight, there was also a small kitchen to cook in, hidden behind a curtain. It was shabby and cramped and cold in the winter. It wasn't comfortable by any standard, but strangely enough, she didn't hate it.

"It's been almost a year, hasn't it?" she said. "Since you became a Promoter and met Enju."

"It's *only* been a year," he replied. "We're still not even halfway to our goal."

Kisara tilted her head slightly to the side and smiled. "Satomi, you really have changed since you met Enju. You've started to smile more, and you can cook now. I never would have imagined you could turn out this way."

Rentaro turned his head sulkily. "I'm not *that* different."

"Hey, Satomi. What's your goal now?"

"Huh?" His heart suddenly skipped a beat.

"To find Enju's parents for her? Satomi, have you given up on your own mother and father? You said it a lot when we were kids, didn't you? That your mom and dad were definitely still alive and that you'd find them. But I haven't heard you say it recently. Do you really still believe it even now?"

She wasn't particularly angry or blaming him, she was just looking at him. But Rentaro couldn't bear it any longer and shook his head. "It doesn't matter, does it?" He tried to speak calmly, but a harshness remained that sounded like he was spitting out the words. "You just have to know everything, don't you? It's fine. I know that my parents are dead for sure."

*Damn it, now I've done it*, thought Rentaro as he trudged down the night streets.

On the way, a lady from the cabaret on the second floor winked at him and said, "Stop by sometime."

Then, on the first floor, a brawny man with a shaved head and goatee from the gay bar winked and said, "You'd be the best 'top.' Stop by sometime." (Rentaro wasn't really sure what a "top" was, but it seemed to be a gay term.)

And then a little ways from the building, the loan shark from the Hiroshima yakuza greeted him saying, "Yo, Rentaro, today was hot, huh?"

But Rentaro could only give a halfhearted reply to each of them.

When it came to his family history, he was never good at controlling his feelings, but he didn't think that it would make him do something as dumb as taking it out on the people around him. Rentaro put both hands in his pocket and tilted his head as far back as it would go, gazing at the night sky sprinkled with stars. There was no helping it. Tomorrow, he would go back and apologize without becoming too emotional.

Rentaro headed straight for the hospital that was part of Magata University. He had never seen the lights off in the lab building next door to it. Magata University had many departments, from computer science to farming, on its vast grounds. It made the school Rentaro attended, Magata High School, look like a miniature garden. Next to the main school building was the university hospital, although it was actually a slight distance of about three hundred meters away.

The receptionist knew Rentaro and let him in without any questions. The front entryway was open, and the smell of disinfectant hung in the air. The people passing Rentaro in his school uniform (which, because of his chronic cash shortage, also served as his casual clothes and work uniform) all seemed to have unpleasant looks on their faces.

*What? You got a problem with me?* Rentaro thought at them, but he still bowed silently as he passed.

Once he got to the north side of the building, the number of people around dropped suddenly, and there was an abrupt dead end to the hallway where there appeared to be a square hole cut into the ground. At first glance, it looked like a pitfall, but when he looked carefully, he could see that there were steep stairs attached to it.

As he walked down the stairs, he thought about the look people would have on their faces if they heard that a mysterious individual had added a morgue to the university hospital without permission and was living there alongside the corpses. He was sure that the slight chill he felt wasn't just because the temperature had dropped.

A strong mint fragrance wafted through the air as he pushed open the door engraved with grotesque demons with breasts that were probably meant to keep people away. Inside, it was dimly lit but surprisingly spacious. The whole floor was covered with green tile, and even though it was slightly eerie like an operating room, if he looked carefully, he could see underwear and lunch boxes and a chalkboard covered with German or some other foreign language, which gave it an overall lived-in feel.

However, the person this space belonged to was nowhere to be seen.

"Doc, where are you?" Rentaro called out.

"Over here," said a voice.

Turning toward the voice, Rentaro gave a start. In front of him was a naked muscular body over 180 centimeters tall with sunken eye sockets. On the cleanly shaven head were fresh scars from where the skin had been extracted. It was the corpse of a man Rentaro had never seen before.

"Woah!" he shouted. No matter how he thought about it, the voice seeemed like it was coming from this man, but he knew corpses couldn't talk. Rentaro was not very good with scary stories of this genre.

"Boo." From behind the corpse was a woman in a white lab coat who he *did* know, and relief made his knees weak.

"D-don't scare me like that, Doc!"

"Hey, Rentaro. Welcome to the Abyss." She spread her arms wide to complete the performance. She was wearing a tight skirt with a white lab coat so long it dragged on the ground. Her skin was an unhealthy pallor, and her presence was so faint that she seemed like a ghost. She didn't bathe and let her bangs grow so long that they covered one eye, but underneath it all, she was a beauty.

Sumire Muroto. Head of the forensics lab and a Gastrea researcher. She was the queen of this dimly lit basement room and had severe social withdrawal to boot. If left alone, she would stay here for as long as her stockpile of food lasted.

"Who is this man?" Rentaro asked her.

"Charlie," she answered. "I forget his real name. He's my lover."

"Didn't you have a woman named Susan here before?"

"Unfortunately, she is no longer here. He is her replacement. Corpses are great. No idle chatter from them. They are the only ones who understand my feelings." Saying that, she lovingly applied embalming liquid to the corpse's cheek.

Even though he had already given up on trying to understand her, Rentaro scratched his upper arm as he watched the scene with dreary thoughts. Because of her extreme dislike of coming into contact with other people, she was openly ostracized within the school. Her favorite motto was, "In this world, there are only people who have died and people who are going to die."

He needed to take care of his business and leave as quickly as possible. Rentaro started to open his mouth, but Sumire was faster.

"The Stage One Gastrea you defeated was just brought to my lab," she said. "Do you think you can kill a little more cleanly next time? The impact of the bullets injured the flesh. On top of that, the bullets were all over the place. Nobita is a perv and lazy and weak, but at least he's a good shot. You're a perv and lazy and weak and a terrible shot on top of that. You're the worst. Honestly, why haven't you already committed suicide? It's not like you have a hope left in this world, do you?"

"I'm not that hopeless!" Rentaro sighed. This depressing beauty was actually entrusted by the government with the dissection and research of Gastrea, and even though she didn't look it at all, she apparently had a high IQ and was once the darling of the academic world.

"By the way, did you eat dinner yet?" she said.

"Huh?"

"Dinner."

"Not yet…"

"Then eat this, my culinary creation." She stood up and took out a plate from the microwave, unwrapping it. At first glance, it looked like completely white porridge, but it was half-solid, or rather oatmeal-like, and when scooped with a spoon, the closest word to describe it would have been *gloopy*. Rentaro wondered how it had gotten to the point where it smelled like it had gone bad.

Involuntarily, large drops of sweat beaded on his face. "Doc, do you know the food called Tastee Wheat from the movie *The Matrix*?"

"Yeah, that looked delicious, didn't it? Guri and Gura's pancake, Laputa bread, and Tastee Wheat. You could call them the top three on my list of 2-D foods that I want to eat."

"Isn't one of those things not like the others?"

"Huh? Wait, even though a TV screen is flat, *The Matrix* was a live-action movie, so should it be counted as 3-D? What do you think?"

"Oh, I know! Let's talk about work."

"Hurry up and eat. If you don't eat it, I won't tell you anything."

"S-seriously…?" Rentaro looked at the dim ceiling, then gazed at the Tastee Wheat, puzzled. A bubble rose to the surface and popped with a "glop," almost as if it were sneering at him. Chanting a prayer, he put it in his mouth.

*It was unexpectedly good!*

No, that was a dream that could not be. Instead, the next instant, he felt a piercing pain and the collective outrage of his senses. "Gahhh, my throat itches!"

"How is it? Is it good?"

"Does it *look* like it was good?"

Sumire used her thumbs and forefingers like a photographer to form a frame. Peeking through it, she gave a thoughtful nod. "If I were a photographer, I would call it 'Anguish: Trapped Between Hell and Purgatory.'"

"Ugh, on top of being sweet, there's also a gross sourness. What the heck is this?"

"Oh, it's half-melted, but it started as a donut. It came out of the stomach of a corpse."

Rentaro pressed a hand over his mouth.

"The sink is over there."

He tried to throw up all the contents of his stomach. Gagging, he said, "W-wasn't that evidence?!"

"No, the case was already solved. When I asked the inspector in charge if I could eat it, he gave his consent right away."

"That's definitely a lie!"

"You're too concerned about the details."

"It is not! A detail! At all!"

"Oh, I know," she said, changing the subject, "since we've finally got three people here in these wonderful catacombs, let's do something like the Oath of the Peach Garden from the *Three Kingdoms*! 'Even though we were not born on the same day, when we die, let it be on the same day, at the same time.' Oh, but Charlie is already dead." She laughed, amused at her own joke.

*What should I do?* Rentaro thought. *I seriously want to go home.*

"For the cast, Charlie is Guan Yu, you're Liu Bei, and I'll be Zhang Fei. Hey, that unhappy-looking Liu Bei is terrible. I don't sense a shred of personal virtue. It's terribly miscast."

"But a Zhang Fei that can only love corpses is okay?" Rentaro's whole body felt tired. His shoulders drooped.

Sumire laughed happily as she took notes. "All right, let's get down to business. Did you want to hear my autopsy report on the organism you killed?"

"Doc, the source—I think it's probably the same Model Spider Factor, but there have been no eyewitness or extermination reports. At this rate, there will be more victims. I want to exterminate it as soon as possible. If it were to go into hiding, where do you think it would be?"

"Let's see." Sumire started to play around, spinning in her chair and crossing and uncrossing her legs. "One possibility is that it opened the lid of a manhole and went underground, shutting the lid firmly behind it."

Rentaro raised his eyebrows. "With those spider's legs?"

"It's got twice as many limbs as a human. Wouldn't that actually make it easier?"

"'Gastrea are not intelligent organisms. They are simply lower life-forms that act on their natural instincts.' Isn't that what the textbooks say?"

Sumire shook her head, as if saying "Oh dear" and spread her hands. "For some reason, it's become the accepted theory in Japan that Gastrea are not intelligent, but it's been proven that this is mostly wrong. In the West, the opposite is the accepted theory."

"Well, that's what I think, too...," said Rentaro. "But while your hiding underground theory seems to be on the right track, I don't think that's quite it. Recently, even the sewer system has security cameras equipped with night vision. If it's as you say and the Gastrea ran underground, it would've been caught by those devices."

"Oh, when did Japan become so advanced? I suppose being down here, I don't know enough of what's going on in the world. Hmm, the DNA of the source of the infection this time was overwritten with that of a jumping spider, huh...?" She looked at him. "Now that I think of it, you know a lot about animals in general, don't you?"

Rentaro scratched his head and looked down, muttering to himself. "Well, I just know a little about natural science and ethology, that's all. It started because I liked Fabre's *Souvenirs Entomologiques*, and it kind of continued from there..."

She laughed at him. "I get it. You were the type who had no friends, so you watched bugs instead, right? You were pleased when you submerged an anthill with water, weren't you?" Her voice changed a little. "'Hah, drown! It's Noah's great flood! Know the wrath of God!'"

"Is that supposed to be me? Don't just make stuff up!"

Sumire rested her chin on her elbow, which was on the armrest, and grinned broadly. "Anyway, you're a real wimp. With such a gloomy hobby, you won't be able to catch Kisara's eye. If you like her, you should make her yours by sheer strength."

Rentaro scowled. Why'd she start talking about this? "Doc, didn't you know? Kisara is a master of the Tendo Martial Arts Sword Drawing Style. I'm only at the beginning level, so I'd just be killed. Her kidneys are failing, though, so she can only move for short amounts of time and does mostly office work now."

When they were little, Kisara often protected Rentaro, who was bullied a lot by her older brothers at the Tendo house, but he didn't like

how she'd treated him as a servant ever since then. Even though he'd gotten strong enough to protect her now…

"Oh? Ah well, let's get back to the topic at hand," said Sumire. "Do you know the distinguishing trait of a jumping spider?"

"Its coloring, isn't it?" said Rentaro. "And it's famous for jumping to catch its prey."

Sumire pulled out her own Tastee Wheat from the microwave and suddenly thrust a spoonful into her mouth. *Eww!* Rentaro thought as he watched her.

"That's right," she said. "You know, of course, that even if it became human size, the jumping spider, which uses its powerful jump to capture prey, would not be able to maintain the jumping distance of ten times its body size, right?"

"Yeah—uh, wait, really?"

"Hey now, get yourself together," said Sumire. "They say that if a flea were human size, it would be able to jump as high as the Tokyo Tower, but if a flea were actually to become that big, never mind its jumping ability—it wouldn't even be able to support its own body weight with those legs, and it wouldn't be able to get enough oxygen through cutaneous respiration. It's the same thing. Based on the law of gravity and the principle of scale, it's pretty obvious that such a creature should not exist. But the Gastrea virus turns that idea on its head."

The woman in the white lab coat stopped talking for a moment and smiled enigmatically.

Rentaro remained silent, urging her to go on. This wasn't entomology anymore, it was physics. There was no place for the layman Rentaro to interrupt.

"When a Gastrea transforms, the hardness of its exoskeleton and its body functions increase to match its size. That's why the larger the Gastrea, the harder and stronger it is. The Gastrea virus, which redesigns living organisms, is a threat. In principle, it is very similar to the reverse transcription of a retrovirus, but it doesn't just replicate copies of itself—after analyzing its host's DNA, it reconstructs it into its most suitable form.

"The problem is the speed at which this occurs. The corrosion speed of a Gastrea virus overwriting DNA is outside of the standard of all the living organisms on the Earth. Dawkins would probably piss his pants. If you told me that that it's not from this planet, I'd believe you.

"And once its corrosion exceeds fifty percent inside the host's body, the host is no longer able to maintain human form, and goes through the process of shape collapse, resulting in the host becoming a Gastrea. Through that process, some individuals gain original abilities that should not exist. Get it? It's an evolutionary leap through mutation."

Before Rentaro knew it, Sumire's plate was empty. *What in the world is wrong with her sense of taste?*

"That was a long tangent, but the missing source could possess some sort of new ability, you know," she said.

"Since we haven't been able to find it, could it be some kind of optical camouflage?" Rentaro suggested.

"It could be a simpler mimicry camouflage, like a chameleon. If it really had the ability to distort light, Tokyo Area could be annihilated by a Pandemic tomorrow, even."

"Don't worry. Enju and I, as Initiator and Promoter, exist to prevent that from happening."

"Enju, huh?"

"What is it?"

"I find the Cursed Children especially creepy. Especially once I found out about their origins. Ten years ago, at almost exactly the same time the Gastrea virus first appeared in the world, children in the womb with Gastrea-controlling factors were born, as if to oppose them. At first, a big deal was made of them being a gift from God to control the Gastrea, but in the end, that was completely wrong."

Sumire looked like she was dreaming as she squinted in the air and let her gaze wander.

"The only way for an ordinary person to contract the Gastrea virus and become a monster is through the blood. Aerosol, or airborne infection, is not believed to occur. There were also many experiments that confirmed that infection did not occur orally or through sexual intercourse.

"However, when the virus entered orally, it did not die immediately, and if it happened to enter a pregnant woman's mouth, then the child in her womb stored up the virus before it was born.

"The Cursed Children had red eyes when they were born, but appeared normal otherwise. In other words, even though they were infected with the Gastrea virus, the progress of the disease was extremely slow. If we think about the fact that normal people who are infected with a large amount of Gastrea virus at once change shape almost immediately, the fact that these girls' bodies don't change shape for years is miraculous. It is extremely interesting. See? I explained it without using a lot of technical jargon. Even an idiot like you can understand the gist of it, right?"

"Yeah, I wish you'd always talk like that…," said Rentaro.

She'd stuck in plenty of nasty asides, but he was able to understand the general concept, thanks to her. *Mimicry camouflage, huh?* No matter what you might say about her, she was pretty amazing.

"Well, I'll be going then, Doc."

Sumire smiled as she gave a light wave to see him off. "Come again, FBI Agent Starling."

"So we're gender-bending now, Dr. Lecter?"

"Rentaro, you are late!"

When he returned to his dear apartment, the window of the second-floor bathroom suddenly opened, and out with the bath steam came Enju, leaning her upper body out of the frame. He was glad that she was welcoming him with her face wreathed with a smile, waving her hands, but he couldn't condone her doing so while she was obviously naked and in the middle of taking a bath.

"Hey, idiot, what if someone's looking?" he shouted back to her. "Close the window."

"Don't worry. My body belongs only to you!"

"Will you please try to understand what I'm saying? I'm saying it's embarrassing for *me*!"

Rentaro ran up the stairs and thrust his key into the door of the corner room on the second floor. He flew into his eight-tatami, one-room home, and when he got to the changing room, he could hear the sound of the shower and see the silhouette of Enju's slender body. It was a modest bodyline, but thin and supple and very beautiful.

He was flustered for a moment, but when he noticed the piece of paper that said "You can peek if you want" in Enju's messy handwriting taped to the bathroom door, his strength left him all at once and he sank to the floor.

He could hear a voice from the bath. "You are late. Were you doing something naughty with Kisara?"

Rentaro plunked down and crossed his arms. "Shut up. She beat me up and told me to get to work."

Enju laughed. "She would. That's what I thought happened, as well."

"You're an evil freeloader."

"Anyway, is dinner ready yet? My stomach feels like it's caving in."

*Okay, okay,* he thought as he picked up the clothes Enju had shed with abandon and put them in the laundry hamper with his own dirty clothes, then took them to the coin laundry on the first floor. There didn't seem to be anyone else around, so he decided to use the machine that worked the best, the newest one in the back.

Rentaro thought that Enju wouldn't want her clothes to be washed with his, but unexpectedly she had said, "Imagining you getting excited about wearing clothes that were washed with my underwear is fun," and said it was fine. They were being washed with detergent, so there was nothing to get excited about, but it still meant he could wash them all in one load, so he let her believe what she wanted.

Thinking there was no way anyone would steal their clothes, he went back to the room and opened the fridge. He lined up the ingredients they had, including the bean sprouts they had bought, and thought for a moment.

Today, he would make egg-topped rice out of the eggs, braised burdock and carrot out of the burdock root and slightly old carrot, and fry the bean sprouts with the bit of cabbage that was left over. Once he figured out what to make, he knew the rest of the work would go quickly. He put a pink apron on over his school uniform and started cooking at lightning speed. Before he knew it, he was humming merrily away as he manipulated his long cooking chopsticks.

There was one time when Enju pestered him into letting her cook, but the result tasted so bad that he'd wanted to spit it out, so he had firmly sworn that he would never let her in the kitchen again. Sumire's cooking not only tasted bad, but she also used unknown ingredients that gave it an unearthly feel. When Kisara cooked, the kitchen went up in flames.

Why did all the women around him completely lack cooking abilities? Just once, he wanted to meet a woman who could make a miso soup that tasted better than his.

With those thoughts floating around in his mind, the sauce of the last dish, the braised burdock and carrot, turned golden. He turned off the heat, removed his apron, and looked at the clock. It was eight p.m.

As he returned from getting the clothes downstairs, Enju had just finished her long bath. When she saw the kitchen, she said, "Ooh!" and jumped, reacting like the kid she was.

"Wait, don't eat yet," said Rentaro.

Enju turned to look at him like she was about to bite. "Why can't I? When I came home, I gargled and washed my hands!"

"That's not it."

"I took the neighborhood circular next door like I was supposed to, and I didn't doodle on it like last time."

"I said, that's not it."

"I didn't watch more than three hours of TV today!"

"That's not it, either."

"I'm not on trash duty today, am I?"

"That's not it, Enju. Please, just notice!"

The small head couldn't take it any longer and began to roar. "Just give me my food! Are you trying to starve me to death?!"

Enju seemed to notice something at that point, and her face turned bright red as she looked at him with upturned eyes. "Don't tell me you were thinking that an empty stomach would exacerbate my lust, and that this was a roundabout way to tell me you desired to have an ultimate fight with me?"

Rentaro put both hands on Enju's shoulders. "Just put on your underwear. We can start from there."

"Thanks for the food," said Rentaro as he put his chopsticks down and bowed.

"Thanks for the food!" said Enju, imitating him and giving thanks. "The food you cook is delicious, Rentaro. How is it that you can make such delicious food from such plain ingredients? You are like a magician." Enju, who had changed into casual clothes, looked at him with her face bright.

Rentaro thought with a wry smile that she was overreacting. But it didn't feel bad to be praised. "Well, yes, being imaginative and creative is important in every endeavor, Watson."

"Who's that? More importantly, will I be able to learn how to cook like you soon?"

"Uh, well, um, yeah...I'm sure you'll be able to...eventually," Rentaro answered, not meeting her eyes. "Everyone has their own strengths."

"You said too much." Rentaro poked her head gently, and she laughed with a "Tee-hee" and stuck out her tongue.

That was when Rentaro noticed a small cardboard parcel next to Enju. "Enju... What's that under your arm?"

"Oh, it's a new laptop computer! It just arrived."

"How much was it...?"

"I found a cheap place, so the newest model was only 180,000 yen."

"O-o-one hundred and eighty thousand..." Rentaro got dizzy and had to prop himself up with his hands.

Because Enju was also an employee of the Tendo Civil Security Agency, she received a salary that was way too much for a child's allowance. To Rentaro, who was living hand to mouth, Enju cheekily buying expensive things and rubbing them in his face gave him stomachaches.

Seeing the greedy expression on Rentaro's face seemed to make Enju realize something, and a smirk unbecoming of a child crossed her face. "I will lend money to you any time you wish."

"Oh, you little devil. It's your fault that I..."

One time in their poverty, right before they were about to be evicted from their apartment, he went crying to Enju and borrowed money to pay the rent they were defaulting on. However, the next day, Enju spread the story after dramatizing it to make it more amusing. Because of that, the people around him gave Rentaro the blunt nickname of "Lolita-complex pervo living off of a ten-year-old girl" (which spread to residents of the apartment, as well). After that, he made do with his own salary even if it killed him.

As he carried the dirty dishes to the sink, he glanced at the clock and remembered. From the dresser drawer, he took out a needle-less pressure syringe and flicked it open with his nail. "Enju, it's time for your shot."

"Drat, is it that time already?" she said.

He urged her to put her arm out. Enju hated shots, but she grudgingly stuck out her arm, her body stiff and eyes squeezed shut. Rentaro pressed the piston with a bitter smile. The girl's frail body gave a twitch. The soft arm, thin as a small branch, sucked up the transparent blue liquid.

Once a day, it was the duty of all Initiators to get a shot of corrosion-inhibiting medication. If she neglected to do so, the corrosion percentage in her body would increase, and in the end, she would turn into a Gastrea.

The girls were born under special circumstances. Most mothers who gave birth to red-eyed children who were Gastrea factors went half-mad. For a time, there were a slew of infanticides where women would give birth to their children by a river and drown their babies in the water. Kids playing by the river could see the corpses of babies floating down the river. Rentaro also saw one once in the past, and it gave him a feeling of emptiness that was hard for him to describe as a child.

Before he knew it, Rentaro was looking intently at Enju's face, eyes closed tightly, bearing the pain of the shot. Laughing, crying, angry Enju. It had taken a whole year for her to show him this much emotion. He thought about how she was when they were first introduced a year ago, and his heart was pained.

When he first met her through the mediation of the International Initiator Supervision Organization, or IISO, he'd been taken aback by her hostility and distrust of people, as well as her wild eyes. Rentaro had never felt such obstinate rejection in his life.

But now, Rentaro loved her smiles and even how she sometimes seemed too mature for her age. Of course, he loved her as a much-younger sister—or even, if he were bragging, as his own daughter.

"All done, Enju," he said gently.

The girl's wet eyes opened slowly, and her rosy, glossy lips opened slowly as if cramped. For some reason, Rentaro felt guilty and looked down in a hurry.

"What's wrong, Rentaro?" she asked.

"I-it's nothing!" He would never say it out loud, but Enju had grown very pretty recently. If Kisara were a beauty with a dark side, then Enju was her complete opposite.

"All right. We're done with our work for the day. We're done with dinner. Now that we're full, there's only one thing left to do."

Enju looked embarrassed for a second and looked downward, spreading her arms and smiling as if she would accept anything that was done to her.

"Yup, good night." Rentaro pulled the string of the light twice, pulled the blanket over himself, and lay down. After a while, he suffered a blow to the crown of his head that made his skull ring.

"Owwwww!" he groaned.

"Why are you ignoring me?!" shouted Enju. "When a lady makes a demand, it is a gentleman's duty to quietly go along with what she wants."

"Don't be ridiculous. What lady are you talking about? You're a ten-year-old child! Save the sleep talking for when you're actually asleep!"

"Then let me ask you this: What part of me is *not* a lady?" Enju stuck her chest out as far as she could.

"Hah, first of all, a lady is modest and prudent," said Rentaro. "And your chest is completely flat."

"What?!" She turned red as she balled up her fists, shaking. "Th-they will keep growing!"

"Enju, it's important for a person to know when to give up."

"It's Kisara's fault. She stole the part of my boobs that were still getting ready to grow!"

"Kisara has no such weird, goblinlike ability. I can guarantee that from when we used to bathe together as kids." When he said that, he was surprised at his own perverted statement.

"Argh! I shouldn't have bought a computer! I should've saved up to pay for breast implants in the future."

Rentaro didn't like the idea of an elementary school girl thinking about breast implants.

Enju pushed herself up. "However! There are unfortunate men like Rentaro in this world who are unable to love adult women. 'Big brother, pwease give me a shot of love!' That's the kind of stuff you like, isn't it? Sumire told me, you pervert."

His head started to hurt, and he pressed his temples. "Please, don't tempt me with your hellish sorcery. Anyway, where do you keep learning all those words?"

Enju puffed out her chest haughtily. "I learned them from my friend, Gookle."

"That person's evil! How many times do I have to tell you not to hang around with Gookle?!"

"Who cares? Let's just get married. Let's get married today! I will accept all of your perverted desires!"

On top of making him out to have a Lolita complex, she'd decided that he had perverted desires, and thumped around repeatedly, jumping so that it echoed into the apartment below them. Their downstairs neighbor, woken up by the noise, started to bang angrily on the ceiling with a bamboo stick, and the situation became extremely confused.

Rentaro held his head. If it weren't for this, she'd be cute. Tilting his head to look at the clock, he sighed and wondered what time he would get to sleep tonight.

Enju blushed as she turned her head sharply in his direction. "That's enough. I will take off my clothes."

"Leave. Them. On!"

3

Shrinking away from the noisily chirping sparrows outside, Rentaro looked in the mirror at the face of a young man who looked like he didn't want to do anything. There were circles under his half-closed, twitching eyes from lack of sleep, and more than an unfortunate face, it looked like the face of a villain. Fixing the collar on the black suit that was his uniform, he tied his necktie. For some reason, his neck felt itchy.

*I don't want to go to school*, he thought from the bottom of his heart.

The TV had been left on and was showing the day's horoscope. Taurus had the worst luck with money, as usual. To make matters worse, Taurus had bad health today, too. Hopefully the horoscope was wrong.

Turning off the shrilly whistling kettle, he poured hot water into his cup of instant coffee and let himself be enveloped in the aromatic fragrance of morning, closing his eyes and breathing deeply.

Just then, the door to the entrance opened with a violent force. "Rentaro, the landlady said she'd lend us a bike!" said Enju, who flew in, her spirits high despite the early hour.

Yesterday, he had abandoned his bike near the scene of the incident, so even though it was regrettable, he probably would have been excused for being late. But now his excuse to rest longer was going away. He had a contract with the student council president and couldn't skip school without a good reason.

He finished off his coffee and took the remote to look for a better channel. Just as he was about to turn off the TV, a reporter shouted, "Look at this!" and Rentaro and Enju turned their attention to the screen without thinking.

The young reporter gripped the microphone firmly in excitement, standing in front of the grand palace of Tokyo's First District. Anyone would have immediately recognized the distinctive paved road and beautifully pruned trees.

Just then, the camera cut to a girl dressed in white on a balcony. Wearing layer upon layer of pure white fabric as thin as Japanese paper, her head was covered with a veil of the same material, making it seem like a wedding dress. Her clothes looked like a deep covering of heavy snowfall.

Her skin, and even the hair on her head, was white.

"Lady Seitenshi…"

His own voice shook as if his soul were leaving his body with the words.

Ten years ago, Japan had split into five areas. She was the ruler of one of those: Tokyo Area. She was the third Seitenshi, and had been installed in the position after the death of the previous Seitenshi. With her otherworldly beauty and shrewdness that was not just for show, this girl had far more support than the first and second famously bold and heroic Seitenshi.

"Rentaro, look." Enju was pointing at the stern-faced seventy-year-old man standing next to the smiling girl. With his tall, dignified body dressed in formal Japanese *hakama*, from his build, he could have been part of the Secret Service.

"Damn, it's the old man, huh?" said Rentaro.

Kikunojo Tendo, the Seitenshi's aide, managed all of her support. Because Seitenshi was a hereditary position, in Tokyo Area, after they lost the war, that aide position became the political post with the greatest authority. That old man had made the Tendo family what it was.

Not really paying attention to what the reporter was so excitedly saying, Rentaro muttered absentmindedly, "No one has ever implemented a government where there's no ruling class, huh?"

"Oh, really? By the way, won't you be late?"

"Hmm? Oh!" When he looked at the clock on the top right-hand corner of the screen, the time it displayed gave him a start.

As an ordinary student and regular civil security agency employee, he had nothing to do with the government types, and he didn't like the guys in positions of power, anyway. He turned off the TV and urged Enju outside.

"Let's go!" he said to her.

She grabbed onto Rentaro's waist, stuck her legs out from the luggage seat and shouted energetically. It was the pose she called the "Roman Holiday seat."

The bike the landlady lent them was in pretty bad shape. The brakes hadn't been oiled, and let out an ear-piercing sound every time he used them, and the spokes were so rusted that pieces of oxidation fell off as he pedaled. He wondered how many years this antique had been left unused in the shed.

But those things were soon forgotten once he started pedaling. As he strained to put strength into his feet on the pedals, he pushed comfortably through the fresh morning air. Enju gave a cheerful greeting to the students and men in business suits they occasionally passed. If he looked hard enough, he could see the Monoliths in the distance, brightly reflecting the sun's rays. Underneath the trees lining the street that were sparkling with morning dew, the sunlight filtering through the trees changed shape and blinked like a kaleidoscope.

He felt strange.

Ten years ago, material civilization was at the brink of being destroyed due to the invasion of the Gastrea, and a vast number of people were killed or turned into monsters. At that time, the only expressions on people's faces had been despair and loathing that had no outlet. It had only been ten years. Even so, it had been ten years.

Rentaro closed his eyes and breathed the scent of spring deeply into his lungs. Hearing the bell of a departing streetcar in the distance, emotions welled up from the bottom of his heart.

*     *     *

Just as Enju was clumsily shouting, "Rome! By all means, Rome" as Princess Ann, Enju's school, Magata Elementary School, came into view. "All right," she said. "I will now be zealous in my studies. We must part for a while, but don't cry while I'm gone." Enju made her parting farewell with her hand stretched out gallantly.

Looking at Magata High School two buildings down, Rentaro sighed in exasperation. "C'mon, Enju. We're only going to be separated for a few hours. Don't you think that's a little too dramatic?"

"If I had my way, we would be together twenty-four hours a day. Rentaro, won't you transfer to my class? I mean, you are not that intelligent, right? You could take the opportunity to start over from elementary school."

"You say the craziest things out of the blue. Be kind to my pride."

"Hmph," she sulked. "Then be held back and wait for me for six years until I become a second-year in high school. That is my final compromise. Take it or leave it."

"Being a twenty-three-year-old high school student is wrong in a lot of ways."

"I don't see anything wrong with it."

"I do. Anyway, if I get held back that much, they'd kick me out."

"How dare they?! I want to be in the same class as Rentaro…!"

Seeing the female students around giggling as they passed, Rentaro felt the heat go to his cheeks as he shrugged his shoulders.

"F-fine, I get it. By the way, Enju, inside the school—"

As if knowing what he was going to say next, Enju shook her head slightly and finished his sentence for him. "I know already. In order to hide the fact that I'm one of the Cursed Children, I must act with the utmost consideration inside the classroom."

Only when she was saying things like this did Enju show her dead, cold eyes. Rentaro uncomfortably shifted his gaze. "All right… That's fine, then… Sorry."

"Oh, good morning, Enju!" A cheerful voice interrupted from the side. Rentaro saw a girl about Enju's age with frizzy hair.

"Good day to you, Mai. I'm glad you look in good health."

"You're talking funny, as usual," said the girl. "By the way, did you watch *Tenchu Girls* yesterday?"

"Of course. Tenchu Black's nihilism where one could not tell if she was friend or foe was excellent, as expected."

She was probably a classmate. Once the girls started talking about the cartoon, they didn't spare another glance for Rentaro. Even though Enju's attention was taken away from him in a second, and he was relegated to outside the mosquito net, watching the two talk, his face broke into an easy smile. He felt dumb for worrying even for a moment about her school life. "Well, I'm going now, Enju."

Before she could say anything, he turned his back and straddled the bike. He kept going until he reached the bike stand of Magata High School two buildings over. The bell signaling the start of school rang as he parked the bike and put on the U-shaped lock.

Rentaro clicked his tongue. He was late. Looking up at the school with an unambitious expression on his face, he half-seriously considered going home. Instead, he hooked his bag on his back and rounded his shoulders, walking slowly into the school. It was the beginning of another boring day.

He slept through Japanese class, and during math class, he was called on three times, but the teacher gave up after being ignored all three times. During break time, the rodentlike girl who was the class president approached him nervously trying to get a survey that had been completed by everyone but him, but he ignored her, too, and she left, looking like she was about to cry.

Some meddlesome girl who looked like her protector came to say, "Hey, don't you think you were a little mean?" but he ignored her, too. "Fine, do what you want, idiot!" she said, and went back to the circle of girls.

Rentaro could hear someone saying, "Is that guy even trying? Why is he even here?"

Rentaro looked out the window at the faraway Monoliths with a yawn.

Right around when fourth period ended, the phone in his breast pocket started to vibrate. *Who's calling me at this time of day?* he thought as he rubbed his sleepy eyes and looked at the screen. Looking wearily at the caller's name, he waited another ten rings for the caller to hang up, but lost to the persistent ringing of the phone and pushed the TALK button. "What do you want at this time of day... President?"

"Don't call me President when we're not working. Well, I'm calling you about work, though." From the phone's speaker, he could hear Kisara's voice as clear as a bell.

"Is it about the case from yesterday?"

"Yeah, I'll tell you more details in the car. Anyway, just come with me to the Ministry of Defense for now."

"Huh?" He thought he heard wrong. Wasn't the Ministry of Defense responsible for Japan's national defense? Huh? "H-hey, what're you talking about...?"

"Look out the window."

Hunching, he did as he was told and went over by the window. When he did, he saw a jet-black limousine parked in front of the school gates and his breath caught. "Damn it, all right, I'm going."

"Idiot. You're late. I'm behind you."

"Huh...? Woah!" Taken aback, he let out a pathetic shout without thinking. Behind him was someone so beautiful it was bad for the heart when she appeared suddenly. He could tell that the other people in his class were also confused at the sudden appearance of someone from another school.

"Come on, let's go."

"B-but what about school?"

Kisara put her hands on her hips and glared at him as if he was trying to sneak a peek from below. "I left Miwa Academy for this, too, you know. School or work, which is more important? This month, we've had zero income thanks to *someone*, remember? Good-for-nothing Satomi."

Rentaro shifted his gaze away from Kisara. "For some reason, I've come to love work a whole lot..."

"Very good. Now, come."

He tried to find an opportunity to apologize for yesterday, but he completely missed his chance. *Oh well*, he thought, walking hunched over, two steps behind Kisara, who was slicing through the wind with her shoulders. Every one of the students who passed Kisara stopped, gaped, and looked back at her.

*"Isn't that the uniform for Miwa Academy?"*

*"No way, the same Miwa Academy that the Seitenshi attends?"*

"It's a school for rich girls, isn't it? Woah, look at how beautiful she is. Who in the world is she?"

"No way, no way, no way!"

"Hey, who do you think that is walking behind her?"

"Who knows? A servant or something?"

A guy from your class! At least remember my face! Rentaro silently replied to the voices as he followed behind Kisara.

As they exited the school gate, Kisara got into the limousine—or at least pretended to as she turned back and passed it gallantly.

"Hey, fake rich girl," Rentaro called toward her.

"Did you know, Satomi?" said Kisara. "You can call for a limousine on the phone."

"Then why aren't you getting in?"

"If I do, they'll want to be paid."

"Did you prank call them?"

"Don't worry. I pinched my nose and gave them a fake name."

"No, no, that's not the issue here."

"Oh, Satomi, look. It's a stray Chihuahua."

"Listen to me!"

Kisara broke into a run and started playing with the dog. When she leaned over to pat its head, the stray Chihuahua started licking her hand, and she laughed like it tickled. As Rentaro looked at the profile of her face, his heart started beating violently.

"Satomi, do you have something I can feed him?"

"Oh, huh?" he said, startled. "Hmm, yeah, I do have something. A lot of stray dogs come to our garden, and Enju likes to feed them. Here," he said, pulling out a bag of beef jerky from his back pocket and holding it out to Kisara.

Kisara's stomach rumbled with emptiness. Kisara stared at the beef jerky for a while. Before he could react, she grabbed it out of his hand with the force of a purse snatcher, turned around with her back facing him, and then—of all things—she started eating it.

Rentaro gaped, unable to move.

The poor Chihuahua, its food stolen from it, started to tremble, looking up with big wet puppy dog eyes.

Before long, Kisara, who was red up to her ears, turned just her neck to face Rentaro. "What? Do you have something to say?"

"Kisara, that was for the dog."

"I was a dog in a past life!" She'd moved into the "unreasonable" phase of the argument.

"Kisara, shake."

Kisara glared at him with a look that could kill, but before long, she bit her bottom lip and put her own hand on top of Rentaro's palm, looking as red as a boiled lobster, and then turned her head away suddenly.

If she found it so humiliating, why was she giving him her hand?

"Turn around."

Kisara spun in circles.

Somehow, it was starting to be fun.

"Weenie."

"Pervert!"

"Wait, was there a trick like that?"

"You're a pervert, Satomi!"

"Joking aside, Kisara, are you really having that much trouble making ends meet?"

Kisara looked down, embarrassed, and pulled out her wallet, opening it to show him. Looking inside, he suddenly felt the desire to cover his eyes with his hands. He didn't realize she had fallen so low. "Hey, Kisara… You don't have to purposefully pay a lot of money to go to a rich girl's school. You could just go to a regular public school, can't you?"

"Attending Miwa Academy is all that's left of my pride as a Tendo," she said defiantly. "I'm allowed, aren't I? It's the money I made from properly managing the meager assets I have as stocks and exchanges."

"But Kisara, I thought you hated being called a Tendo?"

"How other people see me is a different matter, isn't it?"

"Well, yeah…it is, but…," said Rentaro. He tried a different tack. "Well then, how were you planning on getting to the Ministry of Defense with what's left in your wallet?"

Kisara smiled an extremely charming smile. "Satomi, you withdrew money from the ATM two days ago, didn't you?"

Rentaro looked away from Kisara. His boss was trying to bum off of him!

"Satomi, you withdrew money from the ATM two days ago, didn't you?"

"I did, but…" His voice trailed off.

"Satomi, you're such a hard worker, and so strong, and reliable, too!"

"I thought you called me 'good-for-nothing' and 'weak' and 'unreliable.'"

"That was ages ago. I've long since forgotten about that stuff."

"That was yesterday, wasn't it?"

"That was ages ago. I've long-since forgotten about that stuff."

"I'll expense it."

"I'll pay you back in my next life."

He was appalled to hear this coming from a company president. Rentaro sighed a heavy sigh. "All right, fine! Let's just hurry up and get going."

As Rentaro started walking, Kisara grabbed hold of his sleeve and looked down. Seeing this, Rentaro got fed up. "What, was there something else?"

"Um…," she said. "Satomi, the beef jerky… Is there any left?"

In the end, he gave Kisara the last two pieces of beef jerky, and she ate them then and there.

The stray Chihuahua looked up at Kisara with a betrayed expression on its face.

"It's kind of late for this, but was it okay that we didn't get Enju?"

As the train's departure bell sounded, the doors closed with a rush of air. They were the only ones in the car.

Kisara pulled up her hair so that the nape of her neck was showing and looked at Rentaro. "It's not like we'll be fighting. It's more like something that would just put Enju to sleep."

"Oh, I see." Rentaro understood. So they were going to be asked something about the incident from before. But why wasn't the usual report enough by itself?

"I didn't hear the details either, but I was just told to go. I hate bureaucrats. They've got the nerve to tell the civsec officers who protect the Tokyo Area that they should be grateful they are even getting jobs from them."

"Then you should've just refused them this time."

"No way. If they give even the slightest hint that they won't give jobs to puny people like us, then we have no choice but to obey."

Rentaro sighed. "Even though we're 'civil' officers, we're still attached to the government by a thread, huh?"

"They're jealous. Theoretically, there is no limit to the abilities of the Initiators. A top-class Initiator is supposed to be strong enough to sway the balance of the world's armies. That's why the government generally wants to have all the civsec officers under control to manage them."

"They want to have their cake and eat it, too. But wait, then does that mean that we're about to enter enemy territory, in a way?"

Kisara lowered her long eyelashes and nodded slightly. "Oh dear, you just noticed? That's why I went and got you, my bodyguard. You're the only one I can depend on, so you need to be strong, okay?"

Inside Rentaro's head, only her last words continued to echo, and gradually, deep emotions began to well up.

Just then, a soft weight fell gently on his shoulder, and he gave a start. Kisara was leaning her head against his shoulder. She blinked her heavy eyelids in annoyance. "Sorry… I'm a little sleepy. Let me borrow your shoulder. I'm always like this after I eat. I can't sleep at school, either…"

"You can't sleep?" he asked. "Why not?"

"I…am a Tendo… I'm supposed to be a model for everyone. I cannot show an unsightly side of myself." She reached her limit. As the strength left her body, a weight fell on his shoulder. She seemed to have really fallen asleep.

*Clang, clang,* went the train, rushing along with a pleasant rhythm. The sunlight streaming in through the window changed the shadows and shone on Kisara's expression.

Careful not to wake her up, Rentaro slowly turned his head toward her, and his eyes went to her bosom, where he would normally never look directly. Between her slender shoulder and the largely exposed area around her neck was the beautiful line of her collarbone. The soft swell that pushed up her school uniform slowly rose and fell at a distance that seemed almost close enough to touch.

His gaze went from her eyes and the tip of her nose to her well-featured face, lips, and long hair. A sweet fragrance that wasn't perfume or shampoo intoxicated him. Every time her soft breathing hit the back of Rentaro's neck, he felt like he was being shocked. *She's beautiful*, he thought.

"Satomi…"

He almost answered her until he realized that she was talking in her sleep. But the words she choked out next left his heart hurting.

"Satomi…my revenge…help me…kill…Tendo…"

He paused for a long time before saying, "I will."

Kisara knit her brows and curled up her body, starting to shake with fright.

"Fa…ther… Mother…no…don't die… Satomi…help me…"

Rentaro put his arm around Kisara's shoulder and hugged her tightly without a word.


4


The government building was deserted after lunch. When Rentaro and Kisara gave their names at the entrance, they were led into the government building and taken up in a pristine elevator. In front of a room marked MEETING ROOM 1 the staff member who was leading them bowed and left.

Opening the door in Kisara's stead, Rentaro raised his voice involuntarily. The room was far larger than the small door made it seem. In the middle was a long elliptical table, and the back wall was covered with electroluminescent panels. The problem was the people who were inside.

"Kisara, this is…," he started.

"I didn't think that we were the only ones to be called," said Kisara, "but I didn't expect that so many people in the same business would be invited."

People wearing well-tailored suits who looked to be civsec agency presidents were already sitting in their assigned seats, and behind them were people who obviously specialized in fighting, staying back.

In their hands glittered black chrome Varanium alloy weapons. They were definitely Promoters like Rentaro. He also saw a number of Initiators about the same age as Enju next to them.

*What in the world is about to start here?* The instant Rentaro stepped into the room, the idle talk that had filled it stopped, and bloodthirsty glares shot at him.

"Woah, hold up. What's the deal with the quality of civsec officers these days? Are kids playing at being civsec now? Maybe you've got the wrong room. If you're here for a social studies field trip, you should just turn around right now." One of the Promoters yelled loud enough for him to hear and headed in their direction.

The Promoter's intimidating, iron plate–like chest was obvious even through his tank top. His hair was spiked like flames, and his mouth was covered by a face scarf with a skull on it. The eyes assessing Rentaro's worth were opened wide, with white showing between the iris and the lower eyelid.

He held what could be called a bastard sword—a thick, long broadsword that looked like it weighed more than ten kilos. Of course, it was made of Varanium, so the blade was black. The slender Rentaro would have had a hard time swinging the giant sword. Just the fact that the Promoter was holding it lightly made it clear that he was no ordinary man.

Rentaro mustered his courage and stood in front of Kisara to protect her, but apparently the man didn't like that. "Yeah?" he said threateningly.

"Who the hell are you?" said Rentaro. "If you've got business with me, tell me your name first."

"What do you mean, 'Who the hell are you? If you've got business with me, tell me your name first,' little boy? You're obviously a weakling."

"Civsec officers' true abilities can't be determined by how they look."

"'Civsec officers' true abilities can't be determined by how they look'? You're getting on my nerves. I want to kill you. Seriously." His sticky glare made Rentaro's knees shake and beads of sweat appear on his forehead.

*Damn it, why is there a thug like this guy here?* He didn't want to pick a fight in a place like this. As he looked around wondering what agency the man belonged to, a sharp blow hit his face. Rentaro was blown back and stumbled backward. The next instant, he jumped up, pressing on his face with one hand.

Being suddenly head-butted in the face he was more surprised than hurt. He stretched his hand out to the XD gun in his belt.

"Idiot," said the man contemptuously. "What're ya gettin' all worked up about? That was just a greeting."

Around them were sniggers that seemed to be making fun of him.

*That bastard!* thought Rentaro.

"Satomi, don't get involved with the likes of him. Don't forget what we're here for."

"Hey, bitch, what did you say just now?"

"Stop it, Shogen!"

Their rescuer was a man sitting at the table who was probably the Promoter's employer.

"Aw, come on, Mr. Mikajima!"

"Enough's enough. If there is bloodshed in this building, we are the ones who would be in trouble. If you cannot follow my orders, then get out this instant!"

The man called Shogen looked like he was thinking things over and was eerily silent for a moment. Then he left, with an insolent "Yessir" and a final sidelong glance at Rentaro.

Rentaro relaxed his body and sighed deeply. When he did, this time it was the man's employer approaching them, with his hands wide. He looked to be in his midthirties and had the air of the elite about him. He wore a Christian Dior suit and looked like an intellectual.

"You there," said the man. "Sorry about that. He's terribly short-tempered."

"You can't even properly discipline your pet dog?" said Rentaro.

The man didn't blink an eye at Rentaro's snide remark. "I really do apologize."

"Yeah? Well, I'm used to it, so it's fine." That was the truth. Of the civsec Promoters, the hard truth of the matter was that while there were those who stuck to their philosophical beliefs, there were also many who just wanted a place to run wild, or who were criminals who used the position as a cover.

The man turned to face Kisara. "It is a pleasure to meet someone so beautiful."

"My, aren't you a sweet talker," said Kisara.

The man showed no sign of turning in Rentaro's direction again. Even as he seemed calm and collected in his expensive suit, he also gave an air of nervousness.

Kisara wrapped things up with a sociable smile, and she was moderately pleasant as she sat down in a tall-backed chair.

"We're in the lowest seat, huh?" said Rentaro.

"There's no helping it," said Kisara. "In terms of strength, we're the lowest in rank."

Looking around again, Rentaro saw those invited were all big names who practically oozed with capability.

"Then why are weaklings like us even here?" Rentaro whispered quietly in her ear as he looked at the guys from before sitting across from them. "Also, who are those guys?"

Kisara pulled out the business card she had exchanged with the man earlier, still facing forward. There was a watermark on the back that said in gold letters, MIKAJIMA ROYAL GUARD, REPRESENTATIVE DIRECTOR, KAGEMOCHI MIKAJIMA.

Rentaro gave a small groan. Even among the major players, this was a huge name that even Rentaro had heard of. It was a large civsec agency that employed many capable pairs. "That means that Promoter is also extremely skilled, huh?" he said.

"Someone said 'Shogen' earlier, so he's probably Shogen Ikuma," said Kisara. "His IP Rank is 1,584."

"He's on the thousands board, huh?"

IP Rankings, which were regulated and published by the International Initiator Supervision Organization, were rankings based on the number of Gastrea defeated and the battle results. There were problems with individual differences in compatibility, but the rank assigned by the IISO was basically thought of as the basis for measuring a pair's strength.

Rentaro wiped the sweat from his palms onto his pants. If that man had come at him in a rage earlier, Rentaro would have been knocked flat, no doubt about it.

"By the way, Satomi, do you remember the IP Rank assigned to you and Enju?" said Kisara.

"I don't remember exactly, but...around 120,000 something, right?" said Rentaro.

"I don't remember the exact number either, but it's about there." Kisara peeked in Rentaro's direction and sighed affectedly. "And that corporation employs pairs that are even stronger than him. I'd love a Promoter that strong in my office. Even though my Initiator is extremely gifted, my Promoter is a good-for-nothing idiot who's ranked lower than me, and is hopelessly weak, at that."

Rentaro pretended he didn't hear her, but inside his heart, he felt that Kisara's words had hit the nail on the head.

How well-known a company was was directly linked to the quality of its Initiators and Promoters. In other words, if a civsec agency was famous, it was because it employed a number of strong pairs. Enju was strong. With an adequate Promoter, she could probably make it into the thousands board. If she was stuck in the 120,000s middle zone, it was natural for her partner to be called incompetent.

Just then, a bald man wearing a uniform entered the room. All at once, the company presidents in the room, including Kisara, stood up, but the man urged them to sit with a wave of his hand. He was too far away for Rentaro to make out his badge of rank, but he was probably a self-defense force staff officer.

"The fact of the matter is that we have gathered you civil officers here today because we have a job for you. Feel free to assume the job comes from the government." The bald man seemed to be waiting for something as he paused for a beat and scowled as he looked around. "Hmm, one absentee, I see."

Now that he looked, Rentaro could see that the only empty seat was six seats down from them with a triangular nameplate that said OSE FUTURE CORPORATION on it. He had met them once before on a job. The fat president had been accompanied by the lanky secretary who briskly took care of whatever the president needed. They seemed like a comedy duo, somehow. He wondered what had happened to them.

"Before explaining the contents of the job, if there is anyone who does not wish to take on this job, please stand up and leave the room now. Once you've heard what the job is, you may no longer turn it down."

Rentaro sighed inwardly. What was the difference between a job you were forced to take and a task you were ordered to do? He looked around, but as expected, not a single person stood up.

The elliptical table that was not quite round had over thirty people seated around it, including Kisara. Kisara, who had come straight from school and was still wearing her school uniform, stood out like a sore thumb, but she herself didn't seem to care.

And behind the company presidents were the Promoters. Their clothes were all over the place. There was a woman who was wearing all red, with a red bodysuit and even dyed-red hair, and a tall, gangly man with bandages on his face who brought to mind Giacometti's statues. The thought that "I'm going to a government building, so I should wear formal clothes" didn't seem to have crossed a single one of their minds.

Shogen Ikuma stood by himself with his back to the wall.

*Huh?* Rentaro noticed a girl standing close to Shogen. She wore a dull, long-sleeved dress with tights. She had large bright eyes, but there was a coldness to them.

Shogen had left such a strong impression that Rentaro didn't notice her until now, but she must have been his partner Initiator. At that moment, his eyes met the girl's. Rentaro hurriedly shifted his gaze, but he could feel her staring at him. After a while, he moved only his eyes to look in her direction, but she was still looking at him.

He didn't know what she was thinking, but she pressed on her stomach with her hands and looked a little sadly in his direction. At first, he was worried that she might have a stomachache, but he soon realized that the subtle expression on her face meant "I'm hungry." She was an interesting girl to be paired with the tough Shogen.

"Very well, then may I assume that no one intends to refuse the job?" The bald man seemed to emphasize this point by looking at everyone in order. Then, he said, "You will receive the explanation from this personage," and withdrew.

Suddenly, on the large panels in the back of the room appeared the figure of a girl. "Good afternoon, everyone."

Kisara opened her eyes wide, and then stood up with force the next instant. At almost the same time, the other company presidents also stood hurriedly.

Rentaro, too, looked at the panels with unbelieving eyes.

With her pure white clothes that made it look like she was covered in snow and her silver hair—it was the Seitenshi, the ruler of Tokyo Area after Japan's defeat in the war. At a distance not too far and not too close was Kikunojo Tendo, who accompanied her like a shadow. It looked like a live feed from a Western-style room somewhere. For just a moment, Kisara's and Kikunojo's eyes met, and sparks flew. Knowing the feud between them, Rentaro was scared.

The Seitenshi sat comfortably in an art nouveau–inspired chair of delicate craftsmanship, and expensive-looking paintings and a canopied bed could be seen behind her. It was probably her private room in the Seitenshi's palace.

Rentaro started to feel a strange uneasiness at the sudden appearance of such a person of authority. He had a hunch that they had become involved in something dangerous.

"Please be at ease, everyone," said the Seitenshi. "I will now explain the circumstances."

Not a single person sat down.

"That being said," she continued, "the job itself is extremely simple. The job I have for all of you civil officers is the elimination of the source Gastrea who infiltrated Tokyo Area yesterday and infected one person. In addition, please safely recover the case thought to have been taken by said Gastrea."

*Case?* thought Rentaro.

A separate window opened on the EL panel, and a photo of a duralumin silver case popped up. The number that appeared next to it was the reward money for completion of the job. Seeing that price, obvious bewilderment filled the air.

Mikajima suddenly raised his hand. "May I ask a question? May we assume that the Gastrea either swallowed the case or the case became engulfed in it?"

"That is correct," said the Seitenshi.

Being "engulfed" referred to a phenomenon that occurred when a victim became a Gastrea, and ripped clothes, skin, or anything the victim might have been wearing would be surrounded by the skin portion and thus adhere to the Gastrea. If that happened, the only way to remove them was to defeat the Gastrea first.

"Does the government have any information on the Gastrea's shape, type, or current location?" said Mikajima.

"Unfortunately, those details are still unclear," said the Seitenshi.

Next, Kisara raised her hand. "May I ask what is inside the case that you would like us to retrieve?" In the commotion that followed, it became clear that the agency presidents around them were excited. Unexpectedly, it seemed that Kisara had asked what was on everyone's minds.

"Oh? And you are?"

"My name is Kisara Tendo."

An expression of slight surprise crossed the Seitenshi's face. "I have heard of you... Even so, that is a strange question, President Tendo. Because it concerns the privacy of the client, of course, I cannot answer."

"I cannot accept that. If, according to common sense, the source Gastrea is the same type as the infected person, then the source Gastrea is also a Model Spider. Something of that level could be defeated by my Promoter by himself." After she finished addressing the Seitenshi, she turned toward Rentaro with a look of uncertainty in her eyes and added, "Probably..."

What a rude president.

Kisara continued. "The question is, why is such an easy job being presented in such an unprecedented way—and why ask all the top-class civil officers? That is what I do not understand. Isn't it only natural, then, that I am left to assume that the danger that merits such compensation lies in what the case contains?"

"There is no need for you to know that, is there?" said the Seitenshi.

"Perhaps not. However, if you insist on keeping your cards hidden, then we will withdraw from this case."

"If you leave now, there will be a penalty involved."

"I am prepared for that. I will not expose my employees to danger with such an unsatisfactory explanation."

In the tense silence that followed, Rentaro thought about the unexpected outcome. On the train, Kisara had said that she could not refuse a job from the government, but—

Just as he thought he should say something and opened his mouth, shrill laughter suddenly filled the room.

"Who's there?" asked the Seitenshi.

"It's me." Everyone's gazes, including Rentaro's, went to the speaker. Rentaro was startled at what he saw.

In President Ose's previously empty seat, the mysterious man in a mask, silk hat, and tailcoat sat with his legs on the table. The CEOs on both sides of him were so surprised at his sudden appearance that they screamed and fell off their chairs.

Rentaro knew who he was. In fact—"You're... No way..."

"Oof," said the man, as he bent his body and jumped up, stepping on the table with his shoes on. The agency presidents watched dumbfounded.

Once the man got to the middle of the table, he confronted the Seitenshi.

"Tell me your name," said the Seitenshi.

"Oh, excuse me." The man took off his silk hat and folded his body in half to bow. "I am Hiruko. Kagetane Hiruko. It's a pleasure to meet you, miss incompetent head of state. To put it bluntly, I am your enemy."

The chills running up his spine made Rentaro draw his gun. "Y-you..."

The man who called himself Kagetane turned his neck with a violent force toward Rentaro. "Oh ho, have you been well, Satomi? My dear friend."

"How did you get in here?!" Rentaro demanded.

"Oh ho, the correct answer to your question is: from the front door, like everyone else, I suppose. There were some annoying little flies that kept coming at me, though, so I killed a few of them. Oh right, this is the perfect time to introduce you to my Initiator. Kohina, come."

"Yes, Papa."

Before they could turn to look, a girl walked up between Satomi and Kisara. Rentaro felt the hairs on the back of his neck stand. How long had she been behind them?

She had short, wavy hair and wore a frilly black dress. From the length of the two scabbards that crossed her back, they probably held short swords.

"Whoopsie daisy," she said as she lifted her arms and legs and climbed up the table with effort, going to stand beside Kagetane and curtsying, holding her skirt in her hands. "I'm Kohina Hiruko, ten years old."

"She is my Initiator and my daughter," said Kagetane.

*Initiator? This man is a civsec officer?*

Kohina slowly looked left and right with a sleepy look on her face. After a short while, she tugged on Kagetane's sleeve mild-manneredly. "Papa, everyone's looking. It's embarrassing, so can I kill them? Also, that guy is pointing a gun this way. Can I kill him?"

"There, there," said Kagetane. "But you can't kill them yet. Have patience."

"Aw, Papa..."

Seeing blood dripping from the scabbard on the girl's hip creating a stain on the table, Rentaro shuddered. Continuing to hold his gun ready, he used his free hand to move Kisara behind him. "What do you want?" he demanded.

"I came to greet you all today," said Kagetane. "I just wanted you to know that I am also entering this race."

"Entering? What are you talking about?"

"I'm saying that we are the ones who will take the Inheritance of the Seven Stars."

The moment she heard those words, the Seitenshi squeezed her eyes shut for a moment in resignation.

"The Inheritance of the Seven Stars?" said Rentaro. "What's that?"

"Oh? You were all really being made to take this job without knowing anything, huh? You poor things. It's what's inside the duralumin case you were talking about."

"So yesterday, you were in that room because—"

"That's right. I followed the source Gastrea into the room, but what I was looking for had disappeared somewhere, and as I was hanging around, a police squad broke the window and came in. They surprised me, so I ended up killing them quite by accident." He laughed from deep in his throat as he held his mask to his face.

Rentaro felt hatred for the laughing Kagetane. "You bastard..."

Kagetane spread both arms wide and turned on the tabletop. "Ladies and gentlemen, let's review the rules! This is a race to see who can find the source Gastrea and get their hands on the Inheritance of the Seven Stars first. The Inheritance of the Seven Stars is surely engulfed in the Gastrea's body, so all you have to do to get ahold of it is kill the Gastrea. How about we bet your lives?"

"I can't listen to your yapping any longer." The muffled voice came from the other side of the table. It was Shogen Ikuma, with his bastard sword and his skull-face scarf. "You're talking too much. Basically, we just need you to die right now, right?"

Rentaro thought Shogen had disappeared, but the next instant, Shogen had buried himself into Kagetane's chest. He was fast. "I'm gonna kill you."

"Oh?" said Kagetane, amused.

Surrounded by a sudden surge of wind, the great sword swung like a tornado. Its deadly timing was perfect, leaving no margin for escape. But then—it was repelled with a thunderous clang, and the next instant Shogen's sword flew in a different direction.

"Wha…?" said Shogen.

"Too bad!" said Kagetane.

What was that just now?

It was only for a second, but Rentaro saw a bluish-white phosphorescent glow between Shogen's sword and Kagetane.

"Get back, Shogen!" With Mikajima's single roar, Shogen instantly understood and retreated, clicking his tongue.

As if they had been waiting for that instant, all the presidents and Promoters who had gathered drew their self-defense pistols at once and fired round after round. Rentaro fired. Kisara fired, too.

The ear-splitting sound of gunfire came from all directions, 360-degrees around. The thunderous sound came again, and this time, the bluish-white glow was more clearly visible.

It was a dome-shaped barrier. When the bullets hit the barrier, they were repelled in all directions with a shrill sound. The glass in the furniture and on the paintings was blown away, and the sound of bullets competed with someone's war cry.

Rentaro also shot his XD gun as if possessed, but after a while, he was out of ammo and the slide stop popped up, and everyone there had fired all of their bullets. In the strange silence filled with the pungent smell of gunpowder smoke that followed, the cries of the unfortunate people here and there who had been hit with stray bullets could be heard.

"No way…" Rentaro swallowed his bitter spit along with the out-of-this-world sensation that he felt.

In the middle of the table riddled with bullet holes, the masked man and the girl looked down at everything around them. All the high-ranking people in attendance froze as if numb.

Kagetane placidly spread his arms. "It's a repulsion force field. I call it *Imaginary Gimmick*."

"A barrier...? Are you really human?" said Rentaro.

"I assure you I am human. However, in order to generate this, most of my organs have been replaced with Varanium instruments."

"Instruments..."

"Let me tell you again who I am, Satomi. I am Kagetane Hiruko, former member of the Ground Self-Defense Force's Eastern Force, 787th Mechanization Special Unit, of the New Humanity Creation Project."

Mikajima's eyes widened in surprise. "The special unit created to counter Gastrea during the Gastrea War...? It actually exists...?"

"You are free to believe it or not," said Kagetane. "Well, what am I trying to say, Satomi? Basically, I was not fighting seriously at all before. Sorry."

Kagetane came silently in front of Rentaro, and like he was performing a magic show, he used a white cloth to cover the palm of his hand, counted to three, and pulled it away. When he did, a box tied with a red ribbon appeared. Putting it on the table, he lay a hand on the astonished Rentaro's shoulder. "It's a present for you," he said. "And now, I will take my leave of you. Fall into despair, civsec. The day of extinction is at hand! Let's go, Kohina."

"Yes, Papa," said the girl. The two walked calmly to the window, broke it, and jumped down as if this were completely natural.

Everyone in the room, including Rentaro, could not move for a while. No one said a word about chasing after them.

It was the first time Rentaro thought he might be killed with a glance. *Just don't vomit*, he told himself as he bore down with all his might on the nausea that was rising from the pit of his stomach.

Rentaro gave a start as someone suddenly laid a hand on his shoulder. Turning, he saw Kisara with a stern expression on her face. "Satomi, I demand an explanation. Where have you met this man?"

"Well...," Rentaro hesitated.

In the silence, Mikajima's anger got the best of him, and he banged on the table with his fists. "Lord Tendo. The New Humanity Creation Project—was what that man said true?"

"There is no need to answer that." The boulderlike Kikunojo replied immediately, unwaveringly.

As a heavy silence fell, a man in a half-mad state suddenly burst into the meeting room. "It's terrible. The president is…!"

The shrill voice belonged to the lanky secretary who was always with President Ose, who was absent from the meeting. He was deranged, and his shoulders heaved as he panted and his eyes bulged. "The president was killed in his house! Th-the head of the corpse is nowhere to be found!"

Everyone's gaze went to the box that had been set in front of Rentaro. Each side of the box was about thirty centimeters long. Rentaro untied the ribbon with shaking hands, and lifted the lid.

After facing it for a while, he slowly lowered the lid.

He had only met the man two or three times on the job, but in the midst of so many bloodthirsty civsec officers, he was a man who never stopped smiling, so Rentaro remembered privately liking him. His balled up fist shook, and he was filled with so much rage it made him dizzy. "That bastard…!"

"Quiet!" At the Seitenshi's clear voice, Rentaro slowly raised his face that was frozen in an expression of rage. "The situation has taken a rather unusual direction. Everyone, allow me to add a new condition to fulfilling the job. Please retrieve the case before the man trying to get the case does so. If you do not, terrible things will happen."

Kisara glared at the Seitenshi. "You will explain just what is inside the case, won't you?"

The Seitenshi closed her eyes and bit her lip lightly. "Very well. Inside the case is the Inheritance of the Seven Stars. It must be sealed. If misused by wicked people, it could destroy the Monolith barrier and cause a Great Extinction in Tokyo Area."

# BLACK BULLET CHAPTER 02

---

## THE CURSED CHILDREN

---

1

As the morning light filtered through the clouds in beltlike shapes, the sparrows chirped and frolicked on the branches. In the vacant lot behind the apartment building where Rentaro and Enju lived, eight boys and girls were gathered, looking up at Rentaro with bright eyes. Rentaro thought they looked familiar, and it turned out that they were all Enju's classmates.

Stifling a yawn, Rentaro stood stock-still in the vacant lot with his bed hair. Uncomfortably, he fidgeted and moved his body, sending his gaze to the heavens. "What, so basically you want to be my disciples?"

"That's right!" said the kids.

Looking askance at the kids who responded with voices loud enough to overpower him, Rentaro, at a loss, started at Enju, looking pleased with herself next to him. "Hey, Enju... I want to politely send these kids home, so what should I do?"

"Aw, don't be like that," she said. "You can train them a little."

The disheartened Rentaro sighed. Apparently, this had all started when Enju had spread word around her school that Rentaro was a martial arts master. Thanks to that, Rentaro had been shaken awake early in the morning, and he had to give up the morning of a rare day off. Normally, this was the time when he could stay in bed and try to go back to sleep.

"Master! Is it true that you can shock a grizzly to death with just your eyes?" said one child. The truth had been embellished with surprising momentum.

"Master! Is it true that you annihilated a whole marine battalion with your bare hands?" said another child. Apparently, he also killed marines.

"Master! Is it true that you stopped a nuclear warhead and threw it back?" said yet another. Rentaro shot a reproachful look at Enju. *Just how hard are you trying to make this?*

When their eyes met, Enju gave him a thumbs-up and an earnest look with complete faith in him that said, "Rentaro can do anything!"

Rentaro wanted to sigh again. The problem with Enju was that part of her seriously believed that he could do anything. Rentaro scratched his head. Everyone went through a phase where they projected themselves onto their favorite superheroes. It wasn't like he didn't feel the need to protect the dreams of innocent boys and girls. He nodded decisively and prepared himself. First impressions were important in times like these. Anyway, kids were no problem. Easy. "All right you guys, thanks for coming. I am the great Rentaro Satomi!"

Silence.

Rentaro couldn't take it anymore, and he blinked his eyelids rapidly, sending a call for help to Enju.

Enju grinned and waved at him. It was almost refreshing how the message didn't reach her at all.

"Um, well, you guys, the concept of Tendo Martial Arts was created by the originator, Sukekiyo Tendo. To put it simply, the basics of Tendo Martial Arts are the First Style punches, the Second Style kicks, and the Third Style that covers everything else. Sorry to dash your expectations, but I'm only a beginner and can't do that much. There are many hidden secrets that I can't teach you yet—"

"Master! We don't care about that. Just teach us your special move!"

"Dang it, I guess I have no choice." Disconcerted by the children's short attention spans, Rentaro went to stand in front of the single maple tree in the vacant lot. He lowered his hips, shifted into the basic Infinite Stance, and inhaled deeply. "Tendo Martial Arts First

Style, Number 3"—he exhaled sharply and dispatched a punch with a twisting circular motion—"*Rokuro Kabuto!*" His fist hit the tree with a heavy thud, and the maple shook as leaves fluttered down. Rentaro exhaled and returned to his stance. Then, he turned around abruptly. "H-how was that?"

"What? It was too fast. I couldn't see what was going on!"

"It was just a punch."

"Seemed kinda lame."

"Right?"

"Make the tree fall down!"

"I want my money back!"

"*Asshole, asshole!*"

Rentaro was at his wits' end. *What should I do? I just wanna punch these kids.* "W-well, you know. This was just a warm-up. I have a technique I've been saving. One of the Tendo Martial Arts hidden secrets, Second Style, Number 11: *Inzen Kokutei.*"

"Ooh!"

"That one sounds a little cooler."

"It's just the name, idiot."

"We won't be able to tell until we see it, right?"

Thinking, *I'll show them this time,* Rentaro turned back to the tall tree, jumping with enough spirit to kick down the tree. "Tendo Martial Arts Second Style, Number 11—"

Abruptly, Rentaro's consciousness was drawn back to the incident in the meeting room the day before. Going around and around in his head was one of the phrases Kagetane had let slip. *New Humanity Creation Project.* Questions filled his mind.

The Seitenshi had said, "As I am sure you all know, currently, Tokyo Area is protected by the barrier of the Monoliths. I will omit the details for now, but if the Inheritance of the Seven Stars is misused, it could create a large hole in a corner of a Monolith. If that happens, Tokyo Area will be overrun by a storm of death. Time is of the essence. You must retrieve the Inheritance of the Seven Stars."

Rentaro narrowed the corners of his eyes. No matter what, he could not lose to that man—to Kagetane Hiruko.

Tightening his lower abs, he fixed his glare on the trunk. "Here I go. Hidden secret—" At that moment, out of the corner of his eye, he could see a boy who had gotten bored and was playing with a soccer ball kick the ball right for Rentaro. "Argh!"

The start of his move was easily shut down, and Rentaro fell out of position and into a ditch headfirst. The sound of laughter filled the air. He couldn't meet Enju's eyes as he held his temple and shook his head.

"Lame! Super-lame! He couldn't kill a beetle with that weak kick."

*A beetle...?*

"I've had enough. Let's go home and play Playstation."

"Yeah!" the other kids chorused.

"H-hey, wait, you guys—" Rentaro's pose was in vain, and Enju's classmates left one by one, leaving Rentaro and Enju by themselves.

Enju started stamping her feet too late. "Drat it, come back! Rentaro really is amazing! He's amazing at night, too!"

"G-give me a break..." Checking the time, Rentaro saw that it was still morning. But after all that, he didn't think he could go back to sleep.

"Enju, is there anywhere you want to go?"

Enju's face brightened in an instant, and she jumped up and down with joy. "Shopping!"

"Okay, okay. We'll go, we'll go!"

Getting off the crowded train that smelled of sour sweat, Enju pulled Rentaro's hand and he stumbled forward as she dragged him to the toy store. And it wasn't just any toy store—it was a large-scale toy store that rented out a whole floor of a large electronics store. Because it was a weekend, it was crowded, and there were many people who brought their families.

Looking at a child who screamed coquettishly sandwiched between her parents, who were holding her hands, Rentaro wondered how he and Enju looked to other people.

Rentaro played around with a toy block puzzle sample, and as if his hands remembered the sensation, he was gradually filled with a sense of nostalgia. "It was a long time ago, but I used to play with stuff like this with Kisara. It's kind of unexpected that you'd like this sort of thing, too."

"My business is with these things over here." As she said this, she pointed her finger at the cartoon merchandise section where an extra-large IMOD display stood.

Rentaro could read the words *Tenchu Girls* written in a decorative font. Now that he thought about it, wasn't Enju talking to her classmate about this show yesterday?

"What's this show about?" he asked.

He then regretted asking about the show even though he wasn't actually interested because Enju turned to him and said, "Wanna know?" with glittering eyes.

Summarizing what Enju told him triumphantly, the story was about Oishi Kuranosuke Yoshiko (magical girl), whose foster father, Asano, was killed. Swearing revenge, Yoshiko gathered forty-seven warriors (magical girls) from around the country to raid the Kira estate. Apparently, it was an epic, long-running cartoon.

He had heard something about how "Ako samurai magical girl shows" had become popular recently. "Even though it's a magical girl show, it's a story about revenge?" he said.

"Aha, but that is what's good about it," said Enju.

"I-I see…" He looked toward the sword in the special section. It was a sharp, silver Japanese sword where only the handle had been made to look like a magical stick. Apparently, it was called the Stick Blade. Watching the trailer, he saw the atrocious face of the heroine, Tenchu Red, as she screamed, "Dieeeee!" and swung her large war sword.

Rentaro couldn't tell what they were going for. Besides, they didn't use magic at all. Looking at the price tags of the Stick Blade and magical girl costumes in the most prominent part of the display, he involuntarily let out a groan. "Why are they so expensive…?"

"Expensive? They seem normal to me. I will buy it with my own money, so you do not have to worry about your wallet." Enju said just that over her shoulder and then started looking through the large piles of merchandise.

"What do you think of this?" What Enju eventually brought to show Rentaro was a bracelet. It had chrome silver-plating over an engraved design. It was probably made of aluminum or something, since it felt very light when he held it.

"What's that?" he asked.

"It's the bracelet that the Tenchu Girls wear. It's proof that the forty-seven warriors are friends, and it cracks when a friend tricks another friend or lies to them, so they can tell when a friend is lying."

"Oh? Sounds like the folktale of the broken mirror."

"What's that?"

Rentaro explained. "It's a story I heard from Doc a long time ago. It's a folktale about a couple who lived apart, so they broke a mirror in half and each took a piece as proof that they would meet again. However, the wife broke her vows and cheated on her husband. And so, the mirror broke and turned into a bird that flew to where her husband was, and in the end, they divorced. Now, Aihara, what is the moral of this folktale?"

"It's to not get caught cheating, sir!"

"Huh?"

Enju put her chin in her hand. "But they are kind of similar. That broken mirror thing must have stolen the idea from Tenchu Girls."

"It doesn't matter who stole the idea from whom. By the way, how much is that?"

"6,980 yen. It's so cheap!"

"That's expensive! That's two months' worth of food for me." Rentaro didn't even have a chance to stop her before she went to the register and bought it.

"Here, Rentaro. Put this on your arm, too."

"What, me, too?"

"It's a pair of bracelets. Who will wear it with me if not you, Rentaro?"

Seeing that Enju put it on her right wrist, Rentaro also started putting it on his right wrist, but then changed his mind and put it on his left.

Enju smirked as she looked at him.

"Wh-what?" he said.

"We match now, like a couple. Now you cannot deceive me or lie to me. Cheating with another woman is forbidden. If you become charmed by Kisara's breasts, the bracelet will crack, as well."

"What? I, Rentaro Satomi, *love* Enju Aihara...," he said sarcastically. "It didn't crack."

"That's because it's the truth."

"Damn it, is that how you're gonna take it?"

After they left the department store, they walked hand in hand talking about nothing in particular. It was mostly Enju nattering on about something, and Rentaro nodding and agreeing with her, but he felt the gloom from the day before lift just from talking to her.

Rentaro stopped suddenly, seeing the Seitenshi on one of the TVs in the street. It looked like recorded footage from a news show, and her stern expression was completely different from the day before. She was talking about how she was planning to propose another bill to respect the basic human rights of the Cursed Children, the much-talked-about New Gastrea Law.

Rentaro wondered if the bill would pass. He fervently hoped that it would. Rentaro squeezed Enju's hand, which was still in his.

Just a short while ago, it was normal for Cursed Children to be delivered in secret alongside a river, then killed before they could even open their eyes, and because of their incomplete regeneration abilities, they often became the target of their parents' extreme abuse. It was also said that parents with Gastrea shock—an aftereffect of the war where a person would go into shock if they saw red eyes—could not even look their own children in the eyes. Also, because the shape of their DNA was contaminated by the Gastrea virus, even if a paternity test were conducted, it could not be proven that they were related by blood. Because of this, there were those who even went so far as to wonder whether or not they were human.

Since pretty much all of the generation that experienced the Great War, the Stolen Generation, had the potential to practice prejudice against the Cursed Children, there were extremely few who could be called these girls' allies.

Honestly, Rentaro thought the problem was more than he himself could bear. If the top official of Tokyo Area was a person who understood their circumstances, he wanted to welcome her with open arms. In fact, he would rather just leave everything to the Seitenshi.

"Oww, Rentaro. Let go of me," said Enju.

He suddenly came back to the present and let go of the hand he had been holding. When he looked, the news had already moved on to the next topic, and Enju was looking up at him with a confused expression on her face. "Sorry, I was out of it. Let's go."

As he turned, he noticed a crowd had formed on the other side of the street. As he tilted his head, wondering what was going on, he heard an angry roar from the other side of the street that made the ground shake, and the thirst for blood emitted by the gathered onlookers drifted over to where he and Enju were. He didn't know why, but he had a bad feeling about this and stood, unable to move.

The only reason Rentaro, who was completely average in athletic and shooting ability, had been able to survive this long as a civil officer was that his hunches were never wrong. That hunch told Rentaro to get away from this place as quickly as possible. "Enju, it'll take a little longer, but let's go home from the other side—"

"Catch her!" At almost the same time a rough voice screamed these words, the crowd broke apart and a single girl ran out. The girl was carrying a supermarket basket full of food. The logo on the basket was from a large chain that Rentaro had also been to before.

When the girl looked at Enju and Rentaro standing in her way, she stopped suddenly. Rentaro couldn't move, feeling as if he had been bound hand and foot. She was wearing a denim skirt with a leather belt and a tasteful white tunic. However, her face was sooty, and her clothes bore similarly sooty stains that made it unclear when the clothes had last been washed, and there were signs of repairs in many places. Like the food she was currently hugging close to her, they had probably also been stolen.

He could tell at a glance that she was a child who lived in the Outer District. In addition, the girl's eyes that reflected Rentaro and Enju were wine-red. Like Enju, she was one of the Cursed Children.

The countless hands that reached out from behind ended their long face-off. When the grown men and women used their hands to violently push down her back, even Rentaro could hear the sad creak of her bones clearly. The fruits and vegetables fell out of the basket around Rentaro's feet.

"Let go!" The girl's handsome face, which had been forced to lick the asphalt, twisted, and she bared teeth like a tiger's as she thrashed and raged. Not a single onlooker had pity for her.

"You thief! You're the trash of Tokyo Area."

"All right, good job! Take that, you stupid Gastrea."

"Shut up! Stop screaming, you murderer."

"If only you Red-Eyes didn't kill all my relatives…"

"Go to hell, you Red Devil!"

Rentaro tapped the shoulder of someone near him. "Hey, why is she…?"

"What do you mean, why? That brat stole food and then half-killed the security guard who tried to stop her!"

Looking at Enju's face, it was pale, as he expected, and she was shaking. At that moment, the girl whose name they didn't even know looked at Enju.

As long as one of the Cursed Children hid her red eyes, she looked just like a normal girl on the outside. That was why there was no way she could have known that Enju was one of the Cursed Children by looking at her. But for some reason, the girl looked at Enju and reached out her freed hand, asking for help.

Rentaro quickly brushed that hand away and glared at her. *Stop it. Don't get Enju involved.*

The girl drew a sharp breath and looked at Rentaro's expression, her fear clearly showing.

"What in the world are you all doing?" At the moment, police officers cut through the crowd to settle the situation. The pair consisted of a skinny man with glasses and a well-built man with a crew cut. Rentaro calmed his heart, thinking inside that this lynch-mob-like situation would finally end. However, the police officer with glasses let out a cold "Oh" as he saw the now-silent crowd holding the girl down and lording it over her. Forcing the girl to her feet, strangely without even really asking the people around what had happened, he put handcuffs on her wrists.

Giving the dumbstruck Rentaro a sideways glance, the man with the glasses saluted a representative of the crowd with thanks, pushed the girl into the police car, and drove off. Did that police officer really know what crime the girl had committed?

After the girl disappeared, the onlookers dispersed in twos and threes after grumbling to themselves. It all happened in a flash. Afterward, only Rentaro and Enju remained. There was no helping it. There was nothing he could have done about it. Feeling uncomfortable, he pulled Enju's hand to go home. As he did, he looked to his side, surprised. Enju had her hands in fists and was glaring at Rentaro.

"Why didn't you help that girl, Rentaro?!" she shouted at him.

Rentaro was overpowered. Her eyes had turned a pale red. The people who were scattering looked back their way with suspicious expressions on their faces. Rentaro felt shaken but forced it down inside. "It's nothing," he said, willing them to believe him.

Rentaro took Enju's arm and pulled her into an alleyway between two buildings. From the exhaust pipe came a smell that bothered him. "It couldn't be helped, Enju. Under those conditions, if they found out your identity, they would have lynched you, too."

"But you hit away the hand of someone asking for help!" she said.

"There are things that I can and cannot do! Besides, what she did was definitely a crime! Even if the environment of the Outer District is bad, it's still illegal to commit a crime." Without thinking, he replied with logic even though he knew it would only put fuel into the fire of Enju's anger.

Enju shook her head fiercely. "That's just an excuse. If you wanted to save her, you would have been able to. You are a champion of justice. There is nothing you cannot do!"

"Don't force your childish illusions on me. I can't do anything... I can't do a single thing." With that, Rentaro suddenly returned to himself. Enju was holding back her sobs as she cried. As he reached out his hand to her shoulder, she stepped away from him.

"Hey, Enju... Could it be... Did you know her?" he said, unsure.

But Enju nodded as she cried. "When I lived in the Outer District, I saw her around. I never talked to her, but she remembered me, too."

"I can't believe it. But... But when I hit her hand away, I was desperate. I wasn't thinking that deeply into it..." Rentaro couldn't talk anymore after looking at Enju's eyes. He asked the conscience in his own heart. He didn't need much time to make a decision. "Enju, can you go home by yourself?"

"Huh?" she said.

Before he knew it, his legs were moving on their own. He dashed out of the alley, and looking quickly left and right, his eyes rested on a boy riding a scooter waiting at a traffic light. Tapping him on the shoulder and making him turn around, Rentaro immediately flashed his civil officer license. "I'm a civsec officer. A Gastrea has appeared in the area, and I need to borrow your scooter."

"H-hey, wait. What're you talking about?" said the boy.

"Looking at your build, you're still in middle school, aren't you? Think we can settle this peacefully?" Getting agreement from the flinching boy, Rentaro took the scooter from him violently. With a roar of the engine, he made a U-turn and turned it to face the direction the police car had gone earlier.

He didn't put on a helmet, and he ignored the traffic laws. If he were stopped, he could thrust his civsec license in their faces and make them understand the situation, but he would lose a lot of time.

Weaving dangerously through traffic, Rentaro's heart was beating hard with nervousness about a danger worse than a collision. Why did the police take the girl away without asking the girl or the victim a single question? What was behind the excessively simplified procedure? Also, it looked like where Rentaro was heading now was not an important police station or even a local police station. If he kept going this way, he would get closer and closer to the Outer District.

Rentaro prayed to the god he didn't even believe in. *Please let me be worrying needlessly.* Even as he thought this, the Monolith barrier that had looked so far away grew larger and larger, and there were traces here and there of buildings that had been destroyed and abandoned. The dark side of the flourishing Tokyo Area, the Outer District.

Just as he started thinking maybe he had passed them somewhere, he twisted around and discovered a police car parked next to a radio tower that had been bent in half. Rentaro put the brakes on about thirty meters before he reached it in order to keep from making too much noise. Then, he hid the scooter in what appeared to be the ruins of a gas station and approached carefully.

He wondered why he was sneaking around like this, but for now, he trusted his hunch. He approached the police car, going around through the dilapidated buildings in front of him and cutting in. The first floor of one of the buildings he passed through was only exposed steel beams, and the concrete walls inside were scraped away, with wallpaper and wiring drooping like a horror movie. When he touched it with his hand, something plasterlike peeled off and crumbled away. It was hard to believe that it had only been abandoned for ten years. It was dead silent around him, and there was no sign or shadow of people anywhere.

Crouching as he approached the police car, he peeked inside, but as he suspected, neither the girl nor the police officers were inside. Disgusted with himself for being inwardly relieved, he turned his attention to the radio tower facility, and began moving toward it. Going under the broken iron fence, he heard unexpected voices and hurriedly leaned his back against a nearby wall.

Slowly peeking around the corner, he saw the backs of the skinny spectacled officer and the crew cut officer. A little distance away, made to stand in front of the iron fence, was the girl from earlier, unmoving. She must have had some idea of what was going to happen to her, and turned pale and shook with uneasiness.

The officers with their backs facing him turned quiet, and Rentaro gulped in the uneasy atmosphere. As he frowned, wondering what in the world would happen next, the silence was suddenly broken by a gunshot.

Blood gushed from the girl's head, and she fell to her knees. She slowly touched her head and looked at the blood that dripped from it, trying desperately to understand what had just happened. Then, like raindrops came a rush of bullets, and her stomach, chest, arms, and legs were riddled with holes. Her body twitched as if she had been shocked, and she was thrown into the iron fence behind her.

"Shit, she's still alive?!" As the skinny spectacled officer approached her, he shot three more bullets into her head. The girl fell forward onto the ground, and as a torrent of blood flowed out from where she landed, she stopped moving.

Rentaro covered his mouth with both hands, swallowing the scream that wanted to spill out of him.

The police officers looked as if they had been cursed by something and looked left and right, quickly running away from the scene.

With shaking legs, Rentaro walked over to the girl, got on his knees, and put his hands together. *Damn it*, Rentaro cursed inwardly. Holding her upright, he hugged her, not caring about getting his clothes dirty. He could feel her body growing cold from blood loss, and Rentaro shook with the rage that welled up within him.

*Wasn't it the job of the civsec officers to bring justice to the innocent citizens? To protect the innocent citizens? And be a champion of justice?*

*Damn it, why the hell did I just watch? I did nothing while a child was being murdered in front of my own eyes! What is right? What is wrong? Who is the enemy I should defeat, anyway?*

Rentaro succumbed to his unbearable thoughts and shook his head vehemently. At that moment, the girl in his arms choked and coughed up blood. Rentaro opened his mouth slightly. She was alive. She could still be saved. Before he knew it he was running, the girl in his arms.

*IT WAS AROUND 2:00 A.M.*

In the spring night's lingering chill, so unlike the daytime weather, Rentaro staggered home. He didn't know if it was from exhaustion or not, but he had an almost unbearable thirst and a pounding head-ache. A lot happened that day, so it could have been the aftershocks of everything.

Now that he thought about it, holding a thirty-something kilo-gram girl in one arm and driving a scooter took extraordinary strength, but in his desperation, he hadn't felt her weight. It was prob-ably the same as how some people drew out great strength during a house fire.

As soon as the girl reached the hospital, the ER doctors took her, and she disappeared into the operating room. As the operation took place, Rentaro sat on a chair in the hall being asked questions by another doctor. The doctor made an unpleasant expression when he heard that the girl was from the Outer District and had no relatives. Occasionally, if they operated on an orphan from the Outer District with no family registry, let alone insurance, they would not be able to get the operation fee from anyone, and the hospital would have to bear the cost. If Rentaro had not said he would cover the cost at that time, at the last moment, he probably would have been fed the transparent lie that there were no surgeons available.

At the end of the eight-hour-long operation, the girl narrowly escaped death. The fact that the bullets were small in caliber, that they were not Varanium but regular lead shots, that as one of the Cursed Children, she had miraculous powers of regeneration, and that she had a tough skull—if any one of those factors were lacking, she would not have been saved, the surgeon who operated on her explained. Thankfully, the graying doctor was someone who understood the circumstances. He said, "You should tell the police who it was who shot her as soon as possible," but Rentaro only said good-bye with a bitter smile.

He was honestly glad that she had been saved, but he couldn't completely rejoice when he thought of the operation fee and the cost of the hospital stay that he would have to pay later. On the highway in the middle of the night, Rentaro conscientiously stopped at the traffic light, but looking around, there were no signs of pedestrians or even cars anywhere.

After a while, he finally saw his eight-tatami-mat apartment. The lights were off. Of course, Enju would not be awake so late into the night, but he had hoped that maybe she would be, so he felt a tinge of loneliness.

"You seem tired, Satomi."

He drew his gun reflexively and pointed it at the voice. Looking slowly behind him, there was a gun pointed at the tip of his nose, as well.

Before it had been customized, it had probably been a Beretta, and in the gas port at the top, there was a muzzle spike attached for close quarters combat. On the large stabilizer to reduce the kickback at the mouth of the gun, there was a bayonet housing attachment. There was also a long extension magazine with extra bullets. On the left side of the slide, there was a party seal that said, "Give the life with dignity." On the right, it said, "Otherwise, give the death as a martyr." Embedded in the grip was a medallion modeled after the evil god, Cthulhu. Sharp spikes covered the angles of the weapon. And the one holding the gun was—

"That's an evil-looking gun you have, Kagetane Hiruko," said Rentaro.

Kagetane laughed. "Good evening, Satomi." The mysterious masked man in the tailcoat suddenly lowered his gun. Surprisingly, he had another custom Beretta in a different color. "This black one here is the machine pistol, Spanking Sodomy, and the silver one is called Psychedelic Gospel. My beloved handguns."

"What do you want?"

"Actually, I came to talk to you. Won't you lower your gun, too?"

"No."

"Oh, dear." Kagetane snapped his fingers with a click. "Kohina, cut off that troublesome right arm."

"Yes, Papa."

As Rentaro reflexively jumped backward, the sound of wind accompanied a lighting-speed slash that came at the place where Rentaro had been. Before he knew it, a girl wearing a black dress appeared next to Kagetane. Kohina made a troubled face and looked like she was about to cry. "Come on, don't move, or I'll cut off your head by accident," she said.

Chills ran along his back, and he broke into a cold sweat. *Crap, I couldn't see her sword at all. The next time she attacks—*

Again, Kohina kicked up a cloud of dust and disappeared from sight. Even straining his eyes, he couldn't follow her movements. Rentaro thought he was done for and squeezed his eyes shut.

With a clang, two bodies collided in midair and were blown apart with the sounds of scraping. Surprised comments came from both sides.

"I couldn't kick her?" said one voice.

"What? I couldn't slash her?" said another.

"Enju!" Rentaro yelled. Next to Rentaro was Enju, with scorching red eyes.

"Rentaro! Who are they?" Enju asked.

"The enemy."

Kohina stood with her two swords out as if protecting Kagetane. Her personality seemed to change 180 degrees from her earlier timidity, and she stood firmly on the ground with her Varanium blades crossed in her unique stance. "Be careful, Papa. That one over there… She's strong. She is probably a kicking specialist Initiator."

"Oh?" said Kagetane. "You must have a pretty good Initiator for Kohina to think so highly of her."

Kohina screamed, "You little squirt over there. Tell me your name!"

Enju hopped up and down until her face turned red. "You are little, as well. How rude! I am Enju. Enju Aihara, a Model Rabbit Initiator!"

Kohina kept her face down and grumbled softly to herself. "Enju, Enju, Enju… All right, I'll remember. I am Model Mantis, Kohina Hiruko. In close combat, I am invincible." Kohina changed completely

and pulled on Kagetane's sleeve with a sad expression. "Um, can I kill the rabbit? I'll just leave her head, so can I kill her?"

"How many times do I have to tell you, silly girl," said Kagetane. "You may not."

"Aw, I hate you, Papa!"

Kagetane said, "Oh, dear," and fixed the placement of his silk hat, then turned back to Rentaro. "It looks like things have gotten complicated. Do you want to fight?"

Rentaro kept an eye on Kagetane without letting his guard down and looked around. They were in a residential neighborhood, so if they fought here, there would be more meaningless victims. After biting his bottom lip hard, Rentaro lowered his gun. "Hurry up and say what you have to say, moron. I'm sleepy and still have to study for a quiz next week."

Kagetane snickered behind his mask and put his gun back in its holster, holding his arms wide open magnanimously with the moon as a backdrop. "Let me get straight to the point. Satomi, will you join me?"

"What did you say?!"

"For some reason, I've liked you ever since I first saw you. I thought it'd be a waste to kill you. If you join me, then I won't."

"I'm still a civsec officer, you know."

"What of it? I am a former civsec officer myself. Unfortunately, there will soon be a wild storm that will bring Great Extinction to Tokyo Area. At the moment, I have some strong backup. If you become my ally, you can have money, women, power… I will give you anything you want."

Rentaro did not say a word.

"Satomi, have you ever thought you wanted to change this unreasonable world? That the way Tokyo Area works is wrong? Have you ever thought that, even once?"

Before he knew it, the image of the girl whose name he didn't even know resurfaced from the back of his mind. Her head flew back in slow motion, and blood spurted from her forehead. The blood dripped slowly, getting absorbed by the ground. There was the girl, with her eyes refusing to accept what happened, the police officers whose mouths twisted in evil pleasure, and Rentaro, too cowardly to run out to save her because he was afraid he would be killed to keep his mouth shut.

Seeing Rentaro's hesitation, Kagetane pulled out a white cloth from his pocket and covered the ground, counting to three. When he pulled the cloth off, an attaché case appeared beneath it. "From what I hear, apparently, you are not doing very well economically." Kagetane used his foot to slide the attaché case over to Rentaro. When the case stopped in front of Rentaro, the lid popped open. Inside, it was stuffed with stacks of bills. "This is just a small gift to express my feelings."

Rentaro stared at the stacks of bills without moving an inch.

"I hear you make that Enju over there pretend to be human and have her go to school? Why would you do that? Those girls are the shape of the next generation of humans that have gone beyond the current *Homo sapiens*. The only ones left after the Great Extinction will be us, the strong. Join me, Rentaro Satomi."

Rentaro kicked the attaché case back with all his strength and shot it three times with his gun. The case jumped, and the bills were riddled with holes. Some of them floated out of the case like petals.

Kagetane looked at the attaché case riddled with holes for a while. "You have made a grave mistake, Satomi."

"Mistake? If I made a mistake, it was that I didn't kill you when I first met you, Kagetane Hiruko!"

"Fool! Will you insist on completing your jobs till the end? No matter how hard you work for them, they will only keep betraying you."

Rentaro glared at Kagetane. Kagetane glared back at Rentaro. Rentaro wasn't sure how long this went on, but after a while, they could hear the siren of the police car coming to investigate the gunshots.

Kagetane sighed. "We will pick this up again later, Satomi. I don't like doing things this way very much…but see what happens when you go to school tomorrow. You need to start looking at reality." Throwing that last line at Rentaro, he took a big leap backward and melted into the darkness.

Staring in the direction Kagetane disappeared, Rentaro asked Enju, "What do you think of his Initiator?"

"She's strong," she said. "Frighteningly so."

"Can you beat her?"

"I don't know."

"I see…"

The burden of Kagetane's last words to him as they parted weighed down on Rentaro, and he couldn't erase them from his memory.

2

"Is that true?" Rentaro stood as he squeezed his cell phone tightly. A number of his classmates who were idly chatting stopped in surprise and looked in his direction. Rentaro quickly lowered his voice. "I-I'll be there immediately." After folding his cell phone shut, he dashed out onto the school grounds and ran two buildings over to Magata Elementary School.

Hastily taking off his shoes and putting on the visitor slippers at the entrance, he went to the staff room and grabbed Enju's homeroom teacher, who was just about to head to the classroom. His face was pale and thin, and there were large circles under his eyes. He was shorter than Rentaro, but even though it wasn't that hot, he kept dabbing his handkerchief on his forehead, and his eyeballs protruded like he was nervous. "Oh, you're the guardian…"

"What is going on? Is Enju really—?" Rentaro drew closer to him with a threatening look. Even though he knew that it was useless taking things out on her homeroom teacher, he couldn't control his feelings.

The man answered incoherently as he took quick glances at Rentaro. "Yes, the rumor that Aihara is one of the Cursed Children appeared from somewhere. At lunch, the…harassment…directed at her began."

"I can't believe it… But…did Enju…deny it…?"

The teacher looked down as he began to dab his forehead repeatedly with his handkerchief. That was better than any answer. "Satomi, you had Aihara attend this school without telling any of us that she was one of the Cursed Children."

"If I had told you beforehand, wouldn't you all have just found a reason to refuse to admit her?"

The teacher looked away from Rentaro and started wiping his mouth with his handkerchief again. "I had Aihara leave school early because of the shock. I have no right to ask this, but will you go be with her, Satomi?"

Rentaro didn't remember what path he took to go home. Unlocking the door, he entered the apartment panting, and a silent chill touched his skin. Enju was not there. She wasn't anywhere.

His whole body shook with chills, and even taking off his shoes seemed to take too long. He checked the bath and restroom and opened all the closets. She wasn't there. He started to turn pale at the thought that maybe she hadn't even made it home, but opening her clothes dresser, he saw traces that she had at least been there once.

As Rentaro fell into a panic, he let out a deep breath and bent his knees, fumbling around in his pocket to call Enju's cell phone. She seemed to have turned off her phone, so he sent her a few texts. He did not receive any response.

Rentaro took deep breath after deep breath and told himself, *It's all right. This is Enju's only home.* Rentaro kept waiting.

But in the end, Enju did not return home that day.


3


Rentaro opened his eyes slightly at the sound of a soft tapping in the distance. The first thing that came into the field of his blurry and hazy vision was the brown ceiling. The grain of the ceiling changed shape with a twist and turned into a person being chased by a boar. The person was fleeing desperately, but it looked like the boar would catch them soon.

He woke up with a start, and turned his neck to look around the room. He was alone. Enju hadn't changed her mind and come home. His stomach was heavy with disappointment, and a headache that seemed like it was lying in wait attacked, making him crouch where he stood.

Looking out the window, the rain on the glass distorted the view. That was the source of the tapping earlier. His eyelids felt heavy and cramped, and he felt worse than when he went to sleep. He was nauseated now, too. Pulling the clock toward him to look at the time, he saw that it was seven a.m. It had only been about fifty minutes since he'd fallen asleep.

Because he hadn't eaten anything since the incident happened yesterday, his stomach was so empty that it hurt, but he didn't feel like cooking for himself. With his hazy vision and his head feeling like it was full of mud, Rentaro crawled to the fridge and, finding a half-full milk container, drank it dry. It tasted like bitter, half-solidified saliva.

He cracked open a raw egg on the side of the fridge and dumped what was inside into his mouth, then chewed some mustard greens and lettuce in desperation. His own actions shocked him, given that he was usually proud of the fact that he liked cooking.

After he got to the point where he could move around, Rentaro started putting away Enju's clothes, which were scattered around the living room. The previous day, Rentaro had taken all of the clothes Enju left behind out of the closet and slept with them around him. Unlike Rentaro, who was poor, Enju had a lot of clothes in the latest fashions. That was how he felt after spending the whole night with them. Which reminded him, whenever Enju bought new clothes, she would pose suggestively in front of Rentaro, asking him over and over, "Am I cute? Am I cute?" How had he answered her then?

Rentaro picked up the syringe that had fallen in the crack by the dresser. Inside it was cobalt blue medicine in liquid form. Realizing that she hadn't taken her medicine, he became very sad. Nothing would happen if she skipped it for a day or two, but if she didn't take it for a while, the corrosion rate of her body would gradually rise.

"Damn." Rentaro threw the syringe on the floor and held his head in his hands.

Pretty much every day, he took her to and from school, and when they came back to the apartment, Enju would be pestering him for food. She was critical of everything he made, which had motivated him to cook well.

That life had been broken to pieces. Rentaro stood up and looked around the too-empty eight-tatami-mat room. What was he supposed to do now?

He slapped his cheeks hard with both hands. It was obvious. He needed to do something. Taking off the uniform he wore every day, he took a shower, letting the hot rain strike his body and loosen his stiff muscles. After he got out of the shower, he felt a little more like himself. Putting on a fresh uniform and looking in the mirror, he saw that his cheeks were slightly hollow and that only his eyes were glittering, but he decided that it was good enough.

Checking to make sure he still had a close-up picture of Enju's face on his phone, Rentaro took his wallet and went outside. Suddenly wondering how much money he had left, he opened his wallet and laughed involuntarily. He would probably have to walk home, but he didn't care. Rentaro jumped onto the train and got off at the last stop. Since it was early morning on a weekend, the entrance and exits were both empty. Raising his umbrella and looking into the distance to check where the Monoliths were, he walked unwaveringly toward the Outer District.

It had already been ten years since the Monoliths had formed the boundary that separated humans from Gastrea. The Tokyo metropolis was the only place that had remained whole after the Great War. The neighboring Kanagawa, Chiba, and Saitama prefectures all had pieces cut off by the Monoliths. It had been nine years since the Tokyo metropolis absorbed the neighboring prefectures and became Tokyo Area, with its forty-three districts.

The numbering system started from the middle of old Tokyo (the Seitenshi's palace was in the First District), with the numbers increasing as one got closer to the border. The Outer District that Rentaro was heading toward was District 39 on the map. The Outer District referred to the border district connected to the Monolith, a no-man's-land where no one wanted to live at the time.

Slowly, there started being fewer and fewer people, and he started seeing strange things here and there. There were gigantic footprints that didn't look human and chairs that had blood stuck to them that wouldn't come off. Inside a four-wheel-drive vehicle with broken windows that had turned red as though rust bloomed on them grew a mysterious reddish-purple grass out of the space between the cushions, luxurious in its thickness.

A message board created in response to the emergency was still covered with many layers of colorful papers after ten years.

"Sho, this is Atsuko. If you're safe, please contact me here."

"To Daiki Kato—I'm at your grandfather's house."

"This is my number: xxxxx. Koji Aso."

"I'm looking for this boy." There was a picture of a boy about five years old attached.

"To Yoko. Dad and Fuyumi are fine…" The rest was scratched off and couldn't be read.

Rentaro had involuntarily started sweating uncomfortably. He felt like his necktie was tightening around his neck and loosened his collar.

This was a message board created by people who had been separated during the war in order to reunite with loved ones. With transmission base stations destroyed, cell phones were nothing but pieces of trash. This was probably a region that had been caught up in the war. The traces of the Gastrea War that were left behind still seemed fresh.

If he really wanted to remember the conditions from ten years ago, there were plenty of videos uploaded online, but there was no one who could watch them and feel happy about it. Once, a long time ago, Rentaro had watched a video called "Memento Mori," and he remembered running to the sink afterward.

The farther he went, the more he could see, because with the collapsed buildings and dilapidated homes, there were fewer things to obstruct his vision. In the midst of that were conspicuously large factories that looked like they had been newly built. They were facilities for geothermal, steam, water, wind, solar, and nuclear energy. Japan had always been surrounded on all sides by the ocean, so it had strong ocean winds. Besides that, it had about ten percent of the world's volcanoes, so it could make use of their geothermal energy, and because of its complex terrain, there were many extreme rises and falls, so it had strong waterpower, as well.

Now, in the year 2031, solar battery panels had made great advancements in conversion efficiency, and in forty-one districts, they were piloting a new Tokamak nuclear fusion reactor. It could be said that most of the energy for the center was produced in the Outer District. However—

Rentaro looked at the pristine asphalt road compared to the ruined buildings and a bitter expression crossed his face. There were examples from other disasters, too, but when a disaster of this magnitude occurred, the first thing to do was restore roads to transport goods. The next thing was to start securing the all-important lifeline of water, and then to aim for enhancing food, clothing, and shelter.

Why had restoration not moved forward if the roads had been paved so nicely? It was probably because the government had no intention of restoring the Outer District.

There were currently three uses for the Outer District. First, it was a place to manage dangerous nuclear reactions, and second, it was a landfill for the trash created by those in the center of Tokyo Area. Finally, it was where they planted the genetically improved "miracle seed" that was expected to produce large harvests in a small amount of land. Fortunately, powdered concrete worked to lower the acidity of the soil. In other words, it was an abandoned area that was now a field for these three things. None of those three uses showed any consideration for the few residents who lived here.

The Monoliths started to look very big. Surveying the area, it did not look like there were any people there, but Rentaro felt eyes looking at him from somewhere. It was probably not just his imagination. Rentaro gripped the handle of his umbrella hard. Other than the umbrella he was using, he had also brought a child's umbrella with a *Tenchu Girls* character printed on it.

The circumstances this time were more serious than Rentaro had thought. There was no way that it would be resolved easily, with Enju at Kisara's or Sumire's or a classmate's house. If anything, it would make more sense for her to return to her hometown, the Outer District.

Before he knew it, he had reached almost the innermost area. Rentaro relied on his memory to go to a single manhole, and knocked two, three times on the cover.

Shortly after, the cover was lifted open with a heavy sound, and a lisping voice said, "What?" as a young girl showed her face. She was probably around seven years old, and she peered at Rentaro with a puzzled look on her face. Her eyes glowed red.

"I'm looking for someone," he said. "Can you help me?"

"Are you the police? We have no intention of leaving, leaving, leaving."

"No, I'm not the police."

"Then, then, are you a sex offender?"

"Huh? A sex offender? No...that's wrong, too..."

"Then, please leave." The manhole cover shut with a clang, and Rentaro froze with his mouth still open. Returning to himself, he knocked again.

"I hate persistent sex offenders," said the girl.

"Wait, wait, wait! Why are police and sex offenders the only two options you have prepared?!" said Rentaro hurriedly. "And why did you decide that I was a sex offender just now?!"

"It was what I thought after seeing your face."

"You little..."

"By the way, did you need something?"

Keeping his irritation inside, Rentaro put down his umbrella and took out his civil officer license with his right hand and pulled up the picture of Enju saved on his phone with his left hand. "I'm a civil officer. I'm looking for this girl. Have you seen her?"

The girl looked back and forth at the license and the picture and said, "Nope."

"I'd like to ask other people, too. Is there an adult around?"

"That would be the Elder. I'll go get him, so please wait inside."

"Uh, all right..." Pressured by the girl's lilting speech, he went down the ramp and stood in the sewer. It was unexpectedly spacious inside and cleaner than he expected. However, the strong stink of many years of human wastewater had become ingrained in the walls and made his head hurt.

But the girl seemed used to it and said, "Please wait here," and bounced off into its depths. Rentaro looked at her departing back with complicated emotions. Manhole Children. Children who had become orphans after losing their parents and siblings during the war.

As he started looking around after his eyes became used to the darkness, he could hear a clanging sound reverberating from inside a pipe, and a man appeared. He was short, and his hair was white, but his spine was straight. He wore glasses and gave the impression of being intellectual. He used a wooden cane with a rubber end, but he still looked too young to be an Elder.

"I'm Rentaro Satomi," said Rentaro.

When he gave the man his civil officer business card, the man looked at it carefully and then said, "Aha," nodding.

"Are you the guy that strange girl from earlier called 'Elder'?"

"Ah, Elder is a nickname," the man laughed. "I'm Matsuzaki. But I'm surprised, too. Maria said, 'A guy who's a police with his right hand and a sex offender with his left hand is here.' I thought it was some kind of riddle."

The girl from earlier appeared to be called Maria. It would probably be hard to make her understand the difference between a police officer and a civil officer.

"Excuse me, but what do you...?" Rentaro ventured.

"Oh, I look after the children here."

Rentaro was silently moved. The man wasn't homeless but probably lived here of his own accord. He couldn't help looking a little shabby, but when he smiled, his gentleness shone through. Rentaro thought he must have once worked as some kind of educator.

The man pushed up his glasses with his middle finger and looked into Rentaro's eyes. "It's warm in here compared to outside, isn't it?"

"Yeah, now that you mention it." Rentaro had actually noticed when he entered. He thought the sewer would just block the wind and rain, but with this warmth, it would not be hard to live through the winter.

"It's because most of the drainage from the power plants is hot."

"Oh, that makes sense. But it's easy to get sick with this sanitation environment...right?" After he said it, he thought it was probably rude and added the last part.

But the man laughed loudly. "That's not true. The girls are actually more resistant to this environment than us normal people, thanks to the Gastrea virus. Even in the past, when this area was flooded with Gastrea, the Gastrea didn't come all the way to the sewers, so this is a pretty comfortable place to live."

Rentaro looked into the water pipe where the girl named Maria had disappeared. "So, is she one of the Cursed Children, too? She lifted that sixty-kilogram manhole cover like it was nothing."

"Did you notice? She still cannot control her emotions well. I hope that she will be able to leave here someday and live among normal people, but it's problematic if her red eyes give her away, so she needs to at least learn to control her emotions." The man looked like he was having fun twirling his cane as he explained.

Rentaro thought about the girl called Maria. All of the Cursed Children were female. To begin with, all new lives in the womb are female for the first seven weeks. Then, the embryo's sex is determined, and some become male. The Gastrea virus mutated the gene that determined the sex, so none of the Cursed Children became male.

"Mr. Matsuzaki... Aren't you one of the Stolen Generation?" Rentaro asked.

"That doesn't matter," said the man. "When Gastrea invaded, unfortunately, the virus also infected children in the womb. The girls, the Innocent Generation, are victims."

"If only everyone thought like you…," Rentaro sighed. "I completely agree with you."

"It can't be helped. It's not a grudge that will go away in ten years. Everyone has become overly sensitive to the word *Gastrea*, so it's only natural that they would hate having children walking around town who carried the virus in their bodies."

Feeling comfortable with this unexpected sympathizer, Rentaro could have kept talking about this same subject, but then he remembered what he had come for. "Sorry, I'm in a hurry. Did this girl come here? Her name is Enju, Enju Aihara."

He showed the picture to Matsuzaki, who appeared to think a little before shaking his head. "Sorry, I don't know."

Well, Rentaro hadn't expected to find her this quickly. Of course, he wasn't going to get discouraged over something like this. As Rentaro bowed to leave, for some reason, the cane stretched out to stop him.

"Where will you go now?" Matsuzaki asked.

"I'll search all of District 39," said Rentaro. "It's her hometown. I'll look for her until I find her."

"From the looks of it, you are a Promoter whose partner ran out on you."

Rentaro suddenly couldn't speak, and his face looked frantic. That appeared to be enough to confirm Matsuzaki's suspicions.

"Does it have to be this girl?" Matsuzaki asked.

"What…?" said Rentaro, unsure of what he meant.

"When you take care of those girls, you naturally get to know them, but it's not rare for civsec officer pairs to have personality conflicts. If a pair breaks up or if one person dies, you could contact the IISO to form a contract with a new Initiator. Your IP Rank will plummet, but at your age and with your record, it wouldn't be hard for you to bring it back up again."

Rentaro inhaled and exhaled silently and closed his eyes. "I came looking for Enju, but not because I'm a Promoter or because she's my Initiator. You're a good guy, and I thank you for that. But let me say this—don't act all high and mighty without knowing anything!"

Matsuzaki widened his eyes in surprise and dropped his cane.

Rentaro clicked his tongue, thinking that he'd done it now. He had trouble controlling his emotions when it came to these topics. "Sorry… I didn't mean to yell. I'll leave now. Bye."

*    *    *

Matsuzaki looked affectionately at Rentaro's departing back and then turned around slowly, raising his voice into the darkness behind him. "You heard him. He's a nice young man. Are you sure you want to let him leave like this, little lady?"

## 4    *THE NEXT DAY.*

Rentaro was speechless as he hung up the phone. His arm fell limply and he did not recover from his shock for a while. Looking at his surroundings, he saw thin clouds like the previous day's and cherry tree leaves that looked like they were about to be scattered in the strong wind. The sky looked like it might start crying any minute. Outside the school, Rentaro gave a start as he heard the warning bell, but his legs felt heavy and he didn't feel like going to his classroom at all.

During the break between first and second periods, he realized that he had to explain that Enju would be absent to her homeroom teacher, and went behind the school to call from his cell phone.

The response he got was completely unexpected.

Rentaro looked back at the school and went back and forth wondering if he should hurry back to his classroom or not, but in the end, he turned around and headed toward Magata Elementary School once more.

He went to the staff room and met up with Enju's homeroom teacher. The teacher's face looked like he also did not understand what had happened. "Yes, Aihara is at school."

Rentaro searched his memory and only just realized regretfully that her schoolbag and a set of books had been taken out of their apartment. After he left the manhole the previous day, he'd searched District 39 until sunset, but he didn't get any valuable information, and his feet dragged as he went back to the apartment.

The teacher brought Rentaro to Class 4-3's room. They peeked at the situation inside through the window of the sliding door in the back.

There she was. Even though it was break time, she sat alone, looking down resolutely, her eyes staring at the desk, proof of her iron will.

There was extra space between her desk and the others, and her classmates treated Enju as if she weren't there.

Rentaro's heart broke at the pitiful sight. He wanted to yell at her to stop. But this was probably Enju's way of fighting. He had no right to stop it.

"Do you want to see her?" the teacher asked.

He wanted to see her. He had a mountain of things he wanted to ask her when he did. As Rentaro squeezed his chest, he pulled out a syringe with the cap on from his breast pocket and handed it to the teacher. Inside was cobalt blue liquid medicine.

"What's this?" said the teacher.

"It's a special medicine…" Rentaro shook his head. "No, I'm not going to lie anymore. This is Gastrea corrosion-inhibiting medication. Please give it to her."

Saying just that, he turned his back on the teacher, who looked at him questioningly, and cast his body into the violent winds. Would Enju continue to attend school like this? Even knowing that she would only get hurt?

Losing his will to return to his own classroom, Rentaro headed for the university hospital where Sumire was. He had been going to school every day for a while, but he realized with a bitter smile that he was starting to skip classes again.

As he passed the demon-engraved ward-objects and entered the basement, Dr. Sumire was just coming out of the operating room. Taking off her green operating scrubs and mask and throwing them in the trash, she lifted the corners of her mouth and said, "Hey." The queen of this basement room would always be here to welcome Rentaro with her strange smile no matter what, come hell or high water.

"Doc, what were you doing?" Rentaro asked her.

"I had some free time and couldn't take it anymore, so I went to break up with Charlie. Unfortunately, he has been turned into small parts. Oh, while it was extremely stimulating, I feel a little sad because now I have to find a new lover tomorrow."

Rentaro looked at the double doors the fed-up doctor had come out of. The aromatics that were all over the room were only there to mask the intense odors coming out of the dissection room she called her "kitchen."

"It's not much, but make yourself at home," said Sumire.

Rentaro stood in front of the bookshelves that covered the left wall of the room. She was a movie maniac, and she had everything crammed on the shelves. He wasn't sure if it was because she was just the type of person who threw everything on her bookshelves, but next to *The Tenth Dimension vs. the Eleventh Dimension: Settling String Theory!!!!*, a book that looked like it was about quantum theory, was *Forbidden Training 24 Hours: Karin's Big Brother's Pregnant Wife*, an adult game. It was terrible.

"You really are something else, Doc," he said.

"What, you just noticed?" she said.

"Famous universities admit people based solely on their test scores, so they end up as nests of eccentrics."

Sumire laughed. "Don't be jealous, silly boy. I'm a genius because my parents were both geniuses. That brings back memories. When I was young, Mother used to read Dante's *Inferno* from his *Divine Comedies* to me as a bedtime story. This was all she read, and she read it over and over. The misery of a person who is sent to hell…" She laughed.

"So your family's been strange since your parents' generation, huh?"

"I'll dissect you alive."

"No, please, not that!"

"Oh yeah, by the way, the demon to scare people away out front has the face of the fallen angel, Lucifer, or should I say the demon king, Satan? It's related to the *Divine Comedies*. It's an unexpected foreshadowing, don't you think?"

"If I cared less, I'd be dead."

"Now, let's see…what were we talking about again? 'The word *Erromango*, that is the name of the island, Erromango, means "I'm human," but don't you think there's some truth to how it sounds like *erotic*?' Was that where we left off?"

"Stop lying. We weren't talking about that!" Rentaro was disgusted. Why didn't anyone around him listen to what others had to say?

"I was kidding, you stingy, inflexible boy. I can't help but feel bad for your beloved Kisara."

"D-don't say that!"

"Oh, speaking of which, your patron came by earlier."

The hair on the back of his neck stood up, and he looked uneasily from left to right. "She was here?"

"Yeah, and she wasn't happy. She said that since you never visit her in the student council room, she goes to your classroom to look for you, but you're never there."

"It's 'cause I always run away to avoid seeing her."

"Why are you doing that again? She's the school idol, isn't she?"

"Well, she *is* kinda c-cute, but that's just because no one knows what that woman is really like. If she got worked up, she would shoot up the school with a Magnum semiautomatic..." *But,* he thought as his voice trailed off, she was also the one who provided Rentaro the civsec officer with weapons and ammunition free of charge.

It was the natural order of things for civil officers and weapon companies to work together. For example, the Bastard Sword, Mark IV Gibraltar used by Shogen Ikuma was from Escari, the company that supported him. By backing him and having him use their products and be a tester for their new products, they could say "Used by Shogen Ikuma!" in their marketing campaigns, so it was extremely natural for companies like that to be devoted to finding talented Initiators and Promoters. However—

"In what part of me does she detect any promise?" Rentaro said.

"You have such an unfortunate face that she probably just felt bad for you," said Sumire.

"That's ridiculous..." Saying that, he suddenly remembered something and narrowed his shoulders. "Doc, sorry... I actually came today because I wanted some advice."

Putting on the long, white lab coat that hung over her chair, she pulled out a coffeepot and two heatproof beakers, saying "Hmm..." Filling the beakers to the brim with coffee, she slid Rentaro's cup over to him, where it stopped in front of him.

As the hot coffee flowed into his stomach, Rentaro could feel the knot in his chest swell. Rentaro told Sumire everything—about the girl who had been shot, Enju running away, and what he went through to find her.

They arrived at a moment of silence. Sumire, with her chin in her hand, had a grave expression on her face that Rentaro had never seen before. Rentaro suddenly felt uneasy and massaged the palm of his hand. "D-doc?"

"Hmm? Oh, sorry, I was thinking about what to make for dinner tonight," said Sumire.

"Hey, wait a minute!"

"I stopped listening halfway through 'cause your worries are so normal that I was getting bored."

"Wh-what...?"

Seeing Rentaro staring frozen at his beaker, Sumire pushed in to deal the final blow. "Hey, Rentaro, mankind will become extinct one day, you know. It could be in a few million years, when the whole Earth freezes over, or in the far future, when it is swallowed up by the expanding sun. Or the land with the Monoliths could be destroyed tomorrow, and Gastrea could surge in and kill everyone.

"Wonderful movies, famous novels written by literary masters, beautiful buildings—all of them will fall into ruin and return to nothingness in the far future. Do you understand that? From the universe's point of view, essentially, there is no reason for humans to be alive."

Seeing the maniacal smirk on Sumire's face sent shivers down Rentaro's spine. She seemed to be overcome by nihilism.

"Hey, Rentaro, why do Gastrea have to be exterminated, anyway?"

He was caught unawares and faltered for a moment.

"You can't say?"

"No, wait," said Rentaro, finding his tongue. "It's because Gastrea are enemies of mankind who prey upon humans and rewrite their DNA, of course."

"In short, it's because Gastrea are inconvenient organisms for humans to have around, right? But don't you think mankind is a little too spoiled? They rest on their laurels, certain that they are the pinnacle of evolution and look down on other organisms, but that's just because they can't help but feel superior to other organisms based on the consciousness they've acquired.

"But if you think about it carefully, it is our consciousness that is telling us that our consciousness is proof that we are advanced organisms. As long as humans are humans, there is no way to prove that objectively. For example, what about Gastrea? They have the godlike ability to interfere with an organism's genes and redesign them, right? Couldn't you say that *that* is an ability that surpasses our 'consciousness'? It has died down in Japan, but around the world, there are a number of religions that consider the Gastrea sacred. That they are divine messengers who have appeared to purify this corrupt world."

"Really?" said Rentaro, surprised. "Why...?"

Sumire continued. "Humans are using up all the resources and are the cause of the rapid destruction of the world. From the perspective of the spaceship Earth, if Gastrea controlled the world, they would probably be able to steer the ship a lot better. There is that saying that all life is fleeting. The idea that the Earth is just a temporary inn for all living creatures to stay. Aren't we humans leaving the inn too messy? Wouldn't it make sense for us to make the bed neatly before we pass it on to the next generation of governors?"

Rentaro pretended to drink his coffee, lost in thought. "Isn't that the same as the excuse of deep ecologists? With too much ecology, humans end up not being needed at all in the end. Even if there are people out there who affirm Gastrea, I can't agree with them. Anyway, if they're divine messengers, then what are the Cursed Children supposed to be?"

"They are the most fit to be God's substitutes as messengers between humans and Gastrea."

Before he knew it, he couldn't take it any longer and stood up. "Enju is human. She is a human with her own personality and her own will! Nothing more, nothing less."

The coffee that spilled with his movement formed a stream that led to a small river that dripped off the edge of the desk and onto the floor. Sumire playfully spread her arms in approval. "That's exactly right. See? You do understand."

"Oh." She had set him up. When he realized that, he suddenly became embarrassed and collapsed into his chair. She purposefully said things that would rub him the wrong way. Everything she had been saying was to force him to honestly confess his feelings about Enju voluntarily. She had him completely by the nose.

"Hey, Rentaro," said Sumire. "At least you know who you are and where you came from. Enju doesn't even have that."

"Huh?" said Rentaro, confused.

"Most of the kids living in the Outer District were abandoned. Because those girls were born after we lost the war, they don't know their parents' faces, and all they've ever known is the small world of Tokyo Area. They're being spurned by so many people without even knowing anything, being looked down upon with scorn. The first generation of those girls will soon be entering adolescence, and because of those origins, they will definitely agonize over the loss of their identity. It was my hope that you could be there to help lead Enju through that—you guys are family, right?"

Rentaro's mouth opened slightly and he felt shivers going down his spine. Just how far did she...? "Doc, I'm gonna go see Enju after all."

Sumire waved her hand limply and had no further intention of looking at him.

As he left the university hospital, his cell phone buzzed. It was a call from an unknown number. "Hello, is this Satomi."

He knew who it was from the voice.

"Yes, speaking."

"This is Aihara's homeroom teacher. There has been an incident with Aihara... Can you come to the school immediately?"

By the time Rentaro reached the school gates, panting, a small crowded had gathered. There was a donut-shaped wall of people surrounding two people who were having an argument.

Three girls passed by Rentaro.

"What's going on?"

"Remember that girl from Class 3? Apparently, she was a Gastrea virus carrier."

"No way! I think I touched her before. What should I do?"

"I never liked her. She always acted like she was better than everyone else."

Feeling an uneasy sense of déjà vu, Rentaro felt like he was being suffocated and loosened his tie as he drew near to the ring of people. From where he was, he couldn't hear what they were arguing about, but he could hear the loud voices of two people. However, what was unfolding was decidedly one-sided. When someone who sounded like a boy yelled, the crowd around yelled encouragement, but when the girl yelled, all she got were cold, dead stares and a critical silence.

When Rentaro realized that the person inside the circle was Enju Aihara, he felt like vomiting and covered his hand with his mouth. His worst fears had come true. As he started toward Enju again, he heard murmurs around him that made him sick.

*"There really were Red-Eyes around us. Why don't the civsec officers exterminate them?"*

*"Ugh. Her eyes glow red. I wish people like that wouldn't come to school."*

*"Don't come out of the Outer District ghetto."*

*Who do you think is protecting the peace of Tokyo Area?!* Rentaro was overcome with the urge to run into the middle of the wall of people and send them all flying. But seeing their expressions, he had to put down his fist. Most of the people were onlookers or worthless gossips, but there were some pale faces who were seriously afraid that they would catch the Gastrea virus. If they had been educated properly, they would have known that unless they received a large amount of blood from the girl, they couldn't get the virus from her.

Rentaro had seen the boy who was arguing with Enju in her class picture before. His face and closely shaved head looked like it belonged to an energetic little leaguer, but right now, his face was flushed purplish-red, and he was pressing Enju for an answer with a shrill voice. "My dad had been drinking every day and hitting my mom ever since his leg was eaten by a Gastrea during the war! Because of all your killing, my family's…!"

Enju shook her head furiously. "No! That wasn't me. I'm human!"

"That's disgusting, how you pretend to be human."

"I *am* human!"

"Shut up, you monster!"

"I am human!"

"Are not!"

Rentaro looked down, clenching his teeth. It was too hard to watch. This wasn't a conversation anymore—she was just being unilaterally rejected.

*"No matter how hard you work for those guys, they will just keep betraying you."*

This was exactly what Kagetane had told him would happen. Tears of frustration welled up in his eyes. "Enju..."

When Enju noticed him, her eyes opened wide, and she took a step back. "R-Rentaro..."

Realizing that he was connected to Enju somehow, the wall of people parted, and an unpleasant silence descended. Rentaro tread firmly on the sand in the schoolyard with the bottoms of his shoes and walked slowly toward the center. The boy who was verbally attacking Enju faltered and said, "Wh-what do you want?" trying to act tough.

Rentaro passed right by him and when he got to Enju, he hugged her silently. Rentaro closed his eyes and spoke slowly, punctuating each syllable. "Enju, let's change schools."

In his arms, Enju's body moved slightly. Enju's cold body trembled as she drenched the shoulder of Rentaro's uniform with her warm tears. "I...don't want...to give up... I made so many friends, too..."

"They're not your friends anymore."

He heard Enju sniffling. "Is it all over for me? I can't start over anymore?"

"Yeah, it's all over. It'll take some more time before the world is ready to accept you."

"But we have to keep fighting?"

Rentaro paused. "Yeah." Rentaro wiped her tears with his fingertips and put a handkerchief over her face, letting her cry for a while. Finally, he let go of her and made her stand, smiling at her. "Now, at least leave with your head held high."

"But my bag is in the classroom."

"Does that stuff even matter anymore?"

"N-no! You're right!" Enju wiped her eyes on her sleeve and acted cheerful.

*That's right, Enju.*

At that moment, Rentaro's phone vibrated. He thought of ignoring it, but after seeing the name on the screen, he pushed the TALK button.

"Satomi, I know where the source Gastrea's hideout is," said Kisara's voice on the other end. "It's in District 32."

"Kisara, I mean President...," said Rentaro. "How did it get all the way to District 32?"

"Listen to this. It looks like that Gastrea can fly."

He thought he heard wrong and shifted his phone to get a better grip. "The infected became a Model Spider, right? So the source Gastrea should also be a Model Spider. What do you mean a spider can fly?"

"Just hurry and get to the hideout. The other civsec officers are also after the source Gastrea"—she gave a snort of triumph and continued—"but the Tendo Civil Security Agency will get there first. I have your location on the GPS, and I've contracted someone amazing, so chase down the Gastrea with them. In order to get them, I had to use my tuition for next semester. Which means if someone else gets the credit, I'll have to drop out of school! Do you get it? So work hard and do your best."

"Ah, hey, wait, Kisara...?" Hearing the empty dial tone, Rentaro sighed and flipped his cell phone closed. What in the world did she mean by "I've contracted someone amazing"?

At that moment, he could hear commotion mixed with screams in the schoolyard. Rentaro looked in the direction the crowd was pointing. Before long, he could see something that got bigger as it drew near. Finally, it was so close that voices couldn't be heard over the thunderous roar of the rotors, and shock waves blew away the clouds of dust in the schoolyard.

When Rentaro narrowed his eyes and looked up, the sky above him was dyed blue with the polished body of an aircraft. In the middle of the aircraft was the picture of a snake wrapped around a staff. It was the emblem of the god of medicine, Asclepius. Rentaro winced inwardly. Just like a rich girl. She did everything on a large scale.

Looking dumbly into the sky, one of the teachers murmured, "Medevac helicopter..."

5

Shortly after the helicopter flew away, the streaks of rain suddenly got stronger, and it started raining heavily outside the window. Rentaro cupped his cheek nervously in his hand, squirming and checking the passenger seat over and over. Inside the helicopter, it was eerily silent compared to the wild weather outside.

Enju was riding on the flap door in the back where a patient on a stretcher would normally be. Because of the wall between them, Rentaro, riding in the passenger seat, couldn't see Enju, who was riding in the back.

*I should have ridden in the back with Enju.* The more he looked at the Shakujii River rising in the rain, the more he thought so. If he had, then he could have used the time it took for them to get to their destination to talk with her a little more.

Rentaro looked at the glowing GPS dot that Kisara had sent him. Because they couldn't use the satellites in this rain, this was the position from ten minutes ago. It was highly likely that the Gastrea had already moved from this position.

As they neared the Outer District, Rentaro could see the Monoliths blocking their way like a giant mountain range. It was still hard to believe that they were masses of Varanium. One probably had enough for hundreds of thousands of the Varanium bullets Rentaro used. Maybe more.

"I wonder what that is?" said the pilot.

Rentaro saw a flying object below them where the pilot was pointing. He rubbed his eyes and pressed his forehead against the window. About eighty meters in the air, he could see a flying object shaped like an arrowhead. At first, it looked to him like a kite flying in the sky. It looked like a white isosceles triangle floating above the forest. Beneath the isosceles triangle, he could just make out a shadow with eight long, thin legs.

"A spider's parachute…," said Rentaro with realization. "Damn it, so that's what it was. Please go after it, pilot."

"You know what that is?" asked the pilot.

"Yeah," Rentaro answered. "That's the source Gastrea. Somewhere in South America, there is a small spider that weaves its nest into a parachute and uses it to ride hundreds of kilometers on the wind. Since it rides on the wind, it might be easier to understand if you think of it as a dandelion seed. Spider silk is basically a type of polymer, but that Gastrea was able to weave it into the shape of a kite…"

Putting that much into words, he suddenly had a new thought, and his words trailed off. Why did it make it into an isosceles triangle then? Rentaro felt like he was missing something important.

Suddenly, a lightbulb went off in his head. "I see... It's not a parachute, it's a hang glider. If that's the case, then it all makes sense. The front is tapered so that it can cut through the wind and give it lift. That's also why there were no sightings of the source Gastrea. If that's the case, then this is an amazing feat. Because there's no mature spider in the world that possesses this ability."

In any case, he now knew why it wasn't caught by any of the surveillance cameras around town. Outside of the Outer District, the surveillance cameras were meant to watch people from above, so it was normal for them to be pointing down. To capture a Gastrea gliding far above was completely removed from what they were supposed to be used for.

This Gastrea probably dug its claws into the side of a building and climbed to the roof to fly off using the eddies of wind around high buildings. It was smart.

"Wh-what should I do?" said the pilot uncertainly.

"Lower our altitude and match its speed to follow it like this from above," Rentaro ordered.

Just then, there was the violent sound of an iron plate being punched through, and the aircraft lurched to the side. Rentaro hit his head on the glass a few times. "Oww...," he said. "What the hell was that?"

"The door in the back was broken open," said the pilot. "That Initiator you brought did it."

"Enju? No way, we're in midflight right now. What in the world is she trying to do...?" At that moment, Rentaro realized what Enju intended, and his blood froze. "Wait, Enju!" he shouted.

By the time he yelled, it was too late. He could see Enju falling headfirst from a high altitude. Seeing Enju get smaller and smaller as she fell on a path following the law of gravity, Rentaro almost screamed.

Aiming for the spider's hang glider woven from spider silk, Enju crashed into it with the speed of a shooting star. For the Gastrea, it was a violent attack that came from its blind spot directly above it. Enju and the Gastrea fell tangled together into the forest that ran along the banks of the river.

"Lower our altitude," Rentaro told the pilot. "Hurry!" Rentaro quickly looked around and pulled out a vinyl rope he found tucked away to the side of the helicopter. He had no time to think. He pulled

the rope out with all his strength, and doubling it up, he tied it around the side of the seat and pulled it a few times to test its strength.

The instant he kicked open the door, the pouring rain and driving winds that had been absorbed by the thick glass blew into his face. Because both the back and side doors were open and the craft was affected by the winds, the helicopter had not been steady for a while now. Rentaro dangled the vinyl rope, but it was buffeted by the strong winds. In addition, the vinyl rope had a terrible grip compared to a rappelling rope. There was no lifeline or carabiner, either. When he looked down, it was so high that it made him dizzy.

The pilot looked at Rentaro, his eyes wide with surprise. *I wonder at my own sanity*, Rentaro thought. *The hell with it.* He prayed, gripped the rope tightly with both hands and feet, and let his body down into midair.

The vinyl rope, wet with rain, was much slipperier than Rentaro had imagined. He tried to brake, but he wouldn't stop. Just as he was finally able to control his speed by gripping the rope so hard the skin came off his hands, a sudden wind that even Rentaro could hear rocked the rope.

By the time he realized what had happened, it was already too late. With a terrible floating sensation, he was thrown into the air. He spun both arms in panic, but the ground spun as he closed in on it with terrifying speed. *Fall headfirst? No, I need to fix my position. I'll absorb the shock with my legs.*

His brain was functioning at amazing speed, and for just a brief moment, time seemed to slow down. In that moment that felt like an eternity, Rentaro somersaulted in midair and successfully pointed his feet downward. Immediately after, the ground rushed up to meet him. He felt the vibration all the way to his organs. His body was swung about, and after being spun around four times like he was being blown away, he found himself lying on his back in muddy water.

Gasping to get back some of the wind that was knocked out of him, he spit out the disgusting bits of gravel that had gotten into his mouth. He couldn't stand until his head stopped spinning from the damage to his inner ear.

When he felt like his consciousness was focused again, he gave a weak wave at the helicopter that was flying nervously overhead and felt pain in his whole body as he lifted himself up. It had probably been about twenty meters. He had heard that the farthest a human being could fall without dying was about fifteen meters, so he wasn't sure why he was alive himself.

That was when he first realized that the ground he had landed on was muddy from the torrential rains. *Where was Enju? That's right, Enju.*

Favoring his right leg, he stood and walked into the forest along the river. The intense rain pounded down on his face, and his sight was blurred with the water. On top of the uncomfortable sensation of his wet hair plastered against his face, his uniform was heavy from the water it had absorbed. Feeling cold, he rubbed his elbows with both hands.

Beyond the tall curtain of evergreen trees echoed intermittent sounds of battle. When he climbed the small hill that obstructed his vision, supporting himself with his hands on the trees, he saw a battle unfolding before his eyes.

On one side was the Model Spider Gastrea, with venomous fangs bared menacingly, thrusting skillfully with its eight long, thin, and rapier-sharp legs. Just as Rentaro had imagined, in order to fly, its body had been made as light as possible, and other than the yellow-and-black mottled pattern on its body, it looked just like a long-jawed orb weaver.

However, Enju's red-hot eyes saw through the Gastrea's every move. Dodging the skillful thrusts, she swiftly hid herself underneath the Gastrea's abdomen and kicked upward with an iron-hammer-like force that made it seem as if she had Varanium in the soles of her shoes. The kick was only aimed at the Gastrea's abdomen, but its flesh was torn and its chin was crushed to pieces, fangs and all. It flew about ten meters into the air and spun once before striking the ground with its own weight. The bodily fluids that flew out even reached Rentaro's uniform.

Not only were three of its thin, wirelike legs broken, but bodily fluids were gushing out of its abdomen. She had won. "Rentaro, I beat it! We were the first ones here!" When Enju saw Rentaro, she waved her arms excitedly at him.

He sighed with relief. "Don't be so rash. I thought you'd given in to your despair, and I..." As he moved near Enju to put a hand on her shoulder, her face twisted in pain. "Are you hurt?" he asked.

"I-I'm not hurt! I just twisted my left ankle a little. It'll be fine in an hour."

He thumped Enju on the head.

"Hey, what do you think you're doing?!"

"You dummy...," Rentaro said. "You're not fine. Don't pretend it doesn't hurt! You're just a kid."

Rentaro tilted his head and walked over to the Gastrea's corpse, looking dissatisfied. Collapsed with its shrunken appendages, the Gastrea was smaller than he'd expected. Like the information they had gotten said, the duralumin case in question was embedded in the Gastrea's body, stuck to the upper part of the abdomen. When he saw it in the picture, it was hard to tell how big it was, but he could see now that it was about wide enough to fill his arms.

"What is this...?" said Rentaro. There were long handcuffs attached to the handle of the duralumin case. Before the victim had turned into a Gastrea, he probably connected the case to his hand so that he would not let it go. However, the victim's corrosion rate had passed the limit.

The gloomy sound of the rain reached Rentaro. Rentaro held the Gastrea down with one leg and pulled out the case, handcuffs and all, and then took a few steps back. He shivered with a sudden chill down his spine. He didn't care what was inside anymore. He just wanted to hand over the case as soon as possible and get this job over with.

Rentaro turned his neck to look around. There was no sign of anyone even though it was about time other civil officers should have arrived. The fabric of his clothes poked him, and his body prickled all over.

He heard a laugh. "Good work, Satomi."

"Huh?" The second he looked back, there was a white mask at point-blank range. Five long, thin fingers grabbed his face, splashing it with muddy water.

Rentaro choked. He tried to break free, but he was thrown violently into the tree trunk with a terrifying force. He couldn't do anything about the inertia, and at the same time, something sharp crashed into his spine. The air was squeezed out of his lungs, and his vision grew dark as his consciousness faded.

"Rentaro!" cried Enju.

"Found you, Enju." As Enju rolled to the side instinctively, the plants behind her split into three before she remembered to yell and was blown backward. Kohina appeared with her Varanium-bladed short swords, taking a stance that looked like she was about to spread her wings.

Rentaro stood with a fit of coughing, glaring at the man holding onto the mask with one hand while laughing evilly. "Kagetane… Hiruko…!"

Kagetane spoke. "Even though your president's cute, she does some pretty nasty stuff. She was sniffing around my backers without caring about appearances. I'm acting on an order from them. They said to take care of this quickly."

Rentaro felt chills as he held the duralumin case behind him and retreated. Kagetane snorted. "Are you waiting for other civsec officers to show up? You probably shouldn't. I killed almost all of the weaklings nearby on my way here."

Rentaro noticed the splatters of blood coating Kagetane's wine-red tailcoat and shuddered with horror. He drew his XD and fired.

Kagetane was ready. "It's no use. *Imaginary Gimmick.*" As he yelled this, the bullets hit an invisible wall and bounced off in all directions.

The sound of the rain returned to Rentaro's ears. Kagetane opened his arms magnanimously to show that he was unhurt.

*Not yet*, thought Rentaro as he threw the duralumin case away. Pressing down, he stepped onto the ground, focusing his strength. "Tendo Martial Arts First Style, Number 8: *Homura Kasen!*" It was a straight punch with his whole body behind it. However, before it reached Kagetane, it collided with the stubborn bluish-white barrier and was thrown off course, hitting thin air.

Kagetane drew a custom Beretta from its holster, and unfolding the bayonet, he stabbed Rentaro's shoulder and fired off three shots point-blank.

Rentaro groaned. Pushing down on the intense pain in his shoulder, he stumbled. Something hit his back. It was a large rock. He couldn't run away.

Kagetane slowly and deliberately raised his arm and faced Rentaro. "I'll show you one of my special moves—*Maximum Pain!*"

Suddenly, the repulsion field around Kagetane expanded and rushed at Rentaro. It was a side attack that suddenly hit his whole body. With terrifying force, Rentaro was thrown onto the rock and blood gushed from his head. His body sank into the rock, his flesh was crushed, and his bones creaked like they were about to be pulverized. It felt as if his whole body had been run through a press.

As Rentaro screamed, he finally understood. The first time he encountered Kagetane, the police officers who had entered ahead of him had been crushed to death against the walls. This was what he had used against them.

Suddenly, the intense pressure disappeared, and Rentaro fell to his knees, coughing up blood.

"Oh? You're still alive?" said Kagetane.

Rentaro's vision wavered. His head hurt. He felt like he was going to fall apart. This was how strong Kagetane was. In addition to the huge difference between Rentaro's and Kagetane's combat abilities, there was Enju's injured foot. Rentaro's brain calmly calculated the most reasonable combat strategy, and he lowered his head weakly. "Enju, run."

Enju widened her eyes and shook her head. "No!"

Seeing Kohina getting ready to thrust behind Enju, Rentaro fired a shot at Enju's feet. She reflexively leapt into the air.

Rentaro called at her with his eyes. *Bring other civil officers here.*

Enju disappeared into the brush with a sad look on her face.

"Papa! Enju ran away! I want to kill her! I want to go after her!" Kohina, whose duel had been cut short, was on the verge of a temper tantrum.

"No, my daughter," said Kagetane. "If they meet up with other civsec officers, it will become troublesome. Let us finish our job."

Kohina glared at Rentaro, and the next instant, just as he thought that she had disappeared from his sight, he felt a strong impact to his stomach. Two Varanium black blades appeared in there. It took him a few seconds to realize he had been stabbed from behind.

"But you're so weak!" Kohina taunted. "So weak! So weak!"

Blood frothing from his mouth, Rentaro swung backward with his fist, then ran away, firing shots from his gun. With each shot he fired, he felt the recoil in his wounds and almost lost consciousness from the pain, but he gritted his teeth and ran, firing without aiming at anything in particular.

But even though he thought he was hurrying, his steps were extremely slow. His vision blurred. Raindrops stole the heat from his body. It was so cold. He felt like he was going to freeze. Pushing down on his stomach and forcing his way through the curtain of trees, he arrived at a clearing.

It was the flooded river. It was flowing at a speed that was impossible to swim across. Turning slowly, he saw Kohina and Kagetane, along with the muzzle of that custom Beretta, looking at him. The white noise of the rain tapped his earlobe. Rentaro closed his eyes. *Enju, Kisara, I'm sorry.*

"Any last words, my dying friend?" said Kagetane.

"Go…to hell…," said Rentaro.

"Good night."

The Beretta fired into Rentaro's chest, stomach, thighs, not caring where it opened up its small black holes. Letting his gun fall, Rentaro's upper body slowly crumpled. At the edge of his darkening vision, he saw Kagetane crossing himself, as though he were a man of faith.

When Rentaro's body hit the water, the river's flooded current carried him away with amazing force.

It was noisy around him as someone roughly tapped Rentaro's cheek. Someone was calling his name. He opened his eyes with great difficulty, and long fluorescent lights slid one after another on the ceiling. At the edge of his vision, he could see people wearing white coats who looked like paramedics.

It looked like he was being taken to the ER in a stretcher.

His whole body was so cold it felt frozen, and his breathing was ridiculously rough. Inside his mouth was the unending metallic taste of blood, and he couldn't breathe. He probably had blood in his lungs, and he felt like he was suffocating to death.

"It'll be fine."

"We'll take care of you."

The empty words the paramedics chanted as they pushed the stretcher went in one ear and out the other.

With a loud bang, he was thrust into the operating room, and a female doctor wearing green scrubs peered at Rentaro. She looked like skin and bones, overcome with grief, with only her sunken eyes glittering. Rentaro tilted his head, but the instant he saw himself in the mirror in the operating room, he almost screamed.

Rentaro's right arm and leg were torn off, and his left eye had been gouged out. But the most surprising part was that his body had shrunk. It looked like a child's.

*No, that's not it,* he realized. *I see. This is the past.*

The female doctor looked coldly down at Rentaro as if he were about to die, and thrust the pieces of paper she had in each hand at him. "Hey, you're Rentaro Satomi, right? Nice to meet you. And soon, I'll say good-bye. In my left hand is a death certificate. In another five minutes, I would've finished my notes on this, and you would have quickly been erased from your family register. And in my right hand is a contract. This can save your life, but you must offer up everything but your life. Choose. You can just point with your left arm."

Just lifting his arm caused an unbelievably intense pain. His hand was shaking ridiculously, and the blood overflowing from his mouth stained the stretcher. His body trembled like he had the shakes.

Suddenly, Kikunojo Tendo's words replayed themselves in the back of his mind.

*"If you do not want to die, survive, Rentaro."*

As he pointed with his unbelievably white hand, the doctor said, "Good boy," and smiled with satisfaction. Then, Rentaro lost consciousness.

# BLACK
# BULLET
# CHAPTER
# 03

## THE GASTREA THAT
## DESTROYED THE WORLD

1

The first thing Rentaro heard was a scratching sound. He felt like he was wrapped in something very soft. It was warm and comfortable. Then the strong smell of medicine pierced the membrane of his nose. He felt a faint light on the other side of his eyelid. A bitter taste remained in his mouth, and he grimaced.

He returned to consciousness feeling like he was crawling at the bottom of a swamp. He was still surprised that he was even conscious. He tried to open his eyes, but his eyelids were so heavy that his eyelids just flickered. After a while, he could see the ceiling fuzzily. Unlike the wooden ceiling in his apartment, this was a bluish-white ceiling. He was lying in a bed.

Kisara came into his line of sight. She was wearing her Miwa Academy uniform, and her eyes were wet as she looked down at Rentaro. He could smell the scent of shampoo coming from the tips of Kisara's hair that were tickling his nose. It was such a deep, glossy black that it looked tinged with green. Thinking she was pretty, Rentaro gazed at her for a while, his head still fuzzy.

"Hey, Kisara." He tried to make it sound as peaceful as he could.

Kisara squeezed her eyes tightly and bit her lip, her eyelids fluttering, finally smiling earnestly through teary eyes. "Welcome back, Satomi."

Rentaro smiled wryly. "Is this heaven?"

"It's still hell, you idiot."

Rentaro looked at the side table. "You peeled an apple and cut it for me?"

Kisara wiped her eyes on her sleeve. "Do you want some?"

"No, even though I don't think I ate anything, I don't really feel hungry." Forcing his troublesome body to turn his head, he looked out the window and saw that the sky had cleared and a crescent moon was peeking at them.

Rentaro turned back to Kisara. "How long did I sleep?"

"A full day and about three hours. It was a major operation. The doctor was about to give up. But at the very end, your heart started to beat. You hadn't given up on living. You did well." Kisara traced Rentaro's chest with her index finger and tapped twice above his heart. Rentaro's heart fluttered a little.

As he tried to force his upper body up, Kisara held him down, but when Rentaro shook his head slightly, she didn't try to stop him any longer. He checked to make sure he had his right arm and leg and gently touched his left eye.

"You're really supposed to be resting completely," said Kisara.

"Kisara, how did you know where I had been washed off to?" asked Rentaro.

"Because of this." Saying that, she dug in her bag and pulled out Rentaro's gun. The slide stop was raised and the slide lock was on. It was his XD in the "hold-open" position. If he remembered correctly, he had dropped it during the fight. "This had fallen next to the river. That's why I thought maybe you were downstream, so we searched there."

He finally understood the reason he was alive. Rentaro opened and closed his hand to make sure everything was working. Suddenly, he realized that Kisara was peering at him intently.

"A lot happened while you were sleeping, Satomi," she said. "Hmm… Where should I start?" Kisara lifted her chin prettily as she forced her mouth into a smile. "We might die soon."

"What?" said Rentaro.

"More accurately, all the residents of Tokyo Area might die soon."

"Don't tell me Kagetane Hiruko is…"

"All the civil officer representatives were just gathered and told the truth behind this job. Listen calmly. Inside that case is a catalyst of some kind that can summon a Stage Five Gastrea."

He couldn't react right away. Before he knew it, his palm was damp with sweat. "Stage Five—as in the eleven Gastrea who destroyed the world…right?"

"What else is there?"

*I see. That's why there would be a Great Extinction…* Aloud, Rentaro said, "But Kisara, there's no way anyone would be able to just call out a Stage Five!"

"It *is* possible. That was the first I'd heard of it, too. Apparently, someone important from the Seitenshi faction was covering it up."

Rentaro clicked his tongue as an image of the Seitenshi and Kikunojo came to mind. That's why he hated people in authority. "Please, keep going."

"All the civil officer representatives were brave," said Kisara. "No one fainted or fell into a panic, and only a few people rushed to the sink. The rest were quiet."

Rentaro said nothing.

"I heard from Enju that you fought Kagetane Hiruko. How was it?"

"He's too strong… He's not human."

"The Seitenshi's group gave us information about them. Promoter Kagetane Hiruko. Apparently, his repulsion field can repel antitank rifle bullets and stop the iron ball at the end of those tower cranes used in construction. His Initiator is Kohina Hiruko. She is a Model Mantis—in other words, she is an Initiator with the genes of a praying mantis, and with long-enough blades, she is invincible in a close fight. This pair had their license revoked because they caused too many problems, but before that, their IP Rank was 134. You're lucky to be alive."

"They were ranked 134?!" Rentaro's eyes opened wide. No wonder they were crazily strong. It was the first time he had ever seen such a high-ranking pair with his own eyes. He thought again that it was amazing he was still alive.

"Kagetane Hiruko and Kohina have currently run to the Unexplored Territory outside of the Monoliths and are making preparations to call the Stage Five into Tokyo Area. The government is spearheading plans for a large-scale operation."

"I can't believe all that happened while I was sleeping…" Suddenly, they both stopped talking, and they were wrapped in the stillness of the night.

Kisara's eyes narrowed sharply. "Now, Enju, isn't it about time you came out?"

"Huh? Enju?!"

"Perverted bastard!" Rentaro heard Enju's voice close by. At that moment, the blanket in Rentaro's bed was lifted, and Enju appeared. Rentaro was the most startled of them all.

"Woah, hey…you little…don't tell me you were there the whole time…?"

"I slept next to you this whole time. And I heard everything. I heard your love-struck voice. What's so great about Kisara, anyway? Kisara's just a pair of boobs!"

Kisara made a disgusted face at being called a pair of boobs.

"Anyway, I was comatose until just now," said Rentaro. "I can't believe you could sleep next to me like that."

Enju held her head up proudly. "It's because the nurses and doctor were idiots."

"I wasn't asking about your methodology. Don't crawl into my bed. At least let me rest while I'm comatose."

"It's none of your business where I sleep."

"Hey, you little…"

"Rentaro," Kisara cut in. "Don't you have something more important to say to Enju?"

Rentaro paused. "That's right, I'm sorry for giving you that order."

An arm wrapped tightly around Rentaro's neck. Silently, Rentaro hugged Enju's thin body back. "I'm a failure as a guardian, huh?"

"Completely. You are completely hopeless as a guardian." Contrary to her words, Enju looked like she was about to cry. "Do you know how I felt when I thought you were about to die…?"

Rentaro patted Enju's shoulder to comfort her. "I'm really sorry…"

At that moment, Kisara's cell phone rang. Her ring tone was Ravel's *Pavane for a Dead Princess*. After saying a few words, Kisara gave the phone to Rentaro.

"Satomi, it is I."

Rentaro stared at the phone in surprise for a brief moment.

"What do you want now, Lady Seitenshi?" said Rentaro.

"Satomi, the pursuit of Kagetane Hiruko has begun," the Seitenshi informed him. "Many civil officers are participating in this, the largest operation of its kind to date. I am sorry to ask this of you while you are still recovering, but I would like you to participate in this operation."

"There's one thing I want to ask. That man, Kagetane Hiruko, is..."

"I'm sure you've already heard some of it from President Tendo, but ten years ago, he killed many of the staff at a government hospital and deserted. In the confusion following the war, he changed his name and became a civil officer. We, the government, had been covering up the fact that he deserted."

Rentaro gripped the cell phone so hard that he almost crushed it. "Why didn't you take any countermeasures against him?"

"Satomi, the New Humanity Creation Project is a project that does not exist. A soldier who did not exist cannot desert."

"What the hell?! Do you know how many people he's killed? It's all your fault! Why should I clean up after your mess? Like hell I will!"

"Satomi, if you do not fight now, many more people will die. Your dear friends, the people you love. Could you bear that?"

Rentaro hid his face in his hands and shook his head weakly. "Why...? Why me...?"

"You know him best. You are the only one who can stop Kagetane Hiruko."

Rentaro let out a deep breath. "All right. But I'm not doing this for you guys. Don't forget that."

"That's fine. Good luck, Satomi."

Rentaro ended the call and threw the phone back to Kisara. He felt like his arm was being pulled by something, and looking by his pillow, he saw a number of vital sign numbers. Rentaro checked to make sure he wouldn't sound the alarm, then unplugged it, pulling off the electrodes and needles one by one.

When he touched his wounds, he grimaced with the intense pain, but he could do it somehow. It was probably thanks to the latest treatments he received in the ICU. On top of his wounds were recovery patches to promote fast healing, so as long as he took things easy, he should live. Checking to see that it was his own uniform in the paper bag on the shelf, he took off his hospital clothes and started changing. Kisara blushed and called him an idiot before she turned her back to him.

"Satomi, can you win?" she asked.

"I can't lose," he said.

"You'll die."

"I'm prepared for that."

Rentaro could hear a squeak as Kisara bit her lip hard behind his back. "Must you go?" she said. "There's me and Enju, and the three of us together make up the Tendo Civil Security Agency. Isn't that good enough?"

Rentaro paused. "Sorry, Kisara. I…"

"It's all right. I won't ask you anymore. There's something that's been bothering me, as well, so I will look into that. When Kagetane Hiruko went outside the Monoliths to call the Stage Five, information was almost leaked to some of the media outlets. The Seitenshi managed the information quickly and just barely stopped it, though. I'm going to look into this matter some more."

Rentaro thought that was strange as he tightened his necktie. If a Stage Five was about to take Tokyo Area, at worst, that could mean the whole Tokyo Area would be wiped out. If that news was broadcast, regular citizens would probably fall into a panic. Would it help anyone to have that information? Was there still a trump card hidden somewhere after all this?

Rentaro announced that he was done changing.

Righting herself, Kisara flipped her black hair, the moon behind her. "This is an order as your boss. Crush the Kagetane-Kohina pair and stop them from calling the Stage Five Gastrea. Satomi, I need you to work a hundred times harder than you've ever worked for me. And I'm going to work a thousand times as much as I ever did, for you."

"I will definitely stop it," said Rentaro firmly. "I'll do it for you, too!"

## 2     IT WAS 9:00 P.M.

Listening to the wasplike groan of the rotor, Rentaro looked carefully at the dark forest spread out below them. It was the first time he had ever ridden on a helicopter twice in such a short interval. The forest was shrouded in a deep darkness that the moonlight could not pierce.

Rentaro had been in the hospital on the brink of death, so he had missed the Seitenshi's personal briefing, but based on the course of the helicopter, it looked like Kagetane's hideout was around the Boso Peninsula of the old Chiba prefecture. The pilot had pointed out the site of the New Tokyo International Airport earlier, but it was too dark to see. It was probably just ruins that had been converted into plant seedbeds, anyway. Rentaro wasn't really interested.

Other than Abiko, Usui, and some other areas near Tokyo, most of Chiba prefecture had not been surrounded by the Monoliths in time. The helicopter had passed the Monolith border much earlier. They were already in the dangerous area where Gastrea tread, the Unexplored Territory. Somewhere here, a pair that had once held an IP Rank of 134 was hiding. It was about time the other civil officer pairs were dropped off by helicopters or other transport vehicles in the areas they were assigned to cover.

Rentaro tapped his feet nervously as he rubbed his hands together. This was the full force that had been called out to hunt the Kagetane pair down. He had heard that there were many pairs other than himself involved in this operation. Among them, there should be pairs higher ranked than the Kagetane pair, as well. There was an extremely low likelihood that Rentaro would be the first one to find the Kagetanes' hideout and engage in combat with them. Even so, as time passed, he grew more and more nervous. What was this indescribable impatience he felt?

Before they left, Rentaro stopped by the university hospital to visit Sumire. Looking at his face, Sumire threw a large shopping bag at him. Rentaro took it, tottering, and was surprised when he opened it up and looked inside.

"It's from your patron," Sumire said. "She said everything she thought you might need was inside. Is that enough?"

"Wow…it's more than enough…" Thanking the student council president in his heart, Rentaro attached the waist pouch and holster to his belt, filled the pouch with the different tools he needed, and changed the XD barrel for one with a silencer. He tried jumping lightly, and he didn't feel much difference in weight. Since his patron knew that Rentaro avoided wearing equipment like battle dress uniform, headgear, and bulletproof vests, she kept things that changed his appearance or added weight down to a minimum. Miori Shiba, the daughter of the CEO of Shiba Heavy Weapons. She really knew Rentaro well.

"Man, how annoying," said Rentaro. "Now I have to thank her the next time I see her."

"She has high hopes for you, doesn't she?" said Sumire. "Thank her by achieving great things."

He instantly caught what she threw into his chest. There were five small syringes connected together like bells. Inside each was a red liquid, and a cap was on each needle.

"That's my going away present," she said. "It's something I made while researching Gastrea. You know what I'm talking about when I say it's the AGV test drug?"

Rentaro gazed at them in wonderment and kept looking at the drug inside.

"Don't use it unless you have to," she continued. "If you go away, there will be fewer visitors to this basement room, and that'll be problematic."

He didn't know what he could say to thank her, so he just stood still for a moment.

"I have one important piece of advice," said Sumire. "Do you want to hear it?"

"Y-yeah." Rentaro straightened.

Sumire put her hands on his shoulders. "You know…if you die, you should die neatly."

"Huh?"

"I would prefer you to freeze to death if possible. No, no, that's asking too much. In this case, starving to death would be fine, too. I'll pour turpentine down your anus and cover you with natron salts and put you out to dry in the sun."

"A-are you planning on turning me into a mummy and using me to decorate your lab?!"

"You understand things quickly. That's right. Don't worry, as a burial accessory, I'll put a pair of Kisara's underwear on your head and put you up in the university where everyone can see!" She laughed evilly.

"I've just decided! When I die, I'm going to die with a bunch of hand grenades in my arms. I'm gonna rest in pieces!" Asking himself what kind of threat that was supposed to be, he became a little depressed that he couldn't even die carelessly.

"Rentaro, can I just say one more thing?" Sumire sat down and crossed her legs. Rentaro sat like he wasn't going to be tricked by her again.

But he was wrong.

"Ten years ago, from the day Gastrea first started exterminating mankind, my world changed completely. Heaps of bodies, streams of blood, mangled corpses... No matter how many words you used, it would not be nearly enough to describe that hell. However, even if that was the case, what I did to you cannot be forgiven." Sumire shook as she clutched the locket on her chest. Rentaro knew that there was a picture of her lover inside. "My conduct was abnormal at the time. I don't know what I can say to apologize."

Rentaro hesitated a few times and then finally spoke. "Doc... I have never once resented you, ever since that day."

Sumire didn't say anything for a while.

Rentaro snuck a glance at the locket before returning his gaze to Sumire. Rentaro silently put his XD into its holster and turned to leave. As he was leaving, Rentaro looked at her shelves with her Western film collection and suddenly gave a thumbs-up. "I-I'll be back," he said falteringly.

Sumire looked at him blankly for a moment like she didn't know what he meant. Rentaro was suddenly embarrassed, but he couldn't just pretend it didn't happen at this point, so he tried yelling it one more time in desperation. "I said...I-I'll be back!"

The next instant, Sumire was holding her stomach with laughter. "Oh man, you think you have the face of a Hollywood star? Even if I forgave your terrible acting, you need to at least be able to say that without getting embarrassed. And you need to become a man worthy of that line. Don't die."

He was suddenly pulled back to reality by a tug on his sleeve. The sound of the helicopter's rotors returned to his ears.

"What's wrong?" Enju asked. "What are you thinking about, Rentaro?"

"Nothing...," he said.

Enju, bundled up in an extra layer of green flight jacket, was staring up at him. Her mouth had been clamped shut for a while as she fidgeted nervously.

"Now that I think about it, is it your first time going to the Unexplored Territory?" asked Rentaro.

Enju nodded. Rentaro understood. Things that one had to do outside the Monolith were definitely not something you thought about if you lived inside. He braced himself, thinking that he would have to provide her with the best support he could. "Is there anything you want to ask about before we start the operation?"

"What is this helicopter called?" Enju asked.

Rentaro looked around inside the aircraft. "It looks like parts of it have been upgraded, but it's probably the Japanese version of a Black Hawk."

"I know that name! It's one of those weaklings from that retro movie I borrowed from Sumire where two of them crashed. Rentaro, is this going make a nosedive and fall headfirst, too?"

The pilot looked over at them with an unpleasant look on his face. "Hey, idiot! What are you saying?"

Rentaro apologized with a look, and was about to complain to Enju, but when he turned to her, she had such a dark look on her face that he couldn't finish what he was about to say. She was probably trying to get rid of her nervousness in her own way. No matter how much her strength surpassed the human norm, she was still a ten-year-old child. Looking at Enju, sometimes he forgot that. Rentaro decided he would stay with her to the bitter end, and nodded slightly with resolve.

"Do you have any other...questions you want to ask?" said Rentaro.

"Then...what part of this helicopter is upgraded?" asked Enju.

"The helicopter again? You really like helicopters, don't you? The rotor has probably been changed to a newer model that makes as little noise as possible." The sound of the rotors interrupted every break in their conversation.

"It's still really loud, Rentaro."

"We're pretty high up, so from the ground, it should be a lot quieter. Inside a helicopter, you'd normally have to talk a lot louder to hear each other."

Enju looked like she still wasn't satisfied with the answer and swung her legs. "Why do we need to be quiet?"

"So we don't wake the Gastrea. There are some that wake up in the morning and sleep at night like us humans, but there are also nocturnal ones that are active at night. If we make too much noise, we won't just catch the attention of the nocturnal Gastrea, but we'll also wake up the ones that are sleeping right now, and it'll be troublesome. I'll teach you how later, but when we get to the ground, you need to make sure you move without making any loud noises. If not, terrible things will happen."

Enju murmured, "I see," and looked up at him. "What was the Stage Five you were talking about in the hospital room? I thought Gastrea only went up to Stage Four."

"Oh, that?" Letting his eyes look out the window, he could see the ghost town of a city below. Suddenly, he saw a small shadow in the window of a residential house. That was probably some kind of animal, or a former human. Inwardly, he thought, *She's finally asked the question, huh?*

Rentaro answered her. "Where should I start...? Normally, Gastrea start with Stage One, and then move on to Stage Two and Stage Three, growing bigger as they mature, with their skin growing harder, right? In that process, they take genes from various animals, so each one takes on a unique appearance as it matures. Because of that, there is no one way to deal with Gastrea."

"Yeah, I already know all that," said Enju.

"Yeah, I'm sure you do. You could say that the Stage Five is something outside of that general knowledge we have of Gastrea. Normal Gastrea go up to Stage Four—in other words, the complete form, where they are not supposed to grow anymore... But Stage Fives certainly exist. We confirmed their existence ten years ago, when Gastrea appeared repeatedly around the world at the same time. No one knows how they came to be, or where they came from, but anyway, they're so gigantic that they make Stage Fours look like children. Besides that, in order to not be crushed by their own weight, their muscles, skin, bones, and even their organs have been reinforced and are hardened. Doc once said that the Gastrea virus is like a designer that designs creatures, but this is the idea to its extreme."

"But since we have the Monoliths, no matter what Gastrea comes, none can come into Tokyo Area, right? It doesn't matter how big they are, does it?"

"That's a good point. That's where the problem is. The long and short of it is that the magnetic field given off by Varanium doesn't affect Stage Fives."

Enju's eyes widened. She was clever enough to have noticed right away. Mankind made Monoliths out of lumps of Varanium and holed up like badgers in winter, preserving this delicate peace for the past ten years. But there was the possibility that that peace could be shattered.

"That's not all. The most frightening thing is if even one part of a Monolith gets destroyed by a Stage Five. If that happens, Stage One through Stage Four Gastrea will come flooding in through that broken line like an avalanche. If that happens…"

Enju held her breath as Rentaro trailed off, lost in his words. "Wh-what'll happen?"

"We call cases like that Great Extinctions. In the past, it happened in the Middle East and Africa, but in a word, it's hell."

Enju's face paled. In his head, Rentaro critically asked himself what he was trying to do, scaring her like that. After thinking about it for a while, Rentaro shook his head firmly. He couldn't treat Enju like a child anymore. She had a right to know the full extent of the dangerous situation occurring right now.

"You understand, right, Enju? This is the critical moment that will decide whether or not Tokyo Area faces Great Extinction. Even I still have a hard time believing that there's a way to summon a Stage Five to Tokyo Area, but with the government spearheading such a large-scale operation, it is probably possible. And its origin is that duralumin case that was stolen from us. That's why we have to defeat Kagetane and his partner and stop it."

"Are there a lot of Stage Fives?" Enju asked.

"There were eleven that were seen," said Rentaro. "Miraculously, two were defeated. Generally, cells with the Gastrea virus automatically repair and regenerate their telomeres, so theoretically they won't die of old age. The ultimate goal of the civil security agencies is to destroy the remaining nine Stage Fives. No—you could say that's the wish of all mankind."

Just then, the pilot's voice said, "We're here," over Rentaro.

Rentaro stretched his hand out to Enju. "Now, let's go, Enju. Let's save Tokyo Area."

Looking at the helicopter starting its way back after it dropped them off, Rentaro began feeling discouraged. The next time he would ride in a helicopter would either be when they successfully completed the operation, or when his corpse was carried out in a bag.

From here on out, they would need to clear the path themselves.

Rentaro and Enju had been dropped off in the middle of an extensive forest. The tall, dense evergreens grew thick, and the fact that it was nighttime contributed to the low visibility. Because of the torrential rains the other day, the whole forest was wet, and their nostrils were filled with the thick smell of humidity and the night.

In any case, they couldn't keep standing there forever. Rentaro took the lead, and Enju followed him. Rentaro took the bush knife from his hip and cut away the branches that looked like they would get in Enju's way as she followed after him. With Enju's strong regenerative ability, a scratch caused by a branch on her arm would be healed in a second, but she still felt pain, so he never felt like it was acceptable for her to get hurt.

A canopy of tall trees about thirty meters high covered the moon, and the forest was extremely dark. Unexpectedly, the map he had received ahead of time was completely useless. The map was ten years old, so he had naturally expected there to be differences, but it wasn't just a matter of vegetation—even detailed topography had changed.

Rentaro quickly surrendered and was forced to use the light he had brought. He had not wanted to use the light because it would reveal their position to the enemy Gastrea and to Kagetane, whose location they didn't know, but he had no choice.

He twisted the bottom of the switch cover. The 180-lumen circle of light cut through the darkness and illuminated various things. Rentaro looked at the scene and was dumbfounded.

Even though it was chilly, ferns and shrubs that only grew in tropical rain forests stretched as far as the light shone. Among them, there was even a plant he had never seen before that twisted its trunk around the surrounding trees. It was like a strangler fig, but he had never seen one with a mottled black and red pattern.

The strangest part was the sound. At night in rain forests near the equator, it would be noisy with the chorus of bugs, birds, and frogs, but this fake forest was dead silent and seemed as if it had already died out.

"R-Rentaro…" Enju was spooked, too, and drew closer to Rentaro.

"This is my first time out this far away from Tokyo Area," said Rentaro. "Isn't this terrible?"

The distribution of plants and animals in an area taken over by Gastrea was always crazy, but this was the worst Rentaro had ever seen. Of course, there should have been living things that hadn't been made into Gastrea, but perhaps they were in hiding. In any case, they were nowhere to be seen. "Enju, we're gonna get out of here and head to a nearby town."

"Weren't we told to look in this area?" she asked.

Rentaro put his hand on his chin and thought a little. Currently, in the First District of Tokyo Area was the headquarters of this operation being spearheaded by the Seitenshi. Somehow, these government officials had decided that they would use a human wave attack to draw Kagetane out, and as Enju had said, Rentaro had been given instructions to search this area before they left. *But*, he thought as he shook his head. "No, let's go to the town after all. No human in their right mind would want to stay in a place like this for long. I'm sure Kagetane and his partner are somewhere else."

Enju didn't object.

After a while, they found themselves on a forest path. Under their feet, the soft ground changed to paved asphalt. From both sides of the road, the forest looked like it was trying to cover the road. The asphalt was cracked and broken.

Enju started to jump on the road with a strange look on her face. "What lousy work. The Japan Highway Public Corporation is a tax thief."

"Hey now," said Rentaro. "After we humans leave, the roads are more fragile than you think. Weeds start growing soon after, and then cracks develop, and when water gets in there and freezes and melts, the cracks start getting bigger and bigger. It's not necessarily cracked because the government wasn't doing its job."

"I see. Then, let me correct myself. The Japan Highway Public Corporation is a good tax thief."

"What's that supposed to mean?" Rentaro smiled wryly and looked up at the sky. Because there was a lot of oxygen, at least the air was fresh. They followed the road. When they got out of the fake tropical rain forest, they finally saw more familiar trees like dawn redwoods and maples. However, even though it was spring, the maple had red leaves, and the undergrowth showed signs of root rot and was a dark reddish brown, giving off a rank smell. When mankind one day beat the Gastrea, would they be able to find a way to restore the environment that had been destroyed this thoroughly?

"Enju, someone in our line of work said they saw a quetzal in the Unexplored Territory before," said Rentaro.

"A quetzal?" said Enju.

"Yeah, the bird Osamu Tezuka's *Phoenix* was modeled after, the legendary birds whose males are said to be the most beautiful birds in the world. Of course, there aren't any in Japan, so I always thought he was lying, but with the ecosystem this messed up, I think it might actually be possible."

"Rentaro, you really like animals, don't you? Do you wish to see one?"

Rentaro pouted. "What, something wrong with that?"

"No, if you want to see one, then so do I. If they are so beautiful, then they will surely be delicious."

"You want to eat one?! They're legendary birds!"

Just then, there was a growl in the distance, and Rentaro reflexively turned off the light and crouched down. Removing the XD from his hip, he pulled out the one-touch mountable silencer, fixed it on the muzzle of the XD, and slowly approached the sound. He could hear the sound of a small stream in the distance. That sound grew louder as they approached. Moving forward silently for about a minute, they slowly pushed their way through the thicket.

It was closer than Rentaro had expected. He was paralyzed for a moment before he rushed back and crouched in the thicket.

The first thing he saw was the thin pupils in the glowing yellow eyes. Its long, narrow snout was crammed full of teeth. From its head to its long tail, it was covered with a hard armorlike skin that glittered slimily. Placed as it was with only half of its body out of the river and with its thick skin, it looked like a heavy tank.

"It's a gator," said Rentaro. "A gavial...I think? But..." Its long, thin snout was definitely different from that of an alligator or crocodile. But Rentaro still felt uncertain about that conclusion. It wasn't even worth being surprised at the body enlarged by the Gastrea virus, but it had five legs, and there were four extra eyes in places eyes would not normally be.

The Gastrea virus was not perfect. There had probably been some sort of error after the body was designed when the cells were dividing that made it turn into that. Perhaps it could be called God's aesthetics, but most living things were created with symmetry. When that symmetry was altered, it was hard not to be revolted. The long, thin snout of the gavial had evolved into a shape suitable for catching fish, but, it was hard to believe that it subsisted entirely on river fish given the size of its body.

The creature had also noticed Rentaro. It still didn't seem like it was about to attack, but it stared at Rentaro sideways. Cold sweat broke out on his palms. *What should I do? Fight it?* Rentaro dropped his gaze to his gun.

Currently, in order to allow the silencer to work at maximum efficiency, his gun was loaded with what were called "weak charges," subsonic Varanium bullets that used less gunpowder and dropped the initial velocity to below the speed of sound. Thinking about the naturally tough gator skin being reinforced by the Gastrea virus, he thought that he if he aimed at its head, the cranium would probably stop the bullet.

Enju pulled at his sleeve and shook her head slightly with uneasy eyes. He knew that she was telling him to ignore it. That was the last straw. Rentaro held out his gun and stepped back slowly so as not to provoke the creature. He didn't know what the five-legged gavial was thinking, but it kept its eyes on him, watching his every move. As soon as he lost sight of it, he ran as fast as he could away from it. Once he got to a place he thought was safe, he let out a long breath. His heart was still hammering loudly in his chest. He suddenly felt cold and started shivering. He didn't even have enough composure to laugh off his own cowardice.

"If I hadn't stopped you, you would have started attacking, huh?" Enju said in an unhappy voice.

Rentaro couldn't answer.

"Even though you are more fragile than I am, you desire too much to walk in front of me."

Once he thought things through calmly, he realized that there were too many problems with his risk and ammunition management. Thinking about what might have happened if he had tried to defeat the creature like that made him shake his head. "Sorry. I'll be more careful—"

However, before he could finish, the vibration of a low explosion ripped through the air. Rentaro knew immediately what had caused it and clicked his tongue. "That idiot! Some civil officer pair used explosives in the forest... Why did they have to do that?"

At that moment, although it wasn't clear where they had been hiding, from inside the forest, a cloud of bats flew out all at once, calling shrilly and flying above Rentaro's head as if going mad.

Rentaro broke out in a cold sweat. This was the worst thing that could have happened. The forest was going to wake up. Calamity soon appeared. With a thud, a low sound different from before could be felt beneath their feet. It was the rumble of large bodies treading on the ground. It reverberated in all directions, and Rentaro couldn't tell where it was coming from.

Next was a low growl that echoed in his stomach and made him look hurriedly around him. He thought it was the growl of the gavial from earlier, but it was something more twisted and sinister.

Suddenly, Enju's face paled, and she stared at a single point. "Rentaro... What's that?"

Even when he looked in the direction Enju was looking, all he could see was a large shadow. Rentaro turned on the light and then almost dropped it in shock.

From deep within the canopy, a pair of large eyes were fixed on them. Its body was over six meters long. It had the fierce face characteristic of reptiles, with a long neck and a flickering red tongue. Small warts covered its face like boils, and Rentaro and Enju could smell the stink of rotting flesh on its breath wafting downwind toward them. Its body was green, and the bones of its arms had evolved to form wings, so it went without saying that it had mixed with some sort of bird Gastrea.

It looked like a fairy-tale dragon.

There was no doubt that this was a Stage Four Gastrea. It probably had a number of different bird and lizard species mixed in, but with its evolution progressed this far into the stages, it was hard to pinpoint exactly what the original animal was.

Just then, Rentaro noticed that there were what looked like remnants of cloth caught in the Gastrea's fangs, and he let out an involuntary groan. With the government pushing through this operation without regard for material resources, he had known in the corner of his mind that there would be victims sacrificed, but he had blocked that out of his consciousness. Nevertheless, it bothered him.

The dragon started to kick the ground nervously with its right leg, as if it were a runner getting ready to start running before a race.

Keeping his eyes on it, Rentaro fished around in his pouch with shaking hands, but he soon realized that he didn't have a weapon that could work against such a large creature. At that size, without a heavy machine gun or antitank rifle outfitted with Varanium bullets, he wouldn't have a chance.

"Enju," he said, "can you carry me and run?"

Enju showed her understanding with just her eyes.

Keeping his eyes fixed on the dragon, he put his arms around Enju's shoulders. Because of the difference in their heights, he was practically leaning on her, but this was no time to worry about that. "Enju, if you can't get away, leave me."

"I cannot do that!" As she spoke, she kicked sideways with enough force to send them into the air. The cold wind hit Rentaro's cheeks, and when he opened his eyes slightly against the pressure of the wind, they were already in midair. Enju had hopped. She had jumped almost twenty meters while carrying Rentaro on her back.

The cuffs of his clothes fluttered, and they stopped for one brief instant in midair. Right after that instant, they fell on the curve of a free fall, and the forest drew near with intense speed. Enju found a thick branch to land on with both legs on it and then leapt up again. This time, she made short jumps from branch to branch between trees that were about five meters apart, jumping faster than the eye could follow.

Rentaro clung pitifully to Enju. Every time Enju jumped, he was swung about by strong G's and felt like he was about to fall off. Looking behind them, his eyes widened with shock. The fierce hunter was leaning forward in pursuit, trampling the trees in its way. The snapping sound of live trees being torn apart chased after them from behind. The pressure was more than he imagined, and it made him want to scream.

Rentaro fought against the pressure of the wind and opened his eyes narrowly to look behind them. But he realized one thing. Those wings probably didn't function, or, like those of the giant pterosaurs of the past, had only limited functionality. If it could fly, then it would have followed them through the air. If it followed them on the ground, it would eventually hit its limit. It probably couldn't breathe fire like the dragons in picture books, either. Convinced that they could get away, he made a fist.

But then, when he faced front again, he almost lost consciousness with despair. "Enju, it's a cliff."

A cliff rose perpendicularly in front of them, and it was about a hundred meters above the vast forest below it.

"Hang on tight, Rentaro!" said Enju.

"Hey, don't tell me you're gonna—?!"

Enju bent her knees low on the trunk she had just landed on and made a huge jump. Rentaro almost bit his tongue. The scenery passed by with amazing speed, and they leapt over the cliff and into the air. The strong wind whisked by, and Rentaro and Enju experienced a strange climbing sensation for an instant. Inertia and gravity cancelled each other out and they were completely still in midair.

Rentaro's mouth gaped. There was forest as far as he could see. It was like a miniature scene. It was a moment when all his worries, thoughts, decisions, and past travels—nothing seemed to matter anymore. It was the moment he realized his own insignificance. Looking in front of him, the yellow moon seemed closer than usual. Even though he knew what he was doing was foolish, he stretched out his hand to grab it. He gave a small laugh.

Just then, in the space between the forest and the moon, about ten kilometers away, he saw something strange and rubbed his eyes. A long man-made cylinder was stretching smoothly toward the sky. With just the silhouette, it was hard to gauge its size, but it looked to be about two kilometers in length.

*I see. So that's the Stairway to Heaven...?* At that moment, Rentaro felt an unpleasant drifting feeling, and the inertia disappeared and gravity pulled at his body. Rentaro felt like he was about to be torn away from Enju, who was carrying him, and clung on hurriedly. He gritted his teeth and concentrated on not screaming.

Enju was completely calm, and selecting two branches on the ground, she grabbed one as she fell. When the branch bent to its limit, Enju let go and grabbed the branch below it. Enju's thin arms were overloaded, and there was a snapping sound. However, the force of their drop did not decrease, and the two fell like lightning bolts into the middle of the forest.

Countless leaves and branches scratched Rentaro's cheeks, and fresh blood spurted out. Enju landed with both legs on a large rock, and shattered pieces of rock flew in all directions. Thrown by the force, the two of them rolled on the ground a few times before finally coming to a stop.

Holding back his body in a fit of coughing, Rentaro used his hands to push himself up and looked up at the cliff they had fallen from. Far up at the top of the cliff, the dragon looked frustrated at missing out on eating dessert and turned several times before letting out a howl and returning to the forest. Rentaro felt the strength leave his hands as exhaustion suddenly closed in on him in response. He almost collapsed as he let go of his focus.

After all that, Rentaro and Enju didn't start moving again for another thirty minutes. Enju had hurt the joints in her body during the fall and needed some time to recover. Of course, compared to the weak Rentaro, her recovery time was amazingly fast.

He had been planning on walking in front and getting rid of any thing suspicious, but he changed his mind and decided to have Enju help, too. He lectured her as they walked side by side. "You have to be careful of the antitank land mines, the spring-type land mines, the guided mines, and the unexploded cluster bombs. These were scattered by the retreating self-defense force during the Great Gastrea War and left behind, so occasionally civil officers doing jobs in the Unexplored Territory will get hurt." He traced simple outlines of the shapes of the dangerous objects she should be careful of.

"I see," said Enju. "But why did they do something that would mess up their own country so much during the war? Did they not realize that they would be the ones who would have to deal with it later?"

Enju made such a good point that Rentaro was caught off guard, and he pondered for a moment. "You're right... Now that you mention it, that's exactly right, but ten years ago, mankind was cornered and would do anything. Land mines and poison gas were just the tip of the iceberg. At the time, in order to survive, a bunch of inhumane things were allowed, so no one would've batted an eye at things like that."

Looking at the small girl walking next to him, he thought to himself that this was the difference in perception between the Stolen Generation, who experienced the horrors of ten years ago, and the Innocent Generation. He uncharacteristically felt a generation gap.

Enju grinned. "Don't worry. Now there are strong people like me fighting, so everything will be fine. If the enemy finds us, I'll carry you again and jump away."

"Thanks to you, I don't think I'll be scared of the free-fall rides at the amusement park anymore."

"I'm glad. You should thank me."

Rentaro let out a large sigh. She didn't understand sarcasm when she heard it.

"But something seems strange...," said Enju. "Ever since coming here, I've been feeling excited for some reason." Enju opened and closed her hands curiously.

*Of course you would*, agreed Rentaro silently. The Varanium that Gastrea hated also had an effect on Enju and the other girls, who were infected with small amounts of the virus. Most Initiators, when they went outside of the Monoliths, felt temporarily better, or even high. Their wounds also healed faster.

Even as they talked, they proceeded with caution. Even though they were a considerable distance away, the surrounding forest had been woken up once, so they couldn't be too careful. Once in a while, Rentaro would put his ear to the ground and send Enju high up into a tree to check for danger. It slowed their progress considerably, but in the end, that gave them early notice of a light that was burning far away.

As they approached warily, there was a break in the brush, and they could see an obviously man-made stone building. It was a small, one-floor stone building, and at the entrance was a wall of piled sandbags.

It was a pillbox shelter built during the Great Gastrea War. It was dilapidated and had lost most of its function, but it still served as a place to get out of the wind. Light leaked from inside. Rentaro's heart started beating faster at the thought that it could be Kagetane.

Giving Enju a hand signal, he took the gun from his hip and approached from the back. Enju approached from the front. He could hear the crackling of the firewood burning.

Apparently, there was a fire burning inside. From the holes in the pile of rocks, he could see the changing shadows created by the flames. Rentaro stood with his back to the wall and took two deep breaths. Then, he held out his gun and rushed inside.

"Don't move!" he said. Rentaro's XD and the muzzle of his opponent's shotgun intersected at almost the same time.

Rentaro was speechless when he saw his opponent. "You're…"

His opponent panted, looking at him with blank eyes. She was wearing a dark, long-sleeved dress with tights. It was an outfit unsuitable for the hell of the Unexplored Territory. However, his eye was drawn to the painful-looking wound on her arm that blood was gushing out of nonstop. It looked like she had been bitten by a giant beast, and the wound had been gouged out with tooth marks.

Rentaro remembered seeing the girl before.

"If you do not put the gun down, I shall kick your head off." With that cold threat, Enju, who had snuck in from behind, kicked her leg out to lay it on the back of the girl's neck.

"Wait, Enju," said Rentaro. "She's not our enemy."

"Wha…?" Enju looked from Rentaro to the girl a few times and finally put her leg down reluctantly.

Rentaro went to where the girl was sitting weakly and looked her in the eye. "Hey, we met once at the Ministry of Defense. Do you remember me?"

"Yes, of course." The girl spoke as she exhaled painfully.

"Anyway, let's stop the bleeding and get this bandaged up. We can talk after that."

Then he noticed Enju watching them from the side, grinding her teeth. "Wait a moment," she said. "I do not know this woman. Explain your relationship with her, Rentaro."

Rentaro turned back to face Enju. "Oh yeah, this is your first time meeting. She's the Initiator partner for a Promoter named Shogen Ikuma."

3

When they threw the dry branches they had gathered into the bonfire, the fire revived and rapturously scattered orange light on the stone walls. Once Rentaro used his emergency kit to stop the bleeding and disinfect and bandage the wound, the wound started regenerating with help from the Gastrea virus. However, her regeneration speed was very modest compared to Enju's.

Afraid the enemy would approach while he was treating the girl, he had Enju stand watch. However, Enju seemed put out for some reason and pouted, saying, "I don't accept that girl!" and "If it were me, my wound would've healed in three seconds!" as she went outside the pillbox shelter. Rentaro wanted to say that three seconds was too short, but she seemed really unhappy, so he didn't.

The girl's name was Kayo Senju. Rentaro was astounded at himself for not knowing the name of the girl he had thought of as the "hungry girl" until now.

"For some reason, it looks like your partner is extremely angry." The girl spoke with a strangely cool attitude.

Rentaro looked in the direction Enju had gone. "Jeez, why did she suddenly get so upset? Don't tell me she's already at that rebellious age…?"

"I think the reason is obvious…" She spoke as if spitting out her words into space, with a tone devoid of all emotion. Rentaro was at a loss. Because she had a calmness that didn't match her age, it was hard to read her emotions. At the Ministry of Defense, Rentaro had thought she had a better sense of humor than that, but apparently he was wrong.

"Do you think I am strange?" the girl asked.

Realizing that he was staring, Rentaro shifted his gaze. "No, not really…"

The girl closed her eyes and put her hands to her chest. "Do not worry about it. I am used to being treated this way. I am also one of the first generation of Cursed Children. However, because I possess the Dolphin Factor in my body, I have a higher IQ and better memory than normal Initiators. My IQ is at around 210 points."

Rentaro was startled. "You have more than twice my IQ?"

"Well, intelligence tests taken as a child have the tendency to over-estimate." She showed humility even though she was a child.

Rentaro was overwhelmed with a strange sense of defeat. "So then, you take the command and the rear guard with your brains, and Shogen is the advance guard? That's an unusual style."

"That is just because Shogen has muscles for brains and has no patience, so he can't back up anyone. He still gets upset when we get battles taken from us. His way of thinking is old-fashioned and inflexible, which is problematic." The girl broke a thin branch in two and threw the pieces into the fire.

Utterly amazed at the way she did not mince words, Rentaro looked at the shotgun lying beside her. "Let me see your gun."

She thought for a while. "What if I say no?"

"That's fine. If you don't feel gratitude for being rescued, you can do that."

Kayo looked resigned and exhaled through her nose, handing him the gun. "If there's one thing I have learned, it is that when a good deed is done for a reward, it becomes corrupted."

Rentaro pretended not to hear as he examined the gun. Kayo's fully automatic shotgun with a silencer had an add-on-type grenade launcher unit on a 20-mm equipment expansion rail. Both were Shiba Heavy Weapons 2027 models. When Rentaro slung the launcher

out to the right and peeked into the chamber, he frowned. Then he looked up, staring at the girl in front of him. "Why did you use explosives in the forest? This is the empty case of a 40-mm high-explosive projectile."

It was because of that that Rentaro and Enju had been chased by a Stage Four Gastrea and almost died. In the Unexplored Territory, preserving silence was a hard and fast rule no matter what one was doing. A pair whose ranking was far above Rentaro and Enju's should have known this. Kayo hugged her dainty knees and gazed at the fire for a while.

"Shogen and I were caught in a trap," she said. "Thanks to that, we were not only injured, but we were also split up."

"A trap?" said Rentaro.

"Yes. We were also dropped off in a deep forest, and inside the forest, we saw a short flickering light pattern. We thought it was an ally and approached with our guard down." Hugging her knees harder, the girl became smaller. "If we had been more careful, we would have realized that no one would use such a dim, blue, will-o'-the-wisp-like light."

Rentaro gulped. "What was it…?"

Kayo glanced at him and looked back into the fire. "The first thing I noticed was a rotten smell. There was an intense stink of something rotting, and a large swarm of flies had gathered. The Gastrea had disgusting flowers growing here and there, and its tail was emitting light. When it saw us, it trembled disgustingly, like it was delighted. I have seen many different kinds of Gastrea, but that stopped me in my tracks.

"Thinking I would be killed, I used the high-explosive projectile at the spur of the moment. After that, it happened as you imagined. All the Gastrea in the forest woke up, and while we were being chased, I got separated from Shogen. That was also when I was bitten on the arm. Fortunately, only a small amount of bodily fluid was injected, so it does not seem like it will have much effect."

Rentaro put his chin in his hands as he listened to Kayo's story. "This is just a guess, but I think that was a Firefly Gastrea."

"A firefly?"

"Yeah, fireflies live on pollen and nectar, but did you know that there are fierce carnivorous fireflies, too? They imitate the light patterns of other fireflies and prey on the fireflies that approach them. In order to prey on humans, it probably evolved specially to emit a light pattern it thought would draw humans. You guys fell right into its trap. The plants surrounding it were probably orchids. I've heard that there are species that give off smells like mold, urine, and rotten meat in order to lure flies and small winged insects to them to carry their pollen... It probably synthesized a smell that would draw humans. It's unusual to see a Gastrea mixed with a plant type. With a specimen specially evolved that much, it is probably a Stage Three."

Kayo's eyes widened. "Is that possible?"

"Gastrea do that in order to outwit mankind. Humans wouldn't lose to dumb organisms."

Kayo didn't say anything for a while. However, when the tension in her shoulders was finally released, she let out a slow breath. "Anyway, you did a good job guessing the type for a Gastrea you didn't even see. Are you a fan?"

"Ugh... Don't call me that."

"You seem like you had a gloomy childhood where you were pleased when you submerged an anthill with water. Were you like, 'Hah, drown! It's Noah's great flood! Know the wrath of God!'? I imagine you had fun, huh? I understand."

"Yeah, that's right, that's how it was. I killed a ton of ants, I'm sorry, all right?"

Kayo looked amused for the first time and crinkled the corners of her eyes. Then she dropped her gaze back to the fire. "But it must be nice. I do not think I would be bored if I had a Promoter like you. I am just a little jealous of Enju."

Rentaro tried to act as nonchalant as possible as he asked, "Do you have fun with a Promoter like Shogen?"

She paused. "Initiators are tools used to kill. That is all there is to it." Kayo did not answer Rentaro's question. "Enju has probably never killed a person before, has she? I can tell by looking at her eyes."

"That's true, but you have?"

"Yes. I killed a pair that we met along the way here."

At first, Rentaro thought he had heard her wrong. "Why did you do something like that...?"

"Shogen ordered me to. When we were lured in by the firefly's light, if it had been another pair of humans and we had the chance, we probably would have done the same then, as well. According to Sho-gen, 'I won't let anyone else kill that jeering masked bastard.'"

Rentaro made a fist. "You don't think anything of killing someone?"

"I was scared. My hand shook. But that was it. This was my second time. I think I will get used to it eventually."

Anger flared inside him. Before he knew it, Rentaro had grabbed at Kayo and pushed her down. "Don't joke around! The scariest thing about killing someone is getting used to killing. When people realize that they won't get punished for killing someone, that's when they forget that it's a sin."

"Is that something you can say because you have stained your hands with murder before? You have mysterious eyes, Satomi. It seems you have had a complicated past. They are kind, but extremely frightening eyes…"

Rentaro paused. "Hey, do you know why Enju speaks so pompously? It's because she thinks she is doing the important job of protecting mankind that she is able to speak proudly with her head held high. Simple, isn't she? Once, there was a time when Enju half-killed a has-been Promoter. Enju moped around the operating room the whole time, and when she heard that he had survived, she was happy the whole day and even went to visit him in the hospital. I think that's just fine."

"Satomi, that is just lip service." Kayo looked up at Rentaro with a strange look in her eyes. The orange from the bonfire was reflected in her eyes.

Rentaro got up slowly and turned away from the girl. "Sorry. I don't know why I'm saying such self-important things. Damn."

"Why are you apologizing?"

Something grabbed the sleeve of Rentaro's uniform tightly.

"Huh?" said Rentaro.

"Why are you apologizing even though what you are saying is right?" asked Kayo. "You are right. Please have more confidence in yourself. I feel odd right now. I do not understand this feeling. Even though I immediately thought of dozens of rebuttals to what you said, I do not want to deny the words you spoke… This is the first time I have ever felt this way."

"Kayo…" A strange emotion welled up in Rentaro's chest. The impression Rentaro had of her from their first meeting had not been wrong after all. As she quickly wiped her eyes on her sleeve, the chink in the armor he saw in the weak ten-year-old girl went away.

"Do you want something to drink?" Kayo said as she pulled out a kettle and some instant coffee from her pack and started boiling water.

Listening to the popping of the firewood, Rentaro looked at the ceiling. A sharp crescent moon shone in the sky that peeked in from the roof of the pillbox shelter that had collapsed in the wind. Looking around inside the house again, he saw the ruins of rusted small arms left behind by the self-defense force during the Great War.

Rentaro picked up one of the bullets that was lying by a 9-mm gun and held it above the bonfire. Deep beneath the thick rust and dirt, the brass shone, lit by the orange light. "Do you know what this is?" he asked her. "It's called a 9-mm Parabellum. A Parabellum is—"

She cut him off. "I know what it is. It came from the Latin that meant 'prepare for war,' right?"

Rentaro shot a glance at Kayo. "As expected of someone with an IQ of 210. You know everything, don't you? Yeah, it means, 'If you seek peace, prepare for war.'"

Kayo poured some coffee into a paper cup and handed it to Rentaro. His palms gradually warmed up. Kayo held her cup with both hands and blew on it to cool it down.

"Is this the result of preparing to fight?" she asked. "Large numbers of land mines in the Unexplored Territory, large numbers of unexploded cluster bombs scattered everywhere, and after all that, all we won was this small miniature garden, far from peace."

"It was a time when they couldn't worry about appearances, that's why," said Rentaro. "But in these past ten years, they have been able to carry out proper restoration."

"Is the restoration they are doing these days really a healthy restoration?"

For some reason, he was startled by her question. "Why do you ask that?"

"I am part of the Innocent Generation who did not know the Great War. However, in the hearts of the Stolen Generation, whose children were devoured before their eyes and whose lovers transformed into ugly Gastrea, I can see glimpses of frank hatred. Public morals and sentiments are in disorder, and there are many weapons that are made especially for slaughter, like the Stairway to Heaven."

Looking up in the direction Kayo was pointing, he could see a ladder-shaped object that was moving behind thin clouds.

"This is no more than the tip of the iceberg," she continued. "You have also heard of the New Humanity Creation Project, right? The project was abandoned once people realized the fighting abilities of us Cursed Children, but there were experiments in the past to create the ultimate soldiers using the power of the Varanium alloy. I heard that they were even performing experiments on people. This is something that no one would have been able to imagine in a Japan before the Great War."

Rentaro listened without moving a muscle. Kayo stopped talking and took a sip of her coffee. "Well, the latter part I thought was just an urban legend until I saw Kagetane Hiruko," she added.

"Relying on that kind of power is something cowards do," said Rentaro.

"Satomi?"

Rentaro didn't know what to say and put his coffee to his lips instead. He grimaced involuntarily at the bitterness that filled his mouth. Suddenly, he was startled by the static and roar of a rough male voice that came from the black receiver next to Kayo.

It appeared to be a radio. When Kayo turned the knob that was sticking out, the sound became clear, and turned into the voice of a man he couldn't forget even if he wanted. "C...ome here. Hey! If you're alive, reply!"

Kayo signaled Rentaro with her eyes. She was probably telling him not to talk. Rentaro nodded silently. It was true that it would be hard to explain to Shogen why he was here with her.

"I was worried because there was no contact from you," she said. "I am glad you are safe, Shogen."

"'Course you are! More importantly, Kayo, I've got some good news." Shogen Ikuma stopped talking for a moment, as if about to make an important announcement. Through the radio, Rentaro could imagine him smiling under his skull-patterned face scarf. "I've found the masked bastard."

Rentaro's and Kayo's eyes met.

"Where did you find him?" Kayo asked.

Rentaro pulled his map out of his pocket and spread it out on the ground. He quickly found the location Shogen described. An urban area near the coast? It was pretty close.

"Right now, the civil officers nearby are gathering to launch a joint surprise attack. I really want to jump the gun and act first, but well, he *is* ranked higher than us, and the Initiators seem reluctant. We finally decided on the plan I just told you right now. If we all split everything equally, it won't be interesting. You should hurry up and meet up with us, too." He disconnected without even waiting for Kayo's answer.

Rentaro had heard rough voices and laughter behind Shogen. The attack plan was probably progressing as he had said.

Kayo immediately started packing and putting out the bonfire.

"So you're going?" Rentaro asked her.

"Yes," she said. "In spite of it all, he's still my partner. What about you, Satomi?"

Rentaro became uncertain of his own feelings. If the other civil officers could take care of it, then he was inclined to rely on them to do so. He had acted cool in front of Kisara, but the fear of being half-killed by Kagetane without being able to lift a finger was only a little over a day old and wasn't something he could forget yet. He shook his head softly. No, he had to do it himself.

Rentaro put his own personal feelings aside for a moment and analyzed the strategy objectively. The problem was how good those people Shogen had joined forces with were. Their ranks were unknown, but it didn't seem like there were only one or two pairs behind him. There were probably at least a little under ten pairs. And among them, they even had the battle god, Shogen Ikuma, with an IP Rank of 1,584, who could fight without the assistance of his Initiator. Whether Kagetane won or the civil officers team won, it would inevitably be a fierce battle.

"How's your arm?" Rentaro asked.

When the girl took off the bandage silently, he could see that the wound was still in the process of healing.

Rentaro looked in the direction of the town. At the very least, he should see how this battle turned out.

*4:00 A.M.*

Rentaro called Enju back, and the three of them left the pillbox shelter. Compared to Rentaro and Kayo, who had been snug inside with the bonfire, Enju, who had been standing watch for a long time, had better night vision by far, so he had her take the lead.

After walking for a while, there was a break in the forest, and they found themselves in an open field with a good view. If they continued that way for a few more kilometers, they would find themselves in the town, but Rentaro deliberately went around and headed for a small hill. There was nowhere to hide in the straight path to town. He decided that they needed to proceed with caution here.

As they walked, the smell of water was carried to their nostrils. The ocean was close.

Partway there, there were traces of a night camp in a place that was surrounded by tall undergrowth. They must have been afraid that there would be smoke, so there was no sign of cooking, but pouches from portable food were scattered around. It was a bigger group than he had expected.

Rentaro started to panic. Since Shogen had said they would launch a surprise attack, that meant that it would likely be a night or early-morning attack. There were only two hours left until dawn. If they had left here, then he could safely assume that they had already started their operation.

Taking their careful detour, the three of them reached the small hill where they could look down on the town. Below them, the town was eerily quiet. A countless number of fishing boats and small boats were moored in the bay bent like a crescent moon.

It was a small town that was probably worried about its decreasing population even before the Great War. Just as he thought that there would of course be no light, he saw a single light atop a white building that looked like a church. That must be the place.

Suddenly, he heard the sound of guns and gulped. The first shot signaled the start of the battle, and bursts of gunfire and the shrill sound of swords clashing continued. It had begun.

"Rentaro!" Enju screamed.

"All right," said Rentaro. "Let's go."

"I will stay here," said Kayo.

Turning in surprise, Rentaro saw Kayo with her back facing him. "Why?" The moment he called out, a four-legged beast appeared in the path where they had come, shooting out like a bullet.

Kayo released her power and clashed with it face-on, holding back its rush. Rentaro was startled. It was a deer Gastrea. There were horns piercing through its skin all over the top half of its body. Getting pierced by a number of those horns, Kayo forced her shotgun into the Gastrea's mouth and pulled the trigger in a flash.

The Gastrea let out an eerie scream as it was blown away and stopped moving.

Kayo turned as if nothing had happened, despite the blood flowing from her stomach. "It looks like they followed us. Also, did you not hear the noise, Satomi? If no one stays here to hold them back, everyone will be wiped out whether we win or lose."

Looking behind him after she said that, he heard low growls and shrill whistles from the thick forest they had just come out of. Awakened by the gunfire from town, the Gastrea were communicating with their friends through various frequency bands.

Kayo thrust her fully automatic shotgun into the ground with extreme calm, put down her knapsack, and took out all her extra magazines and started lining them up on the ground. She was preparing to resist to the bitter end. The wounds in her pierced arm and stomach were regenerating even as she did this.

"Then, we'll stay, too—" Rentaro started.

Kayo rested the shotgun on her shoulder and fired a shot into the sky. Some of the shots found targets, and silhouettes that looked like monster birds gave a cry as they dropped into the forest.

"Satomi, are you stupid?" Kayo said. "The die has been cast. You two must cross the Rubicon River. In return, when you finish, please come back to assist me."

Rentaro closed his eyes and inhaled deeply, then exhaled. If he remembered correctly, a superior commander had to make decisions in five seconds based on the ever-changing state of the war. "We'll leave this place to you. Stop the Gastrea. But don't try to do the impossible."

"Do not worry. Once I am at a disadvantage, I will run away, so please take care of Shogen."

"All right. Come on, let's go, Enju."

"O-okay, got it," said Enju.

Rentaro started running. The town slowly got bigger. Seeing that the houses and small buildings had kept their original form, Rentaro could tell that the people here had abandoned their town before being attacked by Gastrea and had taken refuge in Tokyo.

Their original forms had been preserved, but not completely. Normally, in houses or buildings where the heater stops being used, when they undergo large temperature changes, after expanding and contracting over and over, the walls start to crumble. In the case of this town, in addition to the usual expansion and contraction, the salty ocean wind also corroded the base material, so the situation was even more serious.

Looking at the ruined town, Rentaro could plainly feel the weakness of a man-made environment. As Rentaro entered the town, he weaved through the shadows of the buildings. The countless moored boats were also completely rusted, and the fishing boats had been transformed into a bizarre state that made it easy to mistake them for haunted boats. Every time the wind blew, these darkness-colored silhouettes made a grating sound.

Rentaro and Enju gradually approached the vicinity of the gunshots. Rentaro's heart pounded. His skin, which had become as sensitive as a radar, prickled every time the wind blew.

He wondered what had happened. He hadn't heard gunshots for a while now. If they had defeated Kagetane, then someone would have given a shout of triumph. Why was it so quiet? *Notice, Rentaro Satomi.*

Removing the silencer that was now just an impediment, he held the XD in his right hand and the light in his left. Crossing his arms, he proceeded with the backs of his hands together. He waited to turn on the light. When he met the enemy, he could turn the light onto the enemy's face and destroy his night vision as he fired off one-sided shots. It was a close quarters gun-battle technique called the Harries stance used by professionals.

Eventually, her feet hit something, and as Enju groped around to pick it up, she let out a short scream. An upper arm had been graphically cut off still holding a gun. It was so fresh, it looked like it would still give off steam. At that moment, a thump came from a one-story house, and Rentaro almost fired.

"My sword… Where…is my sword…?"

"You're…Shogen…Ikuma…?"

The man with the skull-face scarf who was plunked down on the stool of the general store recognized Rentaro and slowly stood, making his way unsteadily toward him. He seemed to have lost his sight.

"'Scuse me...," he said. "Do you...know...where my sword is...? As long as I have that, I can still fight..."

Rentaro gaped as he looked for a long time at the enormous broken sword stuck in Shogen's back. When Shogen passed by Rentaro, he fell to his knees, coughing blood, and then fell to the ground. He did not move again. The situation was so different from what Rentaro had imagined that it took a while for his brain to process everything.

Shogen was dead? One of the highest IP rankers, with a ranking of 1,584? Rentaro gripped his XD and apologized to Kayo in his heart. Finding Shogen's backup gun at his waist, Rentaro examined it quickly. A Smith & Wesson automatic gun, Sigma. Seeing that it was fully loaded with .40-caliber Varanium bullets, Rentaro tucked it in his belt and stood up. He stopped at the corner that led to the street. "Enju, we're going out onto the street. However, no matter what you see, you cannot scream."

"How much worse can it get, Rentaro?" she asked.

Rentaro did not answer. Because they were downwind, he had been smelling the rich smell of blood for a while now. Holding his gun ready, he ran out into the street.

Enju gasped. "Rentaro... What is this...?"

The closest thing was only a few meters ahead. It was the head of an Initiator that had been cut off and rolled onto the ground. It looked at them with a permanent expression of shock. Farther down was a pile of Initiator and Promoter corpses piled on top of each other. These had been killed quickly with a gun. The street had turned into a sea of blood. Among the corpses, Rentaro saw a few faces he had seen at the Ministry of Defense. Rentaro bit his lip and tried desperately to stay upright in the midst of the choking stink as his knees threatened to give way.

Another hundred meters ahead, he could see an open door leading into the church. The candlesticks on the wall burned brightly with flames. The holy cross hanging overhead looked coldly down at the picture of hell below.

At that moment, he heard a familiar voice come from the pier. "Papa, I'm astonished. He really is still alive."

The Kagetane pair was standing at the tip of the pier, gazing at the surface of the ocean. One had two swords at her waist and was wearing a black dress. The other was the mysterious man wearing a wine-red tailcoat, mask, and silk hat.

Rentaro could not believe his eyes. That pair had intercepted many skillful attackers and had eliminated all of them, yet neither had a single scratch. Rentaro was tormented by an intense regret and took a step back.

Why didn't he wait until he could call for the support of other civil officers? He had faced the pair a number of times and had been plainly shown their superhuman strength each time. Even if he hadn't, the outcome of the battle was clear when Shogen Ikuma was killed without being able to do a thing. At that time, Rentaro could have still turned around and run away.

After wasting both chances he had, he was now in the worst possible situation. It was too late to run now. "Kagetane…," he said. "Where is the case…?!"

"I knew you would come." A lukewarm wind blew on Rentaro's skin. With the moon behind him, Kagetane Hiruko turned around with a gun in both hands, opening his arms wide with benevolence. "The final curtain is near. Let's settle this, Satomi."

# BLACK BULLET CHAPTER 04

THOSE WHO WOULD BE GODS

## 1    *4:10 A.M.*

A silent electronic eye watched the confrontation between Rentaro Satomi and Kagetane Hiruko from an altitude of eight hundred meters.

At the operation headquarters in the First District of Tokyo Area, the Japan National Security Council, or JNSC, used the various data transmission technologies that unmanned surveillance drones were equipped with in order to display the events on the monitors in the meeting room practically in real time.

A dead silence had descended on the operation headquarters. Sitting at the long table, the Chief Cabinet Secretary and the Minister of Defense kept looking at each other's faces furtively. Just moments earlier, they watched the footage of fourteen pairs and one person—twenty-nine civil officers in all—who jointly challenged Kagetane Hiruko and had the tables turned on them.

Currently, they had footage from above as two pairs of four people faced each other silently, waiting for the battle to start.

Sitting at the head of the long table, the chair of the JNSC, the Seitenshi, sighed as she looked at the Minister of Defense. "Currently, what other civil officers are in their vicinity?"

"Er, even the closest pair would take over an hour to reach them." The bulldog-faced Minister of Defense seemed at his wits' end as he started dabbing his face with a handkerchief.

The Seitenshi looked at the vice-chair, Kikunojo Tendo. With his boulderlike countenance, Kikunojo returned her look with a nod. "Your decision, Lady Seitenshi?"

After a moment's contemplation, the Seitenshi stood up from her chair. "Very well—"

Suddenly, the sound of the raised voices of the security police who were standing guard outside the meeting room could be heard. The door to the situation room was suddenly thrown open, and a number of people surged into the room. The Seitenshi saw the girl at the front of the pack, and her response was delayed for a moment.

"What is going on?" the Seitenshi demanded.

The black-haired girl at the front of the pack and president of the Tendo Civil Security Agency, Kisara Tendo, swaggered into the middle of the room, cutting through the middle to thrust a piece of paper in the faces of everyone sitting there. The paper in Kisara's hands was covered with circles, and outside the circles, like a collection of autographs, were handwritten signatures and stamps of signature seals.

The Seitenshi peeked at the paper and gulped involuntarily. It was a compact under joint signatures. If she remembered correctly, long ago, during the Peasants' Revolt, they used this in order to form a strong contractual bond among the group and hide the ringleader at the same time.

The gazes of everyone around very naturally turned to the person whose name was one of the many on the list—the Minister of Defense. The other high-ranking government officials drew away from him.

"Good afternoon, Minister Kutsuwada," said Kisara.

"Wh-what kind of joke is this?" said the Minister of Defense.

"Your subordinate had this very interesting piece of paper, you know. It's just as it says on the joint compact. You are one in a group secretly maneuvering behind Kagetane Hiruko. In addition, you are also the one who stole the Inheritance of the Seven Stars and tried to leak that information to the media."

"Th-that's not true…"

Kisara put her hand to her chin and put on a show of tilting her head. "Handwriting a compact under joint signatures is a very old-fashioned thing to do. Thanks to that, I can round up everyone responsible at once, which saves me the extra trouble."

The Seitenshi narrowed her eyes. She could not continue to listen silently. "This meeting room is a place of the law that bears the burden of this country's defense. It is problematic for you to enter rudely like this."

"Th-that's right. You are no more than a filthy civil officer dog! I don't know where you got hold of such a thing, but you need to get out of here!" The minister howled, riding on the Seitenshi's coattails.

However, Kisara remained composed. "Lady Seitenshi, I agree completely with what you say. However, when I discovered these facts, I could not wait another second to share this with you and hastened to this place. Lady Seitenshi, you must also feel the need to dispose of the spy before continuing with the proceedings, do you not?" She was very eloquent.

The Seitenshi signaled Kikunojo. Kikunojo looked coolly at the Minister of Defense. "Take him away."

"W-wait…Lord Tendo!" The minister had a pleading look on his face. "I'm… I'm…!" The security officers lifted the man by both arms and took him screaming out of the meeting room.

"Then, I will take my leave here," said Kisara.

"President Tendo, I cannot let you do that," said the Seitenshi.

Kisara, who looked like she had been about to turn on her heel, stopped her movement and turned back halfway. "Why not?"

"I'm sorry, but I cannot have you leave this building until this operation is completed successfully. I will have you informally confined to this room for the time being."

Kisara pretended for just a moment to put her hand to her chin and think. "If that's the case, then I suppose I must stay."

"Kisara…I cannot believe you would show your face here." Kikunojo did not do anything to hide his wrath.

However, Kisara just flashed him a calm smile. "Good afternoon, Lord Tendo. It has been some time."

"Have you returned from hell for your vengeance?"

"I have just come to exterminate a cockroach that was crawling around my bedside. It was only coincidence that I happened to be here at the same time as you. Don't you think you are being too suspicious?"

"I cannot believe you can joke around like that…"

Kisara's eyes gave off a cold glitter as she narrowed them. "Every Tendo must die, Lord Tendo."

"Y-you little…"

It did not sound anything like a conversation a grandfather would have with his granddaughter. Even just knowing part of the relationship between Kisara and Kikunojo made the Seitenshi frightened.

"Please leave it at that, you two," she said. "President Tendo, if you have been watching the monitor, then you must understand what the situation is to a certain extent. Will you tell us your opinion on the matter?"

*4:15 A.M.*

The lukewarm wind blew against Rentaro's skin.

The smell of salt was strong in his nostrils. There was the sound of rippling waves breaking against the concrete wharf. The moonlight made the surface of the water shine like silvery scales, but the bottom of the ocean was so dark that it could not be seen. The smell of the water was mixed with the smell of blood. There was a mountain of corpses nearby. And at the tip of the pier stood the two fighting *asuras*.

Rentaro looked at the spreading sea of blood and asked in a low growl, "Did you bastards do all this?"

"We didn't want the church to get dirty with blood," said Kagetane. "Everything that we could do is over already. I'm sure the Stage Five Gastrea will be here soon. All that's left is to wait."

"Is the case inside the church? And if I go in and wreck all your preparations right now, will the summoning of the Stage Five be stopped?"

"I don't think that's possible, because we are standing in your way."

"Then, I'll destroy you."

Kagetane raised his eyebrows and laughed. "I am the one who will destroy the world. No one can stop me."

"President Tendo, what do you think the Satomi pair's chances are of winning?" the Seitenshi asked.

Kisara's eyes showed no expression as she put her chin in her hand, thinking. "Perhaps about thirty percent? If I am allowed to take my own expectations into consideration, then I believe he will definitely win."

The Chief Cabinet Secretary scoffed and laughed. "President Tendo, it's not that I do not understand wanting to believe in the strength of one's own employees. However, twenty-nine civil officers have just been killed. And one of them is a survivor of the New Humanity Creation Project. He doesn't even have a one-percent chance of winning."

"One of them? No, you are mistaken, Chief Cabinet Secretary."

"What?"

"Secretary, I will spare you the details, but ten years ago, right after Satomi was taken in by the Tendo family, a stray Gastrea invaded my house and devoured my mother and father. Because of the stress of that time, my chronic diabetes worsened, and my kidneys pretty much stopped functioning."

The secretary looked confused, like he could not tell where she was going with this story. "I-I do believe that is an unfortunate story, but what does that have to do with—?"

She cut him off. "When Satomi protected me then, his right arm and leg were eaten by the Gastrea, and his left eye was gouged out. Near death, he was taken to Section 22. The doctor who operated on him was Dr. Sumire Muroto, celebrated as a miracle worker of the times."

"Sumire Muroto, you said? Then, don't tell me he is…"

Thinking that this was a good time, the Seitenshi looked next to her. "Kikunojo, pass out their specs to everyone, please."

Rentaro glared fixedly in front of him. In front of him was the enemy. The enemy he needed to defeat. Closing his eyes silently, he rolled up his right sleeve and pant leg and stretched his arm straight out. "I will stop you, Kagetane…for the sake of those you killed mercilessly, and for Kisara's and Enju's sakes. Kagetane Hiruko, I will stop you!"

With a creaking sound, cracks appeared on his right arm and leg, and artificial skin made of plastic elastomer and silicone warped and peeled off, piling at his feet.

After taking a glance at the materials, the secretary stood up with a shrill cry. "Impossible!" He scratched his head and made his confusion and fear known. "There is no way... What is the meaning of this...? There was one more? Another human weapon born of the Gastrea War?"

Eventually, a jet-black arm appeared from underneath Rentaro's artificial skin. His left leg also glistened with black chrome from the crotch down. Air vents that stuck out like barbs autonomously started peristalsis, and when he opened his eyes, his field of vision widened, and the colors became more vivid. His artificial eye was connected directly to his optic nerve, widening his field of vision and allowing it to capture objects in 3-D. Built into his artificial eye was a nano-core processor made using a graphene transistor. It activated and started operating. The inside of the pupil spun, geometrical shapes emerged, his sense of smell became sharper, and a rich taste filled his mouth.

Kagetane's body trembled. "Artificial Varanium limbs...? Satomi, don't tell me you're one, too?"

Rentaro raised his head slowly. "I will give you my name, as well, Kagetane. I am Rentaro Satomi, former member of the Ground Self-Defense Force's Eastern Force, 787th Mechanization Special Unit, of the New Humanity Creation Project."

"Satomi's artificial limbs and eye are made of the alloy Super-Varanium, made from a base of Varanium in a state of weightlessness and mixing in ten different kinds of rare and common metals. It is a next generation alloy that has many times the hardness level and a much higher melting point than Varanium. The section Kagetane Hiruko was with, Section 16, was tactically concerned with absolute defense and created a repulsion force field to stop the attacks of Stage Four Gastrea. Satomi was with Section 22, which was concerned with the exact opposite. Using the propulsion force of ten cartridges in his arm and fifteen cartridges in his leg, he can attack with superhuman strength. It is the personal armament of a New Humanity Creation Project soldier born of the desire to consign Gastrea to oblivion using man himself."

Kagetane spread both arms and started laughing wildly. "I see, I see! So that's how it was! From the moment I met you, I liked what I saw, but I didn't think we really were the same kind!" The laughing continued.

Enju gave a heartbreaking scream. "Rentaro, I thought you were never to use that again?!"

"It's fine," said Rentaro. "More importantly, you need to settle this once and for all. It doesn't agree with you to stay the loser, right?"

Enju glared sharply in Kohina's direction and then gave a hard nod. Enju's and Kohina's black eyes turned a fiery red at almost the same time as they released their power.

"I am thankful to Kagetane Hiruko," Kisara continued with dignity. "This past year, no matter how much I hounded him, Satomi lazily refused to use that. He hates himself. But right now, Satomi is seriously angry. I have only seen this once before myself, so I cannot predict what will happen after this."

The Seitenshi stood from her chair and looked around as she announced, "I hope you all understand the meaning of this fight. The battle between Rentaro Satomi and Kagetane Hiruko could be called the battle between the ultimate lance and the ultimate shield, the battle of opposites. However, they will be at odds with one another. In this battle, when it is all over, one pair will definitely be annihilated. Please fight, Satomi, and prove that you are the strongest!"

"Please win, Satomi… Please." The Seitenshi heard Kisara murmur under her breath as she clasped her hands together.

The cold night wind blew and teased at Rentaro's uniform. The air was tense, and it seemed sinful to even breathe. Rentaro stepped firmly on the dirt with the bottom of his boots. Sweating in anticipation of the fight and feeling choked, he tore off his necktie.

The enemy was serious. Even when a large number of civil officers banded together, they could not even scratch him.

Kagetane took a stance. He took his two custom Berettas from their holsters, unfolded their bayonet units, and held them out to his sides. Kohina had also drawn her short swords and was holding them crossed in front of her. As the perpendicular swords and guns diffused the moonlight, they formed the shape of a cross of death, ready to engrave God's majesty on those who would die.

"Do you understand, Satomi?" said Kagetane. "Do you understand what it means to challenge me, who once held an IP Rank of 134?"

Rentaro took his stance silently. The Tendo Martial Arts Infinite Stance made him conscious of the eternally limitless existence of the heavens and the earth. "Don't worry. I know exactly what that means, Kagetane. I've lost twice, all my allies have been annihilated, and no backup is coming. This is not the situation I wanted to be in, scumbag! Let's start the fight. I'm going to exterminate you now, you bastard!"

That was the signal to start the battle.

As Rentaro stepped forward, Kagetane came at him first. He swung his arms as if he was going to mow him down. "*Maximum Pain!* I'll crush you...!" The bluish-white field expanded in a fan shape and rammed into Rentaro with terrifying momentum.

"Tendo Martial Arts First Style, Number 3—" The sound of an explosion rang in the air, and the extractor that ran along Rentaro's fake ulnar nerve on his artificial arm picked up empty golden shell casings and kicked them out as it rotated. "*Sokuro Kabuto!*" Rentaro finished. His explosively fast fist, which was sped up through cartridge propulsion, warped the incoming wall and punched through it. The point of impact exploded, and both he and Kagetane were sent flying into the air.

"So you broke through *Maximum Pain*, huh...?" said Kagetane.

"That's not all!" said Rentaro.

Suddenly, Kagetane's knees bent, and he coughed up blood. He wiped the part of his mask around his mouth and looked wonderingly at the blood that flowed out.

"Papa!" Kohina shouted.

"The field couldn't block all of the damage?" Kagetane laughed maniacally, standing on his tiptoes and spreading his arms as he spun around once. "What fun! What fun, Satomi! I am in pain! I am alive! What a wonderful life! Hallelujah!"

Just as Rentaro thought Kohina had disappeared from sight, she appeared in front of him and Enju. She screamed in his ear, "Don't be mean to Papaaaaa!"

Kohina spun once as if dancing with short swords still in both hands. She covered the ten meters between them and slashed with great speed, but other than that swing, her swordsmanship was very random. There was the sound of clashing blades. In the end, a look of astonishment appeared on Kohina's face. The bottom of Enju's shoe was on her right sword, and Rentaro's artificial arm had blocked the left sword in defense.

The perception amplification device in Rentaro's artificial eye calculated the enemy's position and predicted the direction they would move in based on how fast they were moving. As they were locked together, Rentaro used his free left hand to draw the XD from its holster.

However, before he could finish pulling the trigger, Enju's body rammed into his. It was a strong enough force to make him feel the contents of his stomach come up, but in the blink of an eye, the place where Rentaro had just been exploded into a cloud of dust, and Rentaro understood her actions. From the pier, Kagetane had covered for Kohina with his Beretta.

Keeping her hold on Rentaro, Enju jumped toward the ocean, hopping like a rabbit from the top of one moored rental boat to another. The bullets that were following in hot pursuit riddled the boats with bullet holes right after Enju jumped off, sinking the boats.

Rentaro was astonished as he was pulled about by the intense G's. Using only one point of support while shooting two fully automatic guns at once was usually pretty useless if the enemy was more than five meters away. Just being able to follow Enju's movements—which were hard to even see—and control the recoil at the same time was already no small feat.

Enju hopped high in the air and, checking the warehouse district on the wharf, tapped Rentaro's shoulder twice. The signal meant she was going to drop him.

In less than a second, he felt the now familiar floating feeling. This time, the drop was from about five meters in the air, so he used his right leg to break the fall and rolled swiftly into the shadow of a nearby shipping container to hide. He did that all in one movement and turned his neck to survey the place where he had been dropped. There was heavy construction equipment and the like that had been left behind next to evenly spaced-out metal freight containers. Of course, the Unexplored Territory was uninhabited, so the heavy equipment and containers were all covered with rust from the salty ocean breeze.

Rentaro stood with his back to a container, held his gun ready, and inhaled deeply, then exhaled. Jumping out from the shadow of the container, he aimed the XD at Kagetane in the flesh and fired. The stinging recoil flung his arm back, and the .40-caliber Varanium bullet was fired, its empty casing bouncing onto the ground. To fire at the Promoter, who acted as the commander, was a standard by-the-book move for tag-team battles.

However, Rentaro found himself being surprised for a third time. There was a strange noise like someone hitting a cracked bell with all their might, and the bullet disappeared. Kohina had appeared by Kagetane's side unnoticed. It took Rentaro a few seconds to realize that she had cut apart the bullet.

Rentaro's legs shook. *You've gotta be kidding me.* He fired off as many shots as he could. As if ridiculing his efforts, every last one of the bullets was cut down with a crack. Spinning her body like a top as she skillfully used her two swords to repel the bullets, she looked like she was dancing.

Kohina kept spinning in circles with her short swords in hand until she finally came to a sudden stop with her head tilted in question.

"That's impossible...," Rentaro breathed.

In the back, Kagetane flipped up his mask, gripped one of his guns that had run out of bullets in his mouth, and calmly used his free hand to change the magazine as he walked toward Rentaro. Darkness lurked behind the mask, and Rentaro could not see his features. The ocean breeze made the long tails of his tailcoat flutter, and it made Kagetane's body look larger than life. There were not even any traces of him having used *Imaginary Gimmick*.

Enju's face also paled as she drew closer to Rentaro. Rentaro closed his eyes and thought as hard as he could. "Enju, how many seconds would it take for you to defeat Kagetane one-on-one?" Rentaro asked her, his eyes not leaving the enemy.

Enju seemed to realize something and looked worriedly at Rentaro, but she finally faced forward and said, "I'll defeat him in ten seconds!" and dashed off in a blast with the superfast acceleration that could be called a distinguishing trait of Model Rabbits. Kohina came forward to intercept her, but Enju slid to evade her slash and rushed toward Kagetane.

Kohina saw the signal too late and a regretful expression crossed her face, but she soon turned to focus her attention on Rentaro.

It was the story of two rooks aiming for the unguarded kings at the risk of their own lives. At this rate, it was a race to see which Initiator could cut down her opponent first. Enju was definitely not an easy opponent for Kagetane to handle. However, the same could be said for Rentaro about Kohina.

Kohina came at him as fast as a bullet with her body low to the ground. The device in his artificial eye started sparking, and the back of his eyelid stung as if getting burned. He could just barely track her movements. Twisting his upper body to avoid one sword, he used his right fist against the second sword that was aiming low.

*Now*—he thought. An explosion rang through the air, and golden empty shell casings spun as they were ejected. *Tendo Martial Arts First Style, Number 3—"Rokuro Kabuto"!*

"Off with your head!" Kohina shouted.

The quickly swinging fist exchanged blows with the short swords. The force of the shock wave sent a cloud of dust high in the air, and Rentaro and Kohina were both knocked backward with their feet flailing. Rentaro was able to move again first. In no time, he was shooting with his XD as he drew near Kohina. Kohina flourished her two swords as she cut down the bullets with piercing, resounding sounds. Rentaro narrowed the distance between them as he fired. But even when they were less than three meters apart, not a single bullet hit the swordswoman with her twin swords.

Rentaro gave in to his impatience and started firing, aiming at her head instead of her body. Right after he did this, he was attacked by intense regret. As if waiting for this moment, Kohina avoided the bullets just by moving her neck, and moved to close in on him. He got chills when he realized she had lured him in. She thrust the sword blades at him at an impossible speed, and his artificial eye became so hot it burned, as it was forced to to operate at super-speeds. Rentaro avoided the thrusts on instinct alone and pinned her arms to her sides. Lowering his hips, he swept Kohina's legs out from under her, taking a judolike stance.

However, his enemy was not to be taken lightly. In an instant, she used her strength to free herself and ran away, kicking off of Rentaro's back and springing into the air. The sword she forcefully pulled out gave Rentaro a shallow cut. He couldn't believe his eyes as he saw the small girl fly almost five meters into the air with one jump.

However, he predicted where she was planning to land, and then it was Rentaro's turn to shout. "Above you, Enju!"

Enju, who had been playing a seesaw game with Kagetane, alternating between attacking and defending, hurriedly did a backflip to jump out of the way. Kohina skewered the spot where Enju had been with an amazing force as she dropped down.

"Howl, Sodomy! Sing, Gospel!" Kagetane shouted. His two guns fired, making explosive sounds like a rotating saw. One of the shots that followed Enju hit her left arm as she retreated.

"Argh," she said as the arm that was hit by the 9-mm bullet flew up to the left reflexively.

"Enju, get down!" Rentaro shouted as he changed the magazine of his gun in a split second. Drawing the Sigma gun with his left hand, he pointed it at Kohina, pointing the XD in his right hand at Kagetane. With his arms crossed, he pulled the trigger on both at the same time—an impromptu double-gun stance. Immediately after, muzzle fire scattered from both of Rentaro's hands like fireworks, and both arms were thrown back with intense recoil.

Kohina used her swords to repel the bullets as she danced, while Kagetane mumbled something under his breath. By the time Rentaro realized that it was the preliminary setup for *Imaginary Gimmick*, the bluish-white phosphorescent wall had already appeared with a bang to repel Rentaro's shots in all directions.

The Sigma in his left hand ran out of bullets first, so he threw the whole gun away. He took a reinforced steel cylindrical can out of his pouch, pulled the pin out with his teeth, and threw it. As Kohina thought only to clear it away without worrying about the details, Kagetane raised his voice for the first time. "No, Kohina, not that!"

She fell for it.

Exactly two seconds later, the steel can exploded in a blast of light that spread to blow the darkness away.

It was a stun bomb, with an explosive blast of light that was 170 decibels and 200 candelas. When it exploded, the vibrations created by the compressed shock waves of this chemical-throwing bomb would have made someone go deaf in a small room, and it scattered light brighter than the sun.

"Ahhhh!" Kohina writhed in pain as she covered her ears and screamed in anguish. It even had enough of an effect on Kagetane. Enju was not one to let that chance go to waste. The rabbit-footed girl closed the gap between them in an instant and tread firmly on the road with her left foot, creating a deep impression in the ground.

Kohina immediately crossed her short sword to protect herself. There, Enju landed a direct kick. Enju's center kick was strong enough to kick through thin steel plates, and despite breaking one of the short swords, its power did not wane, and she blew Kohina off the pier. Then, kicking the surface of the water and creating tsunamis, Kohina advanced about twenty meters before she sank.

"Rentaro!" said Enju.

Even before Enju called out to him, Rentaro had already started running. He sprang out in front of the remaining man in tailcoats. Before Kagetane's muzzle could be trained on Rentaro, Rentaro used a striker to set off the bottoms of the cartridges he had in his legs. The extractor positioned along the fake hidden nerve pulled onto an empty cartridge and ejected it.

At the same time the explosion sounded, Rentaro's leg flew up with amazing speed, and on top of that, Enju matched the timing of her kick with Rentaro's.

He and Enju's eyes met. "Tendo Martial Arts Type 2, Number 24—'Inzen Genmeika'!" he yelled, with Enju shouting next to him, and they gave two explosive kicks, side-by-side.

When the impact reached Kagetane, a bluish-white light blocked it, and with a large crash, it blew away the air around them. Kagetane was also blown off the pier, landing on the water and sinking. Rentaro checked where Kagetane hit the water and fired a few shots after him with his XD. He ran out of bullets after three shots. As the night fell silent, the quiet sounds of small waves breaking on the shore returned.

That was when he first realized that he had been yelling and taking short breaths. Rentaro gripped his gun firmly with both hands, praying and waiting. Gradually, his breathing calmed down. "Enju," he said. He bent over Enju, who had sunk to the ground, and looked at the wound on her arm. Rentaro frowned.

Enju's wound showed no sign of healing and was still oozing blood. Varanium bullets prevented a Gastrea from regenerating after being wounded, and it was no different for the Initiators who were able to regenerate thanks to the Gastrea virus. Facing Varanium weapons, she was as vulnerable as a regular human being.

Enju's eyes welled with tears and her mouth was turned down at the corners.

"I-it'll be fine!" he said as he patted Enju's head lightly.

"It hurts!" she retorted.

"Dummy, how can you expect to be unhurt after being that reckless?"

Enju looked at the surface of the water. "Did we beat them?"

Rentaro turned his neck to look past the pier, staring at the dark surface of the water. Cautiously, he pulled out a spare magazine for the XD and exchanged it for the empty one. It hadn't felt like he had made it past *Imaginary Gimmick*, but the force was strong enough to rupture the caster's organs. Even if Kagetane wasn't dead, he was probably out of commission.

And because Rentaro thought that, when an arm suddenly appeared out of the surface of the water and grabbed his ankle, he was so surprised that he couldn't react right away. He couldn't hear Enju's scream for a second. He was pulled underwater with an incredible force, and his eyes and nose and all his orifices were filled with cold water and darkness. Seeing a white mask a mere twenty or thirty centimeters in front of him, he almost screamed. The hand holding Rentaro's ankle was glowing phosphorescently. Rentaro gasped as he twisted his body desperately.

Aiming the XD, he fired at point-blank range. He hit Kagetane's shoulder, but the fingers digging into his skin did not let go of Rentaro. Bad things came in threes. The XD couldn't fire properly underwater, and the bullet got caught in the slide and jammed.

Cornered, Rentaro fired off the cartridges in his artificial limbs like explosives. Small explosions burst in the water, and as white bubbles clouded his vision, Rentaro himself was also blown back. He couldn't keep his eyes open in an impact that nearly took off his arms and legs. He felt a strange floating feeling.

He couldn't tell what was up and what was down and moved his arms and legs awkwardly. He couldn't even get into a proper falling stance when his back suddenly hit something hard and the intense pain knocked the air out of him. He couldn't tell what had happened for a moment.

There was the sound of rain as drops hit his arm. Wrenching open his trembling eyelids, a clear starry sky spread provokingly above him. Rentaro was lying on his back on the deck of a small fishing boat. It looked like he had been blown out of the water from the blast of firing all the cartridges in his arm and leg at once and was lucky he had been tossed onto a fishing boat. What he had thought was rain was the spray of water that had been blown up with him.

Using both hands to push his body upright on the deck, he vomited the ocean water he had swallowed and wiped his mouth on his sleeve. Not only were his clothes heavy from the water they had soaked up, but they clung to his skin and felt disgusting. Where in the world was Kagetane?

Suddenly, his vision jerked down. He thought his knees had collapsed under him, but both feet were planted on the deck. At that moment, he felt chills go up his spine. About two meters in front of him saw another moored fishing boat. Staggering, Rentaro went in for the approach and made a long running jump as he leapt into the air. His instinct was screaming that he had to be there.

As the heel of his shoe flew over the dark sea, he landed on another deck. Sure enough, a scene that made him doubt his own eyes exploded in front of him. As small waves rippled on the surface of the water, they were pushed apart and split in two, and with a thunderous roar, they became two enormous waterfalls.

At around eight meters below sea level, Rentaro could see seaweed and old moss-covered tires. The fishing boat that Rentaro had just been on had been pitifully turned upside down, its bow crushed with a sorrowful sound. Rentaro was horrified as he rubbed his arms.

And at the ocean floor, a pair in a tailcoat and black dress stood close as they looked up at him. They had taken some damage. One of Kohina's short swords was broken, and Kagetane had been shot in the shoulder and had lost Psychedelic Gospel. However, they were far from being out of commission. Their narrowed eyes clearly showed a will to continue fighting. The flame of their fighting spirit was still burning. This was what it meant to be one of the highest-ranking pairs.

Rentaro let the XD drop and stepped back. His brain wouldn't process the fact that the ocean had been split by the repulsion field.

"What are you doing, Rentaro?!" Before he knew it, Enju was by his side, grabbing his arm and leaping into the air. They landed on the largest passenger boat anchored in the bay. It must have originally been a café or lounge, and there were a number of table sets with umbrellas lined up on the deck.

Tilting his shoulder toward Kohina, Kagetane also soon leapt onto the stage. Hatred peeked out from behind Kagetane's mask. His arm was stretched straight out in front of him, his fist clenched. "Why are you getting in my way?! Why?! We of the New Humanity Creation Project were created to kill. If the Monoliths are destroyed and the Gastrea War restarted, it will prove that we have a reason to exist. Hatred will not disappear. The war will not end. We will be needed!

"Don't you understand, Satomi? A world where the Gastrea War continues is a win for us soldiers of the New Humanity Creation Project!"

Rentaro felt a shock like he had been hit in the head with a hammer. "Don't tell me…that was the only reason…? You bastard!"

"What if it was? The extinction of mankind is only a trivial matter. If we do not fight, no one needs us. Now, let us have war! And more war! This is my war *for* me, *by* me. I won't let anyone get in my way."

"Even after spilling that much blood, you still want a massacre?"

"This is a grand experiment! In any case, those who are killed so easily by me will not be able to survive in my ideal country. How was the reaction of those around you when your Initiator was exposed as one of the Cursed Children? Were they happy for you? Did they shout for joy with you? Did they hold your arm with delight? Of course not. I was chosen. Kohina was also chosen. You two are also chosen. You should be able to understand my ideology. Now, Rentaro Satomi, I will give you everything you desire. Come with me!"

"Don't be ridiculous, you bastard! I refuse to allow the future you describe!"

"Then, die…!"

Seeing Kagetane point his gun at them, Enju plunged in. However, Kohina predicted all of Enju's movements as she came in to intercept her. Just as the bottom of Enju's foot stopped the side sweeping of the short sword, Kohina continued on to ram Enju with her shoulder. Enju, who had been balanced on one leg, was knocked over easily. Kohina grabbed Enju's leg, and swung her, throwing Enju into Rentaro. Then, Rentaro gasped as he saw Kagetane aiming his gun at them.

A Varanium bullet would be bad. Catching Enju, Rentaro turned his body in a semicircle.

"Howl, Sodomy!" Kagetane cried. A storm of 9-mm Varanium bullets flooded Rentaro's back, and spasms racked his body as if shocked by electricity.

"Rentaro!" Enju shouted.

He gritted his teeth at the intense pain. He was alive. He had avoided instant death. Rentaro put his hand to his waist and pulled out the string of plastic bell-like syringes. Pulling off the cap with his mouth, he stuck it in his abdomen and injected the medicine.

*"Don't use it unless you have to."* Sumire's voice echoed in his head.

His heart leapt with a sudden throb. His whole body felt intensely hot, and he felt the illusion of his limbs extending. With the sound of sizzling meat cooking, the wounds in Rentaro's body healed, and the bullets in his body were pushed out.

It was the AGV test drug, a drug Sumire created while studying Gastrea that made a human's regenerative abilities go through the roof. This dramatic effect could even overcome the inhibiting effect of Varanium. If it weren't for the side effect that twenty percent of the test subjects became Gastrea, Sumire would be so famous that her name would be in textbooks.

In the end, Rentaro had won the gamble. He opened and closed his hands and rotated his arms. His body felt fine. There were no symptoms of him turning into a Gastrea. Kagetane went crazy shooting his fully automatic Beretta. Rentaro's arm went up to protect his head and heart as he shielded Enju. Again, he felt the intense attacks pierce his flesh as blood flew out of his whole body. Almost all the bullets hit their target, but immediately afterward, the bullets were excreted from his body.

Even as Rentaro felt dizzy with the pain, he chuckled inside. As long as he had this—

However, that self-conceit only lasted for a few seconds. Because Rentaro had raised his hands to guard his face, he noticed Kagetane's approach too late. The rear guard was coming in for close combat? Why?

Completely deliberately, Kagetane slowly put the palm of his hand on Rentaro's side. "It's over. I will show you my secret weapon." Rentaro could hear Kagetane's voice deep within his skull. "Endless Scream."

In the blink of an eye, an intense shock ran through Rentaro's body from his toes to the top of his head, and his body floated for an instant.

"Huh...?" said Rentaro. The repulsion field had become an enormous spear and pierced through Rentaro's abdomen.

Kagetane pulled out the spear with great momentum, and Rentaro tottered and stumbled for a few steps. The right side of his abdomen was gone. A circle was cut out of Rentaro's body as if drawn by a giant compass. A cross section of his ribs was visible, and his internal organs peeked out. Rentaro slowly put his hand to his stomach, scared of what he would find. Blood welled up as if it had just remembered it needed to, and his organs and bowels spilled out.

"N-no...way..." Rentaro coughed up blood and fell to his knees. Turning his head and seeing Enju with both hands covering her mouth, he reached out a hand, imploring Kagetane Hiruko, who was looking down at him with cold eyes.

Kagetane crossed himself. "You've lost," he said.

Thinking that the ground was drawing near, Rentaro fell forward. The stain of blood encroached on the deck. The shadow of Rentaro's death was reflected in the puddle of blood. His arms and legs twitched on their own.

No matter how long he waited, the wound in his body would not regenerate. Even with the effects of the AGV test drug, it apparently could not deal with such a large wound. Unable to bear the pain, Rentaro's cells were quickly giving up on their host. Darkness came at Rentaro from all sides and an extraordinary loneliness descended on him.

Enju was desperately shaking his body. Tears poured out of her eyes as she screamed at Rentaro for some reason. He couldn't hear what she was saying.

Then, Kohina kicked Enju's chin away as Enju raised her head. Enju flew into the lounge table and fell loudly, getting tangled with an umbrella. Kagetane aimed at Enju's head with his gun and mumbled something under his breath.

Was he planning on killing Enju? Enju, who had already lost the will to fight?

Enju stretched out her arms at Rentaro, without any consideration for her own safety. The pain seemed to gouge out Rentaro's heart.

"............!"

He couldn't hear. He couldn't hear Enju's voice. He could feel the cold hand of death reaching into his wound.

".................!"

His consciousness disintegrated, and he sank into a deep darkness. His eyelids felt heavy and trembled.

Suddenly, Enju's voice mixed with sobbing flooded in through his eardrum and echoed in his head. "Don't die, Rentaro! We haven't been able to do anything yet. Don't leave me alone!"

*Thump*, his heart leapt, and his eyes opened suddenly. His right hand grabbed the four remaining AGV test-drug syringes in a flash and, holding them between his fingers, he pulled off their caps with his mouth and thrust them all into his abdomen.

With a familiar sound, Rentaro's chest swelled, and his bones rang with a strange sound. His body cramped and boiled, and he felt chills like something was crawling around through him. The hole in his body made a popping sound, and then—

Enju was surprised at the regeneration that started. Blood spilled, flesh bulged, bowels hung out, nerves connected, his body temperature dropped, bones were rebuilt, and cells regenerated as they died out.

Rentaro's body was dying at a terrifying speed and then coming back to life with amazing momentum, a melting pot of contradictions. Feeling an intense pain as if his internal organs were being rearranged, Rentaro writhed and randomly hit his head against the deck.

Then, Rentaro gave a great scream at the sky and stood up. He staggered a few steps as he almost slipped on the blood pooled below him. His vision was severely distorted, and his depth perception bent the world as if he were completely drunk. But he could still see the death god he was supposed to defeat.

His body was hot. It felt like it was on fire. He felt extreme nausea that came with a pounding headache and the urge to vomit. Rentaro himself wondered why he was able to stand. However, his arms and legs could still move, and he was alive.

Kagetane's mouth gaped as he stood, frozen. "Satomi... What in the world are you...?"

Rentaro shot an evil look at his enemy and readied himself. He took the Tendo Martial Arts Water and Sky Stance. The clear ocean and sky became a single, boundless blue. It was a stance that attacked without worrying about defense.

When Rentaro let out a hot breath, it lingered white in the air and then was carried away by the wind. He closed his eyes and then slowly opened them. Then, he kicked the ground. The sound of an explosion rang from his feet, and an empty casing was ejected. He turned his leg's mobility thruster back and let the jet propulsion come out of the back of his leg. His body felt like it was being torn apart, but he bore the pain and sprung out in a second in front of the enemy.

Kohina unfroze and jumped out without a moment's delay. "Off with your head!" she shouted.

"Outta the way!" said Rentaro as he used his right arm to deal with the blade she swung downward with all her might. Three empty casings popped out at the same time as the explosion, and the strong smell of gunpowder filled their nostrils. Kohina's eyes opened so wide that the corners of her eyelids seemed about to split apart.

Tendo Martial Arts First Style, Number 8: *Homura Kasen, Burst.*

Coming at Rentaro from the front again was the fist and the short sword. Intense shock waves pierced his whole body. With his Super-Varanium fist, he broke the remaining short sword into pieces and blew Kohina away like a scrap of paper. She bounced on the deck and broke through the wall to the pilothouse, crashing into the meters and gauges inside. Kohina lay stunned against the wall with a concussion.

Without stopping, he fired his leg and accelerated again with an impact that almost blew him away. He charged directly through a barrage of bullets.

Kagetane lowered himself with a flutter of his tailcoat. "*Endless...*"

"Tendo Martial Arts First Style, Number 15...," Rentaro began.

Kagetane turned and threw away his gun and reached behind him to ready the spear. At almost the same time, an empty casing flew from Rentaro's arm, and he let loose an uppercut with wonderful speed that looked as if it were scooping something from the bottom up.

"*...Screeeeeammm!*" Kagetane finished.

"*...Unebikoryu!*" Rentaro shouted at the same time.

A phosphorescent spear hit Rentaro's fist and a thunderous roar scattered through the night sky. The clash of a strong fist with unparalleled hardness and a bluish-white spear that could repel bullets from antitank rifles lit up their surroundings like midday.

Rentaro gritted his teeth, his leg sinking with the deck. The ship planks on the deck were flying off from the shock. He tasted bitter adrenaline in this mouth.

As the superior spear slowly pushed his arm back, he broke out in a cold sweat all over his body. Rentaro screamed, stuck together with Kagetane, and fired off a succession of cartridges. The first shot pushed the spear, and the second shot made it clear that his arm was shoved into the spear.

The third shot—Rentaro felt his arm suddenly thrown forward. With an explosive sound that deafened his ears, a supersonic uppercut blew the spear and Kagetane's body ten meters into the air. Kagetane looked like he did not know what had just happened.

Rentaro bounded up, changed the thruster angle to the back and fired. Jumping up as high as Kagetane, he half turned his body at the top and, facing downward, he fired off the rest of the cartridges in his leg. "Tendo Martial Arts Second Style, Number 11—"

For a brief moment, everything seemed to be in slow motion.

A shower of empty golden casings shot out as he turned, seeming to pour down in a shower from above, filling his vision in slow motion. In the downpour of empty casings, his eyes met Kagetane's.

Kagetane spoke in a quiet, hoarse voice, as if he had already given up. "I see... So I lost...to you...huh...?"

As the wind whistled by Rentaro's ears, time returned to normal. It was all or nothing. "—*Inzen Kokutei Unlimited Burst...! Fall...!*"

It was an overhead kick of judgment that turned the sky and earth upside down. With his Super-Varanium toes, he ripped through Kagetane's field and crushed his lungs, breaking a few of his ribs and blowing him away. Kagetane's body bounced with amazing speed over the top of the ocean like a skipping stone, going through two of the small boats moored in the bay, blown almost a hundred meters away, where he landed with a pillar of water like a tsunami that rose and sank.

Rentaro couldn't completely negate the force of his own kick and spun in midair as he dropped, landing hard on the ground on his back with a groan. Immediately jumping up, he surveyed the ocean without letting down his guard.

Ten seconds passed, then twenty. The air shimmered with the heat let off from the successive firing of large-caliber shells from his artificial limbs. The enemy remained submerged.

Slowly letting out a breath, he turned toward to Enju to show her a smile. "All right, we won, Enju! Yahoo!"

Enju gaped, flabbergasted.

Rentaro scratched his head. Well, it *was* surprising.

"No... Papa, Papa...!" Turning his head toward the voice, Rentaro saw Kohina on her knees with an expression of despair on her face.

Enju appeared conflicted as she looked up at Rentaro. Rentaro shook his head softly. "She's not an enemy anymore."

At that moment, there was a vibration in his chest pocket, and a tinny electronic sound echoed in the air.

"It seems you're alive, Satomi." He knew who it was just from the voice. Hot tears pricked his eyes when he heard the graceful voice filled with kindness and confidence.

"It's done," said Rentaro. "I won, just like I promised, Kisara."

"I saw. Unfortunately, I have one piece of bad news for you."

"Bad news...?"

Kisara spoke with an unusually gloomy voice. "Listen calmly. A Stage Five Gastrea has appeared."

"What?" Rentaro could only respond questioningly. The words wouldn't sink in and just floated superficially at the surface of his mind.

So it was over for Tokyo Area. Everyone would be killed. No one would survive.

2

Kisara added one thing after another using present progressive tense as the events were happening. According to what she said, at almost the same time the JNSC council room celebrated the defeat of the Kagetane pair, they received the report of the appearance of the Stage Five, and everyone's faces paled.

The instant the nonstandard-size Gastrea's head appeared in Tokyo Bay, missiles, poison gas, and torpedoes were fired, but the missiles and torpedoes barely scratched it, and those scratches healed in a second. The poison gas was a VX nerve gas, the worst known to man, but after taking in the gas, the Gastrea virus analyzed its components in a second and developed a resistance to it. The dependable Varanium armor-piercing ammunition was repelled by the Gastrea's hard skin. Kisara ended by telling him that the people in the meeting room had fallen into a panic.

Rentaro looked from the port to the faraway horizon of Tokyo Bay. It was true that he could see light and hear soft sounds of explosions in the night. The battle had already begun.

From what she said, he gathered that Kisara had somehow been invited into the JNSC situation room. While they were talking, Rentaro could hear frantic screams and angry shouts arguing back and forth incessantly in the background behind her. It was probably only a matter of time before people started trying to run away.

"Is it all over for us? Is there no hope left of saving Tokyo Area?" Rentaro shut his eyes tightly and prayed as he waited for her answer.

Finally, she spoke, her voice with its usual dignity. "It's too soon to give up. When I asked the Seitenshi if the plan I just came up with was physically possible, she said, 'I daresay we can do it.'"

"We can survive...? H-how?"

"We can see you and Enju from here. You can see the answer if you look southeast."

He turned his head in the direction she had given. Then he understood her plan and was taken aback. *No way... It's impossible, Kisara. There's no way it'd work.*

Two parallel rails 1.5 kilometers long stretched out and pierced the sky at an angle of elevation of about seventy degrees. From where he stood, thin clouds were in the way and he could not see through to the tip. A relic of the last stages of the Great Gastrea War, the massive weapon was completed but had not even been tested once before it was unavoidably abandoned and left to watch over the loss of the war. It was called the Stairway to Heaven.

It was also known as a Linear Electromagnetic Projectile Device. It was a railgun module that could accelerate and fire metal projectiles eight hundred millimeters or less in diameter at near light speed.

"You two are the closest to the target location. There's no time to lose. You're going to do it, Satomi."

The electric lights of the facility turned on all at once as Rentaro and Enju approached. Using the power supply network from the mainland, it was the first time in ten years that they had been turned on. Because the thick power cables were securely shielded and buried underground, they did not suffer any damage from the Gastrea running wild aboveground and could still operate now, ten years later.

The facility sat atop a small mountain, and a deep forest spread around it. The pure white outer walls with spikes on top rose sternly to refuse entry, but unfortunately, it did not take into account the jumping powers of a girl with a Rabbit Factor. Enju quickly carried them over the wall, and they went inside.

From the air, Rentaro could see the whole facility for an instant. The giant base of the Stairway to Heaven that was propped up by supports was connected to a round object about a hundred meters in diameter, which was probably used to store power of some kind.

However, compared to the impressive railgun module, the adjoining research facility looked smaller even than the grounds of Rentaro's school, Magata High. The mystery was soon solved when he looked at a map of the facility that had been sent to his phone. The facility stretched belowground like an ant nest, and the building that showed its face aboveground looked like it was just the tip of the iceberg.

"Satomi, hurry," Kisara said from Rentaro's cell phone.

Rentaro dashed inside the facility with Enju. Inside was a tangled, complicated maze, as though its designer had been afraid of guerrilla occupation. The room they were looking for was on the second floor of the basement. Following the map and Kisara's guidance, Rentaro reached the middle computer room, panting.

The dome inside was spacious, with computers and other equipment set up around the room. On the front was a giant angled electroluminescent panel spread out, and surprisingly, even after being abandoned for ten years, there wasn't a speck of dust accumulated on it.

Rentaro hurried to the control panel in the center of the room, stretched out the external connection terminal, and connected his cell phone. When it suddenly asked for a twenty-digit password, he was flustered, but Kisara's clear voice over the phone did not show a moment's hesitation.

He could hear other people's voices behind Kisara. Apparently, in the midst of this confusion, Kisara had been made responsible for this plan. Which meant that the Seitenshi and everyone else present were probably staying back and relaying information to Kisara. The password went through easily and the green bars extended, completing the link. Transmissions between the facility and headquarters began.

"...the electricity supply from the unmanned transformer station underground looks good, and there are no irregularities with the power supply network, either. The vacuum flask for the liquid helium also looks good. This will work. We will carry out the launch sequence on our end."

As they were getting a handle on the condition of the facility, Rentaro fidgeted nervously. Kisara's voice was far away. On top of that, there were fewer transmission signal indicator bars showing up than he had expected. At first, he thought it was because of the large amount of data, but it seemed to be a problem with the signal. But why? A satellite phone was never out of area, so he didn't know why the data would transfer so slowly. He had a bad feeling about this. If his connection to Kisara was cut off right now, it would be all over.

While all this was going on, an alert lamp lit up in the facility and a synthetic female voice echoed through the halls. "We will now commence the activation of the Linear Electromagnetic Projectile Device. Workers in the interlock portion of the superconductor flywheel power storage system should evacuate immediately. Sequence, moving to Phase One. We will now commence energy storage."

There was a circular indicator displayed on the right side of the panel showing the percentage of energy stored. Even though Rentaro wasn't touching anything, the touch-panel screen was tapped and flicked at dizzying speeds. Headquarters was controlling it remotely. A joystick stored in the housing of the control panel suddenly popped out, and movements of an invisible hand firmly pulled and pushed it. The rhythmical movements were like a car's gear changes.

Rentaro swallowed. His skin pricked with the enthusiasm of the people on the other side of the phone with Kisara, and after all this time, he finally understood that this was not a lie or a joke, but that what was happening now was a critical moment for the survival of Tokyo Area.

Suddenly, a shock that made the earth reverberate assailed Rentaro and Enju from below, and they both staggered. Looking at the view on the front panel, he saw that the base of the Stairway to Heaven, which had been fixed at an angle of elevation of seventy degrees, had started to move slowly with a grinding sound. However, the movement was so slow that it made him want to go to the place himself and move it.

Finally maintaining a distance pretty much level with the ground, the feet of the two tripods installed on the lower parts of the long rails on the left and right were brought down with amazing speed into the ground, digging deep into the ground and leveling a hill as they stopped. In order to prepare for the recoil of the blast, the railgun dug itself in deep.

"Changing to online mode, linking data with satellite. Activating the CYCLOPS system. Showing target on the main monitor."

Before long, the front of the three-sided panel changed, and seeing the zoomed-in image there, Rentaro almost had to look away. Just how many tens of thousands of species' genes had been incorporated into that body? The Gastrea's dark brown skin was cracked and had warts all over it that made it look like it had smallpox, and there were objects sticking out of it. Eight sickle-shaped barbs stuck out all over the grotesque body in random places—on the neck, head, right eye, and other places. Its head was swollen beyond strange, and something shaped like a curved beak projected out near its mouth. The remaining left eye was so small that it looked almost sad. On the screen was a horrifying giant walking on two legs.

Based on the scale, it was probably about four hundred meters tall. As it pushed its way through the ocean, it brushed off the flying missiles cutting through the night sky with its feelers. Smoke from the explosions scattered, and the ocean water near it evaporated. But Rentaro could not see anything that looked like damage.

Enju, gazing dumbfounded at the monitor, looked at Rentaro with a pale face. "R-Rentaro, what's that?"

"A Stage Five," said Rentaro, "also known as the Zodiac Gastrea: Scorpion. Ten years ago, it was one of the monsters that wreaked havoc on the world."

It was originally used by the U.S. Department of Defense and the Japanese government as a code name to tell them apart, but before they knew it, it had become a household name that everyone used.

Rentaro made a tight fist and gazed at the repulsive angel of death. If a whale that swam in the ocean was brought onto land, it would die, crushed by the weight of its own body. It went without saying that the same should have been true for something with a frame many times the size of a whale's.

Suddenly an unbelievable view came into sight. Just how tough was that Gastrea, such that it could support that vast body weight and still move? It was probably harder than anything else that existed on earth. There was no way an existing weapon could kill that. As the Scorpion suddenly stopped, the feelers all over its body stood straight up perpendicularly, and it pointed its giant beak toward the sky. The next instant, Rentaro cursed the fact that these facilities were equipped with a sound collection device.

"Hyoooooooooooooooooooooo!!" It was a loud shriek of a monster that seemed to unnerve everyone working hard around Japan. An earthquakelike vibration shook the whole facility, and a cold sweat broke out all over Rentaro's body. There was anger in that howl. The roots of his teeth clattered loudly. He didn't even have a chance to scream.

"Did you hear that? Don't lose focus, Satomi!" Rentaro came back to his senses with Kisara's cry. Even Kisara could not completely eliminate the panic and irritation that were mixed into her voice. "Satomi, listen calmly. We're in a bad situation. There's no Varanium armor-piercing ammunition in the chamber."

"Wh-what do you mean?" Rentaro asked.

"There's nothing that can be shot out of that railgun! In other words, it prob...can't be used...like that. S...plea...secu...it......self......" Suddenly, Kisara's voice became so faraway that he couldn't tell what she was saying. Not knowing what was going on, Rentaro pressed the phone harder to his ear.

"Kisara? Kisara?! What's wrong? Hey, Kisara!" Glancing left and right, he looked suddenly at the control panel and stared at the screen. All the blood suddenly left his face. The indicator bars that had been steadily showing their wireless data transmission had come to a complete stop. The data transmission had been interrupted.

"Right now, we can't enter anything remotely... The transmission is probably...being affected...the supermagne... The rest is up...to yo... Satomi......" Even as she was breaking up, he could pick up what she was trying to say.

Rentaro clutched the cell phone in his hand like his life depended on it and screamed. "Kisara! No, Kisara! Stop! Please stop! I can't do it. Don't leave me alone!"

"Satom...... The world...depen......... please..."

There was static, and then their call was cut off. Rentaro gazed at his cell phone with unbelieving eyes. He was suddenly enveloped with chills. But this was not the end of the terrible situation.

Suddenly, a piercing alert echoed, and when he looked up, the status screen on the left panel seemed to be red with rage. "Coolant leak in power storage system confirmed. Please abort experiment immediately. I repeat—Coolant..."

On top of that, the synthesized voice said, "Fire-control system UNTAC is not activated. Please reactivate it or abort the experiment."

"Railgun firing angle, eleven degrees above ground level. Energy eighty-eight percent filled."

Rentaro forced himself to take deep breaths and calm down. He couldn't let this abort now. He didn't know how much the coolant leak would affect the firing, but looking at the status screen, it was only leaking slightly. He could probably shoot once.

But at the same time, he knew if he missed, he would not have another chance. He prepared himself. Opening his clenched fist, he checked to make sure he could move all five fingers.

He stretched his black artificial arm straight out in front of him and narrowed his fingers into the shape of an arrowhead. With his left hand, he felt around behind his humerus, where his triceps would have been, and pushing a button he found there, his arm turned counterclockwise and popped out. The connection whirred and came loose, and Rentaro's right arm came off from the elbow down.

Rentaro stared for a while at the nerve connector terminal, insulation, shock absorber, and other parts in the cross section of the arm. Finally, he opened the universal bolt connected to the chamber next to the control panel. Rentaro then set his disconnected right arm into it and pushed the LOCK button. His right arm was sent to the chamber and locked into place.

"Rentaro, don't tell me you...?" Enju said, her voice trailing off.

"Yeah, I'm using my right arm as a bullet," said Rentaro. "Super-Varanium should be good enough."

As if approving of Rentaro's sacrifice, the composition analysis results were displayed. This material would be able to withstand up to five percent below light speed.

"Still no response from the fire-control system. Switching to manual trigger control system. Energy one hundred percent filled. Ready to shoot."

Another joysticklike object came out of the control panel. All this stick had was a trigger like that of a gun. Rentaro prayed as he gripped it hard.

The indicator flickered one hundred percent on the screen. The whole facility shook with the powerful energy of a mass of billions of tesla volts of energy looking for an exit. The fire-control system that allowed for automatic aiming to hit the target was not responding, which meant that Rentaro would have to manually hit the target.

He couldn't do it.

Rentaro squeezed his eyes shut. There were almost fifty kilometers between this facility on Boso Peninsula and the target in Tokyo Bay. In the world of shooting, where hitting a target a kilometer away was already considered a miracle, even if the target was large, how was he supposed to hit it from fifty kilometers away? Manually, he didn't even have a fraction of a percentage of a chance of hitting it.

The panel showed the Scorpion trying to land in Tokyo Bay, with a firing line rushing at it as the battle with the self-defense force at the water's edge progressed. Beyond them was the line of jet-black Mono-liths standing silently to protect Tokyo.

At that moment, the Scorpion shot out one especially long sickle-shaped feeler and mowed down all the artillery batteries and missile silos crowded around the coast of the bay at once. Dense clouds of sand and rocks were stirred up and Rentaro could tell that the state of the war was starting to take a dire turn for the worse. Replaying the Scorpion's hate-filled war cry in his head, he gripped the joystick so hard it almost broke. He wiped the sweat from his hand holding the joystick on his clothes.

The coolant loss alert was annoyingly shrill in his ears. It was as if it was urging him saying, *Hurry up, hurry up.*

He heard a ragged sigh come from his own throat that sounded like that of a wounded animal and clenched his teeth. He could not let that organism step on the land of Tokyo Area. If he quit here, what in the world had he been fighting for this whole time?!

*Do it! Do it! You can do it, Rentaro Satomi!*

---

The tips of his fingers seemed like they had solidified and wouldn't move. Rentaro finally fell to his knees, still clinging to the joystick. "It's no use......... I can't do it. I'm......"

He wanted to run away.

Suddenly, a small hand was placed on top of Rentaro's. Surprised, he looked next to him, where Enju was looking at Rentaro with an unusually kind expression on her face. "Rentaro, I am here."

His mouth was parched. The corners of his eyes felt hot, and looking down, he hugged Enju and squeezed hard. "If this misses, it's the end for us."

"It won't miss. You can do it."

"Don't be ridiculous. Of course it's impossible. First of all, how can you believe in a weapon that was inactive for ten years that never even had a test run? One wrong step and the bullet could shoot toward Tokyo Area and cause an unprecedented disaster there."

"But you can do it."

"How can you always say such irresponsible things? I'm..."

Enju suddenly brought her face so close they almost bumped heads. She focused on him with her eyes wide and bit her lip. "I have not said a single irresponsible thing. It is what I always think. You are the only one who can save this world. No one else but you, Rentaro."

Rentaro was surprised and covered his mouth. Closing his eyes, he took a deep breath to calm himself. "Enju…I definitely don't want to lose you."

The tension left Enju's tense body and, at peace from the bottom of her heart, she closed her eyes and put her arm around Rentaro's neck. "Don't worry. I love you, too."

Her body felt so hot he thought he would be burned, but he also felt relief like being wrapped in down. He didn't know how long they stayed like that. Suddenly, Enju let out a strange sound and pressed in on Rentaro's face. "Rentaro, let us be clear. I can interpret what you said just now as a proposal, right?"

"Uh………………… D-d-dummy! Of course it just means I *like* you. Interpret it in a familial way! What does a ten-year-old kid have to say about love, anyway? Besides, before you can even think about feelings, the law says…"

Enju looked dissatisfied as she stared at Rentaro with the corners of her mouth turned down. "Then, do you *love* Kisara?"

Rentaro gave a start. "Don't say that……!"

Enju thrust a victory peace sign in front of Rentaro's nose. "Two years. Within two years, I shall make you like me more than Kisara!"

Rentaro smiled wryly and scratched his head. "When you're twelve and I'm eighteen, huh? The older I get, the more criminal it seems, doesn't it?"

"I can't wait longer than that."

"Okay, okay, I get it. I expect a lot from you."

Enju smiled faintly and slowly peeled her body away from his. "Are you still scared…?"

Rentaro looked at the palm of his own hand and was strangely moved. The trembling had stopped. Rentaro closed his eyes. "No… Thanks. Give me your hand. We're gonna end this."

Lifting his face, he looked at the panel. He even felt pity for the raging Scorpion.

*Sorry we made up a name for you. But I can't die yet.*

The energy that was about to run wild earlier had started shaking like an earthquake right below them.

Rentaro gripped the joystick again, and Enju put her hand on top. They put their fingers on the trigger together.

Rentaro closed his eyes. Strangely, he felt good. He felt like he couldn't miss. "Enju."

"Yeah," she said.

They slowly pulled the trigger.

He felt so light and comfortable that it would be a disservice to compare it to floating. He lost all sense of time.

Finally, everything was enveloped in light, like a blessing.

## EPILOGUE    PUTTING ON A BOLD FRONT

The Seitenshi's palace was, in a word, magnificent. Turning his head, Rentaro could see the forest of marble pillars, the graceful arch of the domed canopy, and the polished floors with mosaic pictures.

Occasionally, he reached up to fix the collar of the unfamiliar white formal suit, scratching his head. How had it turned out like this? It was not the first time he'd screamed this question in his mind that day.

"Tomorrow is the celebration ceremony, so don't be late," Kisara had said the day before, throwing a map and the suit at Rentaro, looking like she couldn't be bothered.

He thought about being extremely late, but in the end, the next morning, Rentaro found himself changing trains by himself. He frowned, thinking something was strange as he looked at the map, but he was not mistaken—the ceremony was in Tokyo Area's First District. He was stunned when he realized that it would be smack-dab in the middle of the Seitenshi's palace.

As Rentaro repeated quietly to himself that this must be some kind of mistake, a guard approached him with eyes that said he thought he was facing a suspicious person. However, the moment Rentaro showed his invitation, it was like he had said, "Open sesame," and the guard's face broke out in a smile as he hit Rentaro's shoulder with friendly, but hard, blows and let him through.

Kisara stood in a dress in front of the large door where the ceremony was being held. She had her hands on her hips and looked unhappy. After seeing Rentaro, all she said was, "You're late," which brought them to the present.

"Satomi, you are the guest of honor today," she said. "Please don't look around like some tourist. As your employer, you are embarrassing me."

"Hey, but Kisara, you didn't say anything about what a big deal this was," Rentaro protested.

"Oh, didn't I? Yesterday, I told you that the Seitenshi herself would be decorating those civsec officers responsible for remarkable achievements, so come dressed in your best, didn't I?"

"No! You threw the map and suit at me like it was too much of a bother to do anything else. That was it."

"Really? Oh well. Oh, Satomi, your necktie is crooked. I'll fix it for you, so stay still."

His heart thumped as hands covered to the elbow with black lace gloves reached for his neck. Kisara was beautiful. After his nervousness faded, he was able to gaze at her again. She was wearing a black dress with frills that looked like bunches of black roses, and she had a matching black ribbon tied in her hair.

She didn't notice because she was crouched over as if in a fight with Rentaro's necktie, but from where he was, he had a perfect view of her full chest in her shoulder-baring dress. Kisara's hair smelled really good. "H-hey...," said Rentaro. "You know you're at a terrible angle right now?"

"Don't talk to me," said Kisara. "Jeez, why are neckties so hard to tie?" Rentaro's fingers opened and closed against his will.

"Maybe like this...?" Kisara pulled at the necktie with amazing force.

"Guh...." Rentaro choked. The tie had tightened around Rentaro's neck with amazing force.

Kisara closed her eyes and shook her head. "It's not working. I'm not good at stuff like this. Satomi, you look just like the Hanged Man card in my Tarot deck, especially with that unfortunate face of yours. You'll just have to tie your necktie yourself."

Right after she said it, she realized how rude it was and covered her hands with her mouth. Kisara looked with conflicted feelings at where Rentaro's right arm used to be and finally opened her mouth to speak. "Your new artificial arm isn't ready yet?"

"No, but I think it's almost ready," he said.

"Speaking of which, I saw Dr. Sumire the other day. She said, 'I can't believe he defeated a Stage Five with a rocket punch. He's seen too many super-robot cartoons. I thought he was just a regular carefree kid, but he's an idiot. He's a carefree idiot. Oh, how funny! How funny!'" She ended with an impression of Sumire's laugh.

"Why is it that even though I saved Tokyo Area, I have to be made fun of this much?"

"How should I know?" Kisara pulled a pocket watch out of her pocket. "It's time. Now, listen carefully. I told you earlier, but I'm going to tell you again. The Seitenshi is taking valuable time from dealing with state affairs to conduct this ceremony, so there's a silent understanding that these kinds of ceremonies should be done as quickly as possible. So when she asks you a question, you should reply with concise answers like *Yes* or *No*. And don't ask any questions. Do you understand?"

"*Yes.*"

"Good answer."

Rentaro stood in front of the large door and took a deep breath. He prepared himself and pushed open the door. It felt cold but was lighter than he expected. Belts of light shone in inside. As he looked back, Kisara smiled at him kindly. "Under the circumstances, you did a good job this time. Good boy. Please continue to work hard and fight, my knight."

Emotions welled up in his heart, and he wanted to say something, but the words wouldn't come out right away. The large door closed, and looking around, he saw a red carpet and a slightly winding marble staircase stretched out in front of him. The Seitenshi sat comfortably at the throne at the top.

It was a spacious room with high ceilings. Next to the honor guard were ladies and gentlemen around a table looking down at them.

"Satomi, thank you for coming." The Seitenshi came down the stairs wearing a slight smile on her face. "Have your wounds healed?"

"Yes, thank you," Rentaro answered formally. "They are a lot better."

"How does it feel to be the savior of Tokyo Area?"

A few days had passed already. Even though it was a plan that deployed a large number of civil officers, the details remained hidden to the public. *For some reason*, a civsec officer *happened to be* nearby to bring down the Gastrea Scorpion that suddenly attacked Tokyo Area with a super-long-range attack.

"The reactions of those around me have changed a little, so it's a little embarrassing," Rentaro said.

"I'm sure it is," said the Seitenshi. "That's not surprising. Just remembering the scene makes me tremble."

The shot that Rentaro and Enju fired at a great speed flew straight into the Scorpion's head and made a giant hole, blowing away its brains.

The Varanium's regeneration interference worked, and it should have died instantly. However, with supernatural strength, right before it died, it swung its upper body and looked in Rentaro's direction.

Its half-closed eye sockets seemed to shake as if making an appeal to Rentaro, and when it finally shut them, it fell sideways into the water, and a giant tsunami broke on the shore of Tokyo Bay.

"I am proud that someone with your abilities was there at that time," the Seitenshi continued. "Satomi, will you offer your assistance to Tokyo Area in the future, as well?"

Rentaro kneeled as he had been instructed. "Yes, even if it means my life."

The Seitenshi raised both hands high overhead and proclaimed solemnly, "To all who are gathered here today, hear my words. The hero here has sworn to fight for the sake of Tokyo Area. He destroyed the Zodiac Scorpion and the Kagetane Hiruko and Kohina Hiruko pair, who formerly held an IP Rank of 134. In light of those accomplishments, after discussion with the IISO, we have decided to consider this a Special First Level Battle Result and promoted the Rentaro Satomi and Enju Aihara pair to an IP Rank of 1,000."

The spectators suddenly let out shouts of joy. The Seitenshi smiled as she shifted her gaze to Rentaro. "Rentaro Satomi, do you accept this decision?"

"Yes, with pleasure," he answered.

The Seitenshi smiled mischievously and continued in a small voice. "The Satomi-Aihara pair originally had a rank of 123,452, so this is a significant promotion. It's probably the first of its kind in history. You might even make it into the *Guinness Book of World Records*."

"Y-yes, ma'am."

"Well then, do you have any final words you would like to say?"

*"No, I don't."* If he had said that, everything would have ended smoothly. Rentaro made a silent apology to Kisara as he raised his head.

"There is," he said.

The Seitenshi's eyes opened in surprise, and the atmosphere in the room suddenly became so tense that his skin prickled.

"Let us hear it," she said.

"I saw what was in that case," said Rentaro.

The Seitenshi's eyes widened again. The people around them could not tell where he was going with this and started murmuring in confusion.

Rentaro remained kneeling as he continued. "I know I shouldn't have. After defeating the Gastrea Zodiac, in the short time before the missiles burned down the church, I opened the case that was recovered and looked inside. I saw…"

Rentaro hesitated for a moment before continuing. "…a broken tricycle inside. What is the meaning of this? How did that become the catalyst to summon a Stage Five Gastrea? No, what are the Gastrea—the enemy organisms who suddenly appeared in this world—in the first place? What happened in this world ten years ago? Please tell me, Lady Seitenshi."

The noise that broke out became so great that it was out of control.

The Seitenshi made her face blank and murmured in a low voice so that only Rentaro could hear. "The Inheritance of the Seven Stars was hidden outside Tokyo Area in the Unexplored Territory, but one of them was stolen during this incident. If that had been destroyed, I cannot imagine what would have happened. The Zodiac came to get it back. I cannot tell you any more."

"What do you mean, you can't?" said Rentaro.

The Seitenshi closed her eyes for a long time. Finally, she exhaled and opened her eyelids. "Those Initiator girls are possibilities. As you know, as civil officer pairs are promoted, they also receive certain rights. You obtain a certain social class, but above all, the access key to top-secret information should be tempting. Because you are currently ranked 1,000, you are now at access Level 3. If you defeat your present rivals and get into the top ten, you will receive the highest access key, Level 12.

"Satomi, please win. Defeat the other eight Zodiacs besides the missing Zodiac, Cancer, and rise in the ranks with Enju Aihara. Then, you will know. You will know what you are and what you were born to do. Please become strong and aim to be the best. If you would call yourself the son of Takaharu and Mafuyu Satomi, then you have a responsibility to know the truth."

Rentaro sprang to his feet and pressed the Seitenshi for an answer. "What are you talking about?! Why are my parents' names coming up now?!"

No matter how long he waited, there was no answer. He became angry and reached out, about to grab the Seitenshi by the collar. Right before he touched her, the Seitenshi shot him a cold glare and his hand stopped. "Stop. If you grab me now, you will be executed for treason."

At that moment, he realized that the room was filled with enough murderous intent to make his blood grow cold, and cold sweat dripped down his cheek.

He didn't know where the source of it was. However, it wasn't a joke or an exaggeration that there was a fighting master who could cut off Rentaro's head or torso in a split second.

Rentaro gritted his teeth. His fist shook as he lowered it. "My apologies..."

He somehow mustered enough strength for that before he threw his body into the large door to open it and left the Seitenshi without looking back.

Rentaro went to the Tendo residence. The main Tendo residence was a luxurious house located in the best residential neighborhood of the First District of Tokyo Area, with Western-style architecture reminiscent of a country house. This was also the house where the young Rentaro had been taken in and raised. Currently, Rentaro was living two people to a one-room, eight-tatami-mat apartment, and Kisara had also left the main house to be independent. It had been a long time since he visited this house like this.

Even though all the citizens of the country were complaining about the lack of land, there was easily a hundred meters between the entrance and the actual building of the house, as if trying to rub it in. The trees in the garden were neatly pruned by the gardener, and they were composed in complete symmetry. A fountain with angels bathing in it was covered with shell inlay.

Going inside with a spare key, Rentaro went straight up to the second floor, heading for the room he had come here for. In the hallway, he passed the elderly housekeeper. Seeing Rentaro, she murmured, "Young master, is that you…?" and looked like she was about to drop the linens she held.

He wanted so much to stop and apologize for not contacting her for so long, but if he didn't hurry, that man would come home. Rentaro lowered his face, pretending he didn't know what she was talking about, and rushed past her.

When he finally came to the door of the room, he pulled out his XD, used his teeth and knee to deftly attach the silencer, and fired a few consecutive shots, breaking off the hinge. Thinking that it really was inconvenient to not have his artificial arm, he took off the silencer, picked up the empty casings, knocked down the door, and went inside.

It was spacious inside, with a warm carpet and a bookshelf covering half the wall. And in the middle was a work desk made of rosewood. Wanting to get it over with as soon as possible, Rentaro opened a drawer and started examining the papers inside.

Rentaro's cell phone chose that moment to vibrate. It was an unknown number. *Damn, why did it have to ring at a time like this?* Rentaro hesitated for a moment but then put the receiver to his ear.

"Hello, Satomi. Good afternoon." A chill ran down his spine. Rentaro tried to calm his wildly pounding heart and let out a deep breath.

"You're alive, Kagetane?" Rentaro's feet felt restless as he remembered what it felt like when he sent Kagetane Hiruko flying with his kick.

After that fight, Kohina had gotten up with a selfless expression, slipping past Rentaro to Kagetane's aid. Kagetane probably did not survive that. That's what Rentaro had thought at the time even though he wasn't sure.

"Yeah, somehow," said Kagetane. "But it was pretty effective. I've been ordered to rest for now. I won't be able to work for a while. It's a bother."

"Work murdering people?" said Rentaro. "Why don't you take this as an opportunity to quit that line of work?"

"No, work my day job. I'm sure we'll meet again eventually. I just wanted to tell you that today. I won't lose the next time we meet."

"Yeah, I won't lose either." In reality, in that fight, Rentaro was only barely able to win because of the pile of clever tricks he'd used to outsmart his enemy. He wasn't sure what he could do if he had to fight a completely prepared Kagetane pair head-on.

"Also, I thought it was about time I introduced you to my client."

*Damn it, that was what it was?* Hearing the sound of a gun cock behind his back, Rentaro threw the phone down and drew his XD without looking back. He pointed it at the sound. Standing up slowly, Rentaro prepared himself as he turned around.

Pointed at his nose was a gun with double Magnum barrels. Rentaro had his finger on his own trigger, at a distance that couldn't be avoided.

"Sneaking around like a thief, Rentaro?" said the man holding the gun.

"You're home already?" said Rentaro. "I thought you wouldn't be back until tonight, Lord Tendo."

Kikunojo Tendo was wearing a formal Japanese *hakama* on his toned body, and stood almost 180 centimeters tall. His back was completely straight, and even though his beard and hair were white, the sharp, glittering eyes that Kisara had inherited were serious. "What are you doing here?" he demanded.

"I was looking for things that could be used as evidence," said Rentaro. "But I don't need to anymore. Asking the person himself is faster. Kikunojo Tendo—on the surface, the recent incident was settled with the reckless behavior of Defense Minister Kutsuwada. But I don't think that was the end. The mastermind behind these events was you, Kikunojo Tendo."

Kikunojo didn't move an eyebrow. However, his finger on the trigger tightened slightly, making Rentaro's heart race faster. With their guns pointed at each other, they moved in a small circle around the fulcrum of the point where their arms crossed. It was a suffocating dance in bad taste that took place on top of the carpet.

"Did Kisara instigate this?" Kikunojo asked.

"I'm acting on my own judgment," said Rentaro.

When he said that, Kikunojo snorted derisively. "Oh? Why did you suspect me?"

Rentaro was taken aback. "You're...not going to deny it?"

Kikunojo's shoulders shook as he scoffed at him. "If I did, would you believe me?"

"No......" But he had still wanted Kikunojo to deny it. He started saying so before he closed his mouth. Rentaro lifted his face. "Defense Minister Kutsuwada died. He hung himself at home while out on bail!"

"I know that. What about it?"

"What do you mean, 'What about it'? I saw the joint compact. It's true that everyone whose name was written on it was arrested... But the real ringleader's name wasn't even on there. I was surprised when I saw the names written on the joint compact. Every single one of them was either in your faction or had been connected to your faction in the past. When I was younger, I greeted all of them at the evening parties held in this house. What is the meaning of this?!"

*"This child seems so wise. Only to be expected from a child adopted by Master Tendo."*

*"I'm sure you'll be an excellent politician when you grow up, Rentaro."*

Thinking back on their words, Rentaro's eyes prickled with tears. His hand shook with anger as he held his gun, and he felt like he could almost pull the trigger.

"Everyone was kind," Rentaro continued. "They all respected you! How could I believe that you, their chief, was the only one not part of this plan? Mr. Kutsuwada hanged himself to stop the investigation against you. The second he died, all the people who were arrested immediately used him as a scapegoat. There's no way I can know what you're thinking. But... But, after all this, you're not embarrassed to continue acting arrogantly, Kikunojo Tendo?!" Rentaro said all this, panting.

But Kikunojo's face only twisted slightly with the faintest bit of self-deprecation. "Why would I do such a thing? Are you saying that my goal was the destruction of Tokyo Area, then? That's absurd."

"I didn't know why at first, either. But when Kagetane stole the case and went to the Unexplored Territory to summon the Stage Five, for some reason, that information was almost systematically leaked. If that happened, Tokyo Area would've fallen into a ruinous panic, and no one stood to benefit from that."

"Did you figure it out?"

"The New Gastrea Law."

Kikunojo's eyebrow twitched in surprise.

"The bill the Seitenshi is pushing to pass despite the resistance from those around her. A law that would improve the social positions of Initiators and allow the Cursed Children to coexist with everyone else. Ever since your wife was killed by a Gastrea in the Great War ten years ago, you've been a staunch advocate of discrimination against Initiators.

"I don't know what kind of deal you made with Kagetane, and I don't want to imagine. However, Kagetane, the Gastrea elite who think it would be disgraceful for humans and Initiators to coexist, shares with you a mutual interest in crushing that bill. If it were leaked to the press that Kohina Hiruko, one of the Cursed Children, was participating in terrorist activities to destroy Tokyo Area, then there would be no one supporting the girls in public opinion. You weren't planning on destroying Tokyo Area from the start, you coward."

Without warning, Rentaro was kicked in the stomach, struck with enough force to make him feel like regurgitating the contents of his stomach. A gun was pressed against his throat, and he was pushed like that into the bookshelf. The moment his back hit, hardcover books began thumping to the floor.

Kikunojo pressed the gun against Rentaro with a look of rage. "Try saying that again!"

"I'll say it as many times as you want!" said Rentaro. "This is how the incident progressed. You had one of your subordinates go to the Unexplored Territory to get the catalyst to summon the Stage Five, what the Seitenshi called the Inheritance of the Seven Stars. He successfully acquired the catalyst and was supposed to hand the case over to Kagetane, thus finishing everything smoothly.

"However, on his way back from the Unexplored Territory, your subordinate was attacked by a Gastrea and took in its bodily fluids. Your subordinate barely escaped alive running back into the Monolith barrier, but there, he unfortunately turned into a Gastrea. He became a

Model Spider Gastrea and infected a human. As evidence, one person whose name was written on the joint compact is still missing even now. I'm sure he was the source Gastrea that Enju and I defeated.

"In the end, Kagetane was somehow able to get the case, but now the information that was supposed to have been leaked was quickly sealed off with a news blackout by the Seitenshi. So in order to make people remember their fear of the Gastrea and crush the New Gastrea Law, you approved the actual summoning of the Stage Five."

"That's right!" Suddenly, Kikunojo yelled like he was on metaphorical fire. "It was all to wake up those complacent fools. How could they forget? How? Ten years ago on that day, the sun set, the earth split apart, and humans were driven out of their own world! Demon brats with the blood of those worms are strutting around town with innocent looks on their faces, you know. Those Red-Eyes are demons who will destroy the whole world. How can you be so calm about it? You want to give them human rights? Don't be ridiculous."

Rentaro took the space of a moment to brush away the hand with the gun. When he did, the sound of a gunshot boomed and the bullet grazed Rentaro's cheek. As Rentaro swept Kikunojo's legs from under him, he drove his knee into the older man's ribs. The feeling was a familiar one to Rentaro, and Kikunojo raised his voice in anguish.

"Everyone's like that!" Rentaro said. "It's true that your wife was killed. But Kisara's parents were killed. You lost your lover. But everyone, everyone lives coming to terms with their past. You're a ghost, Kikunojo Tendo! You're a ghost being dragged along by hatred from ten years ago. Even in your position of aide to the Seitenshi, you try to forestall her. Do you hate the Seitenshi?"

Kikunojo coughed violently as he declared, "Don't say ridiculous things. I regard her with respect and affection. Of all the Seitenshis, she is the only one who could be called a match for the wise monarchs of the past. She is a queen I truly want to serve."

"Then…"

"That's why there are things I cannot forgive!"

Rentaro kept his XD sighted on Kikunojo's forehead as he looked at the man's fiery eyes. He could not see any affectation in them at all. This man held in equal parts devotion to the Seitenshi and hatred for the Gastrea, and it was driving him mad.

"I'm sure Kisara has also realized the truth," said Rentaro.

"I'm sure she has," said Kikunojo. "But you have no proof. You can't do anything."

Rentaro met Kikunojo's eyes for a long time. When he finally moved his knee, Rentaro tucked the XD in his belt and turned on his heel.

"What are you planning?" said Kikunojo. "If you don't kill me now, you'll regret it."

"I'm already regretting it, 'cause you're Kisara's greatest enemy," said Rentaro.

"What about you, Rentaro...?"

"What?"

When he turned around, Kikunojo had on a fierce expression with his wrinkles scrunched in the middle of his face. "What about you, Rentaro? Your arm and leg were eaten, and you lost Takaharu and Mafuyu, didn't you? How can you forgive them? You don't resent them?"

"I do resent them! Tearing them apart from limb to limb wouldn't be enough. I thought I would kill all the Gastrea and the Cursed Children with these hands!"

"Then why?!"

"Have you talked to even one of those girls? They cry at the smallest things, laugh, sulk—they're filled with human warmth. You called them worms? I say they're humans. I, Rentaro Satomi, believe in Enju Aihara!"

"Rentaro... You..."

Rentaro closed his eyes slowly. "You saved my life. You told me, 'If you do not want to die, survive, Rentaro.' So concise, and so very like you. At times when I closed both eyes in despair, I would remember these words, and they would help me push through. I remember every single day what happened that day ten years ago. Thank you... Goodbye, Father."

Rentaro left the house.

"Hey, Rentaroooo! Over heeeeere!" Enju, dressed in a thin hospital gown, was hopping and yelling loudly enough to be heard throughout the district. A surprised old woman strained her back, a three-year-old girl peed her pants, and an old man's dentures and wig were blown off at the same time.

"A-at least be quiet inside a hospital, you dummy," said Rentaro. "Do you know what the word *manners* means…?"

Before he could finish, there was a thud as Enju thrust her face into his chest. "Rentaro, Rentaro, Rentaro! Big news! During the checkup, I got my body measurements, too, and my boobs got a little bigger! Aren't you happy, Rentaro?"

Looking at Enju proudly sticking out her flat chest, he almost let slip a "Huh, where?"

"Don't you think I should wear a brassiere soon?"

"Y-yeah. Maybe in about five years?" Rentaro nonchalantly said something mean.

"How was the ceremony thing? Were you praised? Did they say 'Good job'? My checkup was *so* boring. I wanted to go see, too. Oh, that suit makes you look cool, Rentaro!" Enju's eyes sparkled as she asked Rentaro question after question.

"Enju, what were the results of the checkup?"

Her eyes suddenly glittering, she made a victory sign as if saying, *Listen to this!* "Twenty-four point nine percent. It barely changed."

Rentaro almost involuntarily let out a groan, but he somehow swallowed it. "I… I see…"

"Rentaro, I'm gonna change now, 'kay?"

When Rentaro looked up, he saw the unusual sight of Sumire Muroto out of her basement room beckoning him. "I'm going to go hear what annoying things Doc has to say."

"Then I'll wait for you at the park in front of the hospital." Saying that, Enju raced down the hall. As Rentaro watched her leave, he went to the room where Sumire was waiting.

In the park, there was nothing to block the sunlight, and it was a very comfortably warm day for April. Even though the peak of the cherry blossom season was over, the cherry trees squeezed out the last of their strength to bloom proudly. Rentaro and Enju strolled along a walking path that was scattered with flower petals every time the wind blew. The smell of sprouting plants filled his nostrils.

"Oh ho, so our IP Rank went up that much?" said Enju.

"Yeah," said Rentaro. "They said it was the first time in history anyone went up that fast. We'll get the official notification next week."

As Enju spotted an ice cream stand in the corner of the park, she said, "Can I buy some, Rentaro?"

Thinking that they were expensive, Rentaro reluctantly opened his wallet and let out an involuntary groan. Even if their ranking went up, the inside of his wallet still continued to be as empty as ever.

Rentaro sighed. Grabbing hold of the bill with a shaking hand, he slipped it into Enju's hand. "This needs to cover this month's living expenses, so use it wisely."

"I understand," said Enju. "I should buy as much ice cream as I can with this, right?"

"Why did you take it that way? Hey, wait! Enju!"

Already not listening to the yelling Rentaro's words, Enju ran away. Rentaro looked at her retreating back in shock.

He smiled unwittingly. He was alive. He was hungry. What a wonderful thing.

Enju didn't know. In the peacefulness of Tokyo Area, she didn't know that one more precious life had been sacrificed.

After operating the railgun, Rentaro put Enju, deep asleep, gently onto the floor, and then slipped outside the facility. Looking at the sky, he saw that the night sky was slowly starting to grow lighter. Because of the high altitude, his breath had been white, and he'd kept rubbing his hands as he made his way down the bare rock.

Once he was some distance away from the facility and looked back at the Stairway to Heaven, he could clearly see that the rail part where the projectile was accelerated was crushed. The rail was not strong enough to withstand the sudden acceleration of a projectile after all.

As Rentaro walked, something he had been trying hard not to think about came back into his mind. Gastrea were very sensitive to loud noises. Depending on the Gastrea, there were some that would gather after hearing a sound a few kilometers away.

During his fight to the death with Kagetane, and when he fired the railgun, thunderous roars should have echoed throughout the Unexplored Territory. However, in the end, his duel ended uninterrupted and the railgun's firing sequence ended without being delayed. It was obviously a strange situation. Someone had stopped the large wave of Gastrea that should have surged toward them.

Eventually, the smell of blood grew stronger. Rentaro went behind a large rock, and then he held his breath.

In front of his eyes was the corpse of a giant Gastrea. The body, which was like a Komodo dragon that had been turned ten times as large as normal, was missing its front legs, and its lower jaw had been blown away.

And that wasn't the only corpse.

There were Gastrea that looked like insects, Gastrea entwined with plantlike vines, snake types and frog types, and many others that had been changed so much that their origins were unclear. There were also many different shapes and sizes, from large Gastrea to small Gastrea, Stage One to Stage Four. What they all had in common was that the spark of life was gone from every Gastrea.

Rentaro walked among the dead bodies. Finally, he saw a human leg with its shoe still on strewn casually on the ground. Near it was an empty magazine. A little farther, and he found the remains of a fully automatic shotgun that had been broken cleanly in two. Rentaro desperately held back a sob as he walked through the mountain of corpses. In deathly silence that almost made his ears hurt, all Rentaro could hear was his shoes stepping on the gravel.

And then, he found her. Unfortunately, he found her.

Rentaro shook his head gently. His voice felt like shaky, and his hands were clenched into fists. "Why...? Why didn't you run? Didn't you say you would run when you were at a disadvantage?!"

Kayo Senju, who was being propped up by a large rock, looked up at Rentaro with fading eyes. "I couldn't...do that..."

Her left arm and right leg were missing. Her white dress was stained with blood, and she had bite marks all over. Her injuries were healing unbelievably fast. Not only were they healing, but her missing arm and leg were regenerating, as well. But this was not a welcome situation at all.

"Satomi...I'm...?" she started.

Rentaro forced his pounding heart to calm down and said, "Your body's corrosion rate is probably over fifty percent."

The Cursed Children were constantly taking massive doses of corrosion-inhibiting medication to control the Gastrea inside their bodies, but it still only inhibited and did not stop the corrosion completely. Because the girls carried the inhibiting gene, they did not turn into Gastrea immediately like normal people, but if they suddenly used a lot of their power, or if Gastrea bodily fluids got inside them, then their corrosion rate would slowly increase.

And then, like a normal person, if their corrosion rate went above fifty percent, then the corrosion would start, and they would not be able to keep their human form any longer. There was nothing that current medical technologies could do to change that limit.

Rentaro took his XD gun out and checked how many bullets he had left. He had exactly one Varanium bullet left in the chamber. Rentaro put the silencer on and aimed at her forehead. He knew what he had to do. Kayo Senju could not be saved. She had to die right here, right now.

"Satomi, what happened to Shogen?" Kayo asked.

"He's fine," said Rentaro.

When their eyes met, she lowered her lashes in relief. "Satomi, please. Please let me die as a human."

His breath shook as he exhaled. It wasn't because he was cold. The muzzle of the gun jumped around, and his aim was all over the place. Even though he was so close, there was a possibility that he would miss. What a joke.

Suddenly, remembering the irreplaceable time they had spent together surrounded by firewood and talking, his heart was so filled with affection that it tore at his chest. *Damn it, damn it!*

"Satomi, please, don't cry...," said Kayo.

Rentaro ground his teeth so hard his molars felt like they would break, and he smiled. "Don't worry, I'm not crying. This isn't my first time."

"You affirmed my existence. I didn't want to let you die. That is why I tried hard. My heart is full of gratitude right now. Thank you, Satomi."

Rentaro had no words and could only shake his head left and right.

Kayo continued. "Hey, Satomi, you don't have many friends, do you?"

"Huh?"

"You're hopeless, so I'll be your friend."

Rentaro's and Kayo's eyes met for a brief moment. "Yeah, it's sad how few friends I have. Thanks." His hand stopped shaking. His heart calmed.

"You are my irreplaceable friend. I will never forget you."

He lifted his gun and aimed for the space between her eyebrows. Her eyes were not focused. Her voice was hoarse.

"Satomi, after this… I imagine you will face many trials. If you lose your way and are lost in the darkness, follow the compass in your heart…to…to the light… Satom……save…this…world……"

He pulled the trigger. The .40-caliber recoil made his arm kick back. There was the sound of a muffled gunshot, and a single empty casing was expelled. His slide stop came up and locked.

The girl's transformation stopped. There was an acrid smell in the back of his nose; he must have inhaled some gunsmoke. When he turned around at the sound of a helicopter, he could see the red sunrise shining in from beyond the faraway mountain range. Her fight was over. Another Initiator had died in battle, unseen.

Enju looked like she was still having fun choosing her ice cream. Looking up, Rentaro slowly raised his palm to shade his eyes from the sun and thought as he squinted at the bright light of the sun. *What are humans, anyway?*

They can speak, they walk on two legs, they wear clothes. But that didn't prove that they were human. And humans only had at most twice as many genes as flies.

*Then, what are the Cursed Children?*

Sumire Muroto called them "God's substitutes as messengers between humans and Gastrea."

The Seitenshi had said, "Those Initiator girls are possibilities."

Kikunojo Tendo called them "demons who will destroy the whole world."

Human beings once lived on the earth invincible, proud, and rejoicing that they were the prime of creation. However, that ended with the appearance of the Gastrea. It could be said that about ninety percent of the surviving humans in this degenerate world had latent prejudice against the Initiators.

More and more children were abandoned because, with the contamination of their DNA, their paternity couldn't be proven. Abandoned to the darkness before they could even open their eyes, they rubbed shoulders in a corner of Tokyo Area, children who just wanted to be loved.

The girls faced unending prejudice and ceaseless enmity. Were they just a new classification of human beings?

Rentaro closed his eyes quietly.

Enju Aihara said, "I am human!"

*I will believe Enju.*

Those girls were the ones who'd broken through the human shell and gazed out over the world, looking down at mankind as it trod a path of destruction, humans killing each other over differences in race, religion, or language. The Cursed Children were a "new humanity" that could bring a new perspective.

Kikunojo, who was so torn up by despair that he spit ill omens and cursed everything on earth, could have been Rentaro if he had not met Enju.

Like Kisara Tendo, who could not live without her hemodialysis—

Like Enju Aihara, who could not live without her dose of corrosion-inhibiting medication—

—Rentaro Satomi surely could not live another second without Enju Aihara's smile.

Those girls were definitely not worms.

"Rentaro, are you feeling unwell after all?" By the time he returned to himself, Enju was looking at him with mountains of ice cream in each hand.

"N-no! Look, see? I'm so happy that our rank went up that I'm jumping." He forced a laugh and ran up on a nearby bench and started to jump off.

Enju's eyes widened for a second at Rentaro's strange behavior, but she soon burst into laughter. "Weirdo."

At that moment, the clear sound of something metal hitting the stone pavement stopped time. Rentaro looked back and forth at his own left arm and the ground, dumbfounded. On the ground were fragments of a bracelet. They had chrome silver-plating over an engraved design.

That's right. Enju had bought this for him. If he remembered correctly, it was a toy from a cartoon...

*"What's that?"*

"It's the bracelet that the Tenchu Girls wear. It's proof that the forty-seven warriors are friends, and it cracks when a friend tricks another friend or lies to them, so they can tell when a friend is lying."

Rentaro exhaled with a shaking breath and stared at the fragments of the broken bracelet.

### ENJU AIHARA'S DIAGNOSIS CHART – PRIMARY PHYSICIAN, SUMIRE MUROTO

- Enju Aihara has a Gastrea virus corrosion rate of 42.8%
- An estimated 7.2% left until shape collapse
- Comments from the physician—Extremely dangerous territory. To prevent the patient from being too shocked, I reported a lower number to her. According to regulations, notification of the patient is at the discretion of the Promoter.

This part is written not in my capacity as a doctor, but is my advice as a friend:

Don't let her fight anymore, Rentaro.

## AFTERWORD

Nice to meet you. My name is Shiden Kanzaki. To explain to those reading from the afterword, this book involves the tag battle of a protective high school hero and a ten-year-old Lolita heroine. I have written about this in other places, too, but I had so many uninterrupted publishing offers that—

Actually, this did not happen at all. Rather, I took my manuscript and said, "Please publish this, please publish this," and rolled around on the floor of the Dengeki Bunko editorial department like a cute cat. Thus, I tricked Mr. Kurosaki into coming near me and grabbed hold of his leg firmly, which brings us to the present.

## REGARDING THE TITLE

I didn't think about it too hard and just put together a color I liked and the title of a movie I liked and got *Black Memento*. From the beginning, my editor disapproved of this title, but I was used to calling it that, so I waited it out in a war of attrition and schemed to publish it that way. But then he attacked directly with a phone call in the middle of the night. I realized that he really hated this title and was immediately reformed and settled on the current title.

## REGARDING THE DOUBLE GUNS

The concept behind the double guns of a certain person that come up in the book are "the worst double guns in history." To you double-gun lovers on the other side of the page reading just the afterword in the store, pretend you've been tricked for a second and try reading this book. I'm sure you will realize—little girl heaven, boobs galore, perverted guns, fake martial arts—there are many attractive elements prepared for you here as I await you who will never read it again.

Now, let me be a little serious here. A hundred apologies and ten thousand thanks to the nice guy who found me, my editor, Mr. Kurosaki; the artist who drew the gorgeous pictures, Saki Ukai; the chief editor who helped me when I caused a certain problem; and everyone else who was involved in the creation of this book.

Finally, to you, the reader who is using their precious time to read the afterword: Thank you very much. I am grateful for this meeting from the bottom of my heart. I look forward to the joy that I will receive when you, the reader, read this book. I pray that all of my readers will be blessed.

blog: kanzakisiden.blog.fc2.com
twitter: twitter.com/Siden_K